Kath___n Wallace is an experienced blogger, whose writing care___ innacle to date was when a little blog post she wrote ab___ ___er front bottom's run in with some mint and tea tree O___ ___ Source shower gel went viral and ended up being ___ ___ more than 30 million people globally. #lifegoals

___ time working parent, Kathryn somehow finds the ___ between regularly losing her shit and screaming ___H! HAIR! SHOES!' on repeat to update her blog, ___, *I Need To Stop Talking*, which has around 175,000 ___rs on Facebook and is growing rapidly.

___er spare time, Kathryn likes to lie face down on ___ofa screaming silently into a cushion or attempt to ___ce her children that urination really doesn't require ___dience.

Also by Kathryn Wallace

Absolutely Smashing It

WINNING AT LIFE

Kathryn Wallace

sphere

SPHERE

First published in Great Britain in 2020 by Sphere
This paperback edition published by Sphere in 2020

1 3 5 7 9 10 8 6 4 2

A CIP catalogue record for this book
is available from the British Library.

ISBN 978-0-7515-7501-9

Typeset in Caslon by M Rules
Printed and bound in Great Britain by Clays Ltd, Elcograf S.p.A.

Papers used by Sphere are from well-managed forests
and other responsible sources.

Sphere
An imprint of
Little, Brown Book Group
Carmelite House
50 Victoria Embankment
London EC4Y 0DZ

An Hachette UK Company
www.hachette.co.uk

www.littlebrown.co.uk

For Mummy, for always encouraging me.
For Daddy, for always believing in me.
And for Helen, for always putting up with me!

CHAPTER ONE

'MUM! Ava keeps showing me her vagina.' For approximately the three thousandth time that long, hot day, it appeared World War Three was threatening to break out.

Wearily, Gemma left the dinner she was preparing and headed up the stairs. 'What's going on, guys? I told you, you need to get your stuff ready.'

'And I'm trying to get my stuff ready, but Ava keeps coming into my bedroom with her vagina hanging out, and I don't want her to,' Sam retorted grumpily.

'Ava.' There was no response. 'Can you come here, please. Sam, I'm sure she's not really—'

'It's not a vagina, Sam. Vaginas don't hang out. It's my VULVA,' Ava announced loudly. Not for the first time, Gemma really really wished her seven-year-old daughter came with an inbuilt volume control.

To be fair to Sam, he wasn't entirely wrong, Gemma decided as Ava appeared with rather too much on display beneath the summer dress she had attempted to squeeze herself into.

Gemma ran her hands across her face. 'Ava, what are you doing? Go and find some proper school uniform that fits. And where are your pants?'

'This is my proper school uniform.' Ava looked appraisingly at herself in the hall mirror. 'I think it might be a bit short.'

'A BIT? Ava, you told me last week that you definitely had all your uniform ready for going back to school. So what's happened?'

Ava stared back at her mum mutinously. 'Nothing's happened. I have got all my uniform, and here it is. And I am not wearing any pants, because the only pants left are the ones that Granny bought me, and they're PINK.' She looked appalled at the very concept of pink pants.

Gemma buried her head in her hands and let out a groan. It didn't matter how hard she tried, it seemed she was destined to spend the last day of the holidays trapped in her own personal *Groundhog Day*, as she once again proved herself to be miserably lacking in the key parenting skills of basic preparation and organisation.

She turned her attention to the problem at hand. 'Okay. Ava, you cannot have actually grown that much over the last six weeks. Let's go and have a look in your wardrobe. And Sam: congratulations, now that you're about to start Year 6, it's officially your responsibility to go through the festering hideousness that is the interior of your book bag. Personally, I suggest you tip the whole lot out and put it straight into the bin. Maybe even burn it. Just check there's nothing important you need for tomorrow, yes?'

Taking her daughter by the hand, Gemma walked across the landing and attempted to open her bedroom door.

'Ava, what's the matter with your door? Why isn't it opening?'

'Um.' Ava looked vague. 'Maybe because there is something in the way of it.'

'Like what? There can't be much, can there? You were sent up to tidy your room nearly two hours ago.'

With renewed efforts, Gemma pushed harder on the door, which resisted for a moment longer before flying open with a crash, revealing a scene of absolute chaos.

'AVA! What the hell is all this?' Gemma didn't know where to begin; her daughter's bedroom looked like what you'd be left with if a branch of Hobbycraft exploded inside the Chelsea FC merchandise shop.

'I was making ... stuff,' replied Ava, returning to the spot in the middle of the floor where she'd clearly been sitting. Almost eleven years of parenting had made it abundantly clear to Gemma that, when you asked your child to go and tidy their room, what they would actually do was one of three things:

A – Ignore you.

B – Go and sit vacantly in the middle of the mess.

C – Become distracted by a new toy they had found and end up actually causing more chaos than they'd started with.

In a personal record, it seemed that Ava had elected to combine all three of these options.

'Okay.' Tempting though it was to completely lose it, Gemma had learnt the hard way that all losing it generally resulted in was it taking even longer to achieve the desired outcome. Tentatively, she stepped over two footballs and a pile of Match Attax cards before making it to Ava's wardrobe. 'Let's have a look and see what we can find.'

It transpired that Ava had somehow managed to find one of her old Year R dresses and put it on; to her relief Gemma found two perfectly suitable summer dresses in age 7–8, which would both preserve her daughter's modesty and ensure that she wasn't going to end up hauled in to see the headmistress on Sam and Ava's first day back at school. She found at least five pairs of (non-pink) pants, not in Ava's pants drawer but stuffed down the side of her bedside table.

'Ava?' Gemma looked stern. 'Why are these pants here? They should be in your drawer. I told you to make sure you put your washing away nicely.'

'Well,' Ava put her hands on her hips, 'you tell me and Sam to do that, but then you leave all of your clothes piled up on that chair in your bedroom. So I don't think that's very fair, do you? You are a . . . a . . . you are a hypnotist.'

Attempting to explain to Ava the difference between a hypocrite and a hypnotist, Gemma was caught somewhere between extreme exasperation and laughing so much her pelvic floor was in jeopardy. Finally she cleared a path through the debris covering the carpet so that she could at least get back out of the room without a pair of football studs puncturing the sole of her foot. Anyone who said that football wasn't a dangerous sport had clearly never stood on a sole-up football boot left in the hallway as they'd returned home after one too many Jägerbombs on a night out.

Ava now sorted, Gemma went back to check on Sam. He was sitting where she'd left him; to her delighted surprise he'd actually followed her instructions and had indeed tipped out the contents of his book bag into his lap. She recoiled slightly; was part of it *moving*?

'Great, well done, love. Everything for the bin, yes? There wasn't anything that you needed?'

'Um.' Her son was clearly trying to avoid meeting her eye. 'It's just ... Mum, if I tell you something, will you promise that you won't be cross?'

Ah, the million-dollar question. If Gemma had learnt nothing else over the years, it was that a request from her son to promise that she wouldn't be cross was almost inevitably followed by him telling her something that was going to make her very cross indeed.

'Go on then.' She sighed. 'Hit me with it. What have we not done that we were supposed to have done? Made a scale model of the Eiffel Tower out of vegetables? Taken a trip to Egypt to personally visit Tutankhamun's tomb? Translated the complete works of William Shakespeare into Sanskrit?'

Sam took a deep breath. 'No. It's worse than that. I was meant to write a diary. Every day for the whole of the holidays. I had to write at least a side of A4 about what we got up to each day, and if I haven't done it then I have to go and help out every morning break time in the Key Stage One playground.' He looked appalled at the very prospect. 'Mum, help me. What are we going to do?'

'Or he might get expelled,' Ava said brightly, popping her head around the door.

Oh, fuck Gemma's actual fucking life.

Four hours later, Gemma collapsed on the sofa, exhausted. Having finally managed to get the children into bed – all that could now be heard was the rustle of pages from Sam devouring yet another Tom Gates book, and Ava happily belting out to the neighbourhood she was a 'SWEET TRANSVESTITE' (which would teach Gemma to have added the *Rocky Horror* soundtrack to her Spotify playlist) – she was quite honestly ready for bed herself. Gemma vehemently disapproved of homework, particularly when it required her involvement. She had been all set to send Sam in with a strident note for his teacher, explaining precisely why he hadn't completed his diary, because he had been spending his holiday having fun, and not even thinking about fronted adverbials, or any of the other Government-sponsored bullshit that would no doubt be looming large in his SATS.

Sam, however, had proved surprisingly resistant, saying that he didn't want her to embarrass him; that he just wanted to get on and do the diary. If Gemma had known that the way to get her frequently recalcitrant son to ditch the three hours of procrastinating and actually *do* the work he'd been sent home with was simply to embarrass him . . . she'd have been threatening to run down the street starkers years ago.

The problem was, there were only so many ways you could write 'Today I sat around in my pants and stared at

6

a computer screen' and make it sound interesting. Gemma wanted to throw herself face down on the ground and wail at the very thought of the Competitive Parenting that would be going on via the Year 6 diaries. She had blocked notifications from the class Facebook page over the summer; it had turned out to be an inspired move. Bar the fact that, had she not, she might at least have found out about the requirement for Sam to complete a daily diary slightly more than twenty-four hours before the end of the school holidays.

A quick glance at the Year 6 parents' page showed that she wasn't wrong: Vivienne (Alpha Mummy of Redcoats Primary School) and her coven were falling over themselves to outdo each other with anecdotes of what their various offspring had been up to each day.

'SUCH fun writing up Tartan's diary entry tonight. We jumped on the Eurostar and had a Mummy-and-Tartan day in gay Paree! Simply fabulous! Kiss kiss!'

It had been Ava who had come up with the bright idea that they should simply lie about what Sam had been doing. 'Let's just pretend, Mummy, that Sam is really interesting and isn't just a smelly boy who sits in his dressing gown all day and scratches his HAIRY BALLS. I know, Sam, you can write in your diary and tell Mr Andrews all about your HAIRY BALLS.' At which point Gemma had to physically take hold of her daughter by the shoulders and tell her to sit down and be quiet before she laughed so much she made herself throw up.

Uncomfortable though she was with suggesting to her children that any kind of untruth was okay, Gemma was able to get herself comfortable with the plan by explaining to Sam and Ava that they would treat the diary as a piece of creative writing. 'After all, it's not like most of the other parents won't have used a bit of artistic licence,' Gemma told them. 'When Tartan tells you he's been to Iceland, Sam, it's far more likely that he's talking about the super-market than the country.'

'Yes, and we can think of MUCH more interesting places for you to have gone to, Sam,' shrieked Ava in delight. There was no love lost between Ava and Vivienne's off-spring. Last year, Ava had unmasked Satin, Vivienne's daughter, also in Ava's class, as having been deeply unpleas-ant to Rosie, Ava's friend who lived next door to them. Thrilled at the thought of Sam getting one over on Tartan, she now came up with an increasingly outlandish series of places that Sam could have conceivably visited, from the vaguely plausible Buckingham Palace to the completely preposterous 'backstage at a Beatles concert on an island in the middle of the SOLAR SYSTEM'. Gemma filtered, Sam wrote, and between them they managed to blitz the entire summer's diary in just under four hours.

It would, Gemma declared, go down as one of her all-time parenting triumphs.

Dozing in front of the TV, thinking she really should go and fire up her laptop and answer a couple of emails before going back to work the next day, her eyes snapped open at the sound of a knock on the front door. It would be Tom; he had promised to stop in at hers that night to let her know how the pre-term inset day had gone.

Tom and Gemma had met when Tom had started at

Redcoats last year, as Ava's Year 2 teacher. Persistent efforts by Becky – Gemma's best friend and next-door neighbour – had led to romance blossoming, and the two of them had been pretty much inseparable since Gemma's fortieth birthday at the start of the summer.

'Hello, love.' Tom put down his bag and pulled her into an embrace. 'How was your day?'

Gemma's attempt to reply was interrupted by a stern command to 'STOP HAVING SEX. STOP IT RIGHT NOW', from the top of the stairs. In Ava's mind, the acts of kissing and having sex were somewhat confused, leading to the memorable moment when she'd announced to Gemma's parents over lunch at theirs that 'Mummy and Tom were having sex IN THE STREET' and Gemma's mum had almost choked on her beef stroganoff.

A belligerent Ava was put back to bed – 'but you were having sex with Mr Jones, I saw you' (goodness, Tom was going to have some fun in the school playground tomorrow as Ava regaled everyone she came across with that little anecdote). By the time Gemma returned downstairs Tom had poured them both a glass of wine, and held out his arm for her to curl up next to him on the sofa.

'If that little interchange was in any way representative of your day, I'm surprised there's any wine left in this bottle,' he said with a smile.

Gemma laughed. 'It hasn't been that bad. I mean … there was the minor matter of having to complete an entire summer's homework in the space of four hours.' She looked at him sternly. 'Surely one of the benefits of dating a teacher from your kids' school is that you might think to give me the heads-up on this kind of thing!' Tom had the good grace to look vaguely mortified. 'Don't worry; it's all sorted now. I've even managed to find Ava a school dress that doesn't make her look like a call girl. Frankly, I am absolutely smashing it right now.'

Tom smiled. 'Good. I'm glad one of us is. Because I have had a total fucker of a day.'

Gemma turned in her seat, twisting so that she could look directly at him. 'Why? What's happened?'

Tom took another slug of his wine. 'I don't entirely know where to begin. I arrive at school this morning, and Sharon – Mrs Goldman – is going absolutely out of her mind. As you know, Ava's class were due to be getting a new teacher this year. The Year 3 teacher that the school had employed – a Miss Collins, apparently – hasn't been responding to Sharon's calls or emails. Then today, she simply didn't turn up. I'd say she's decided not to take the job at all, which means Sharon's going to have no choice but to step in and teach Year 3 herself. As you can probably imagine, hands-on teaching is not really her forte. She's beside herself, and I can't say I blame her. One year of that particular class was quite enough for me.'

He winked, and Gemma could see him remembering the time he'd spent in charge of Ava's class, who had once been described by their previous teacher, a Miss Thompson, in an unguarded moment after one too many mulled wines at the school Nativity, as 'feral, like bloody animals'. It was not an unfair assessment.

'Oh, goodness.' Gemma imagined a show-down between her daughter and Mrs Goldman: two of the most strong-willed individuals she'd ever met. 'I guess that must have thrown the day's plans out a bit.'

Tom laughed, a slightly hysterical laugh, and took another sip of his wine. 'Oh no, that's nothing, not in the grand scheme of things. Because you see the other thing that I haven't mentioned to you . . . is that someone tried to burn down the school.'

'WHAT?' Gemma was horrified. 'What do you mean, someone tried to burn down the school? Who would do that? They didn't succeed, though, right? It's still standing?'

Tom shook his head. 'Not all of it, no. Most of the main building's okay, but the Year 3 and 4 classrooms are damaged pretty much beyond repair. You should see the state of them. It's awful. Mr Cook was the first on the scene, as caretaker he called the fire brigade and then did his best with the extinguishers on site, but it would have been like pissing on an inferno. Whoever set out to do it clearly wasn't messing around.'

'So what's going to happen?' Her hand to her mouth, Gemma could hardly believe what she was hearing. 'Will the children be able to go back to school?' Concerned though she was about the future of Redcoats, if she was completely honest, a large percentage of her horror was solely down to the thought she might be stuck with the kids for a few more weeks. Gemma had once had a dream that she had decided to home educate Ava and Sam; she'd woken up sweating and actually screaming out loud for help, and had been too scared to go back to sleep for the rest of the night.

Tom nodded. 'Sharon's arranged for two mobile class-rooms to be set up, so short term, they're all sorted. The site has been made safe. Longer term, though, I really don't know. The LEA will be coming in next week, they need to understand how much the repairs are going to cost and then talk to us about funding them.' He looked worried. 'It's not going to be cheap, that's for sure. Honestly. What a start to the school year.'

You could say that again, thought Gemma to herself. You could say that again.

CHAPTER TWO

'I am going to report you to Childline. And the police. And the ... QUEEN OF ENGLAND. This is NOT fair, I do NOT like you, and I am NOT happy.'

Gemma tried again. 'But, Ava, it's nearly eight o'clock. We're going to be late. Come on, please. Time to get up.'

Ava pulled the covers over her head. 'NO. You always tell me to go to bed; well, now I am in bed, and you are telling me that you don't want me to be in bed. You are being a hypnotist again, Mum.'

Briefly, Gemma hid her face in the neck of her hoody and let out a scream of frustration. Incredibly, it did the trick: Ava actually sat up of her own accord to see if her mum was being attacked by werewolves or zombies, both of which she didn't *think* were real, but Sam kept telling her that they absolutely were, so she wasn't going to take any chances.

'Good. Now up you get.' Gemma passed Ava's school uniform to her and held her gaze until she capitulated and started furiously putting it on. 'Really, Ava: you've been up before seven a.m. most mornings all holiday and have been out in the back garden playing football. Why have you picked today to sleep in?'

Ava stared mutinously at her. 'Because I am DIFFICULT.'

Well, she wasn't going to argue with that one.

The next twenty minutes were predictably chaotic: Gemma stood over Ava to ensure she didn't get back into bed fully dressed and fall asleep again (something she'd been known to do more than once) while simultaneously barking a series of orders at Sam, almost all of which were ignored as he instead concentrated furiously on the latest Minecraft manual and shoved cereal into his mouth using a ladle. (There were plenty of spoons available, had he managed to walk the extra half a step to the dishwasher and open it in order to extract some of the clean cutlery and crockery, but Sam's fear that someone might then assume he was in the process of emptying the dishwasher and insist that he finished the task was such that he simply wasn't prepared to take the risk. Hence the ladle.)

Seeing Gemma standing, one foot on the landing – 'Sam! TEETH! HAIR! SHOES!' – and one foot in Ava's bedroom – 'Ava! GET DRESSED!' – Tom, who'd stayed over last night, took pity on her. 'Listen, love, why don't I take the children into school this morning? Then you can go straight into the office and get a bit of a head start on the day.'

About to say yes, Gemma was stopped in her tracks by Ava, stomping furiously out of her bedroom and staring directly at Tom, who she usually adored. 'NO. You are

NOT going to take me to school, Mr Jones, because then everyone will know that you and my mum are having ALL THAT SEX.'

So that was that then.

Tom headed off as Gemma grabbed her laptop and cor- ralled the children into the car. Parked next to her was Becky and Jon's Range Rover, which Jon was unlocking and gently ushering seven-year-old Rosie into. Ella, just one, was in his arms, making increasingly fretful attempts to grab Rosie's hair, which had been expertly tamed into a French plait by someone. Gemma could just imagine Ava's face if Gemma suggested she French plait her hair; Ava frequently com- plained furiously about how utterly unreasonable it was that the strict school rules prevented her from having a Grade 1 cut all over. ('They tell me that my hair is not allowed to be in my eyes, so I said to Mrs Goldman that I would just cut it all off then, and then she says that I am not allowed to do that either. She is just being difficult for the sake of it, Mummy.') Not that Gemma could have managed a French plait even if Ava had permitted it: her hairstyling abilities were on a par with her ability to get everyone out of the house on time. Shit: she really needed to get moving.

It was clearly Jon's morning on duty with the girls. His wife Becky had started her brand-new job just a couple of weeks ago. She was now the Marketing Manager for a recently formed charity that worked with organisations to make flexible working opportunities the norm, not the exception, with the aim of everyone being able to work in a well-paid and fulfilling role, regardless of whether or not they also had responsibilities away from work.

The length of time it had taken Becky to find a new role made it abundantly clear just how much this charity was needed. When she'd been offered the position, Jon had agreed to reduce his hours in his high-profile sales role, so that they could share the childcare between them. It had been a great move for them, both as a family and for their relationship.

Although Jon didn't appear to be thinking that right at that moment in time. He gave Gemma a strained smile as she waved hello. 'Morning, Jon! Did you want me to take Rosie in with me?'

'That's all right, thanks, Gemma. I promised Rosie I'd take her, as it's her first day back. Bit of a mad one, isn't it?' There was a slightly hysterical light behind his eyes. 'Still, we're getting there. I think I might just be getting this parenting malarkey down to a fine art.' Said at that precise moment Ella suddenly decided to vomit congealed porridge . . . all over the top of her appalled big sister's head.

Jon having refused her offers of help, Gemma drove off, still laughing when she thought of the look on poor Rosie's face. 'If you ever do anything like that to me, Sam, I will phone up the President of the United States and arrange for him to cut off your HEAD,' said Ava in strident tones.

'No you won't,' muttered Sam, though without conviction. He was never entirely certain what his little sister was capable of.

The school gates were predictably chaotic. Her teeth gritted, Gemma reverse parked into a space she'd have written off as implausibly small just three or four years ago. Being incapable of getting out of the house on time had its benefits: Gemma's parallel-parking skills had improved like she wouldn't have believed. The morning she'd simultaneously squeezed the car into a minute space between a white van and a VW Beetle while responding to Ava's request to tell her how babies were made was still one of her proudest moments.

Tom had told her last night that Mrs Goldman was doing her best to keep the news of the arson attack on the school confidential, but it seemed that that ship may have sailed. Vivienne – who else? – was resplendent in the middle of the playground in a fluorescent yellow reflective jacket that clashed horribly with the turquoise leather shorts and matching top that she was wearing underneath. Clutching a megaphone, she was announcing at top volume to everyone to: 'PLEASE avoid the area marked to the right; this is where the ARSON ATTACK took place, and the Year 3 and 4 classrooms were BURNT TO THE GROUND.' Next to her was a familiar face: Nick the Dick, Gemma's ex-husband, who had ended up in something of an on-off relationship with Vivienne at the end of last term. From the look on his face, he was very much wishing their relationship was more off than on right at that moment. Ava running over to tell him that 'some of Mummy's pants have gone missing and so Sam and I were wondering if maybe you had taken them, Daddy, because your pants are too small for you' was a welcome distraction in Nick's eyes, even if not quite so much in Gemma's.

'Morning, babe!' Nick couldn't have moved any faster to get away from Vivienne. 'Morning, kids!' He held Ava's hand and she skipped happily alongside her daddy as he joined them to walk round to the KS2 side of the school. Fortunately for him, Vivienne was fully absorbed in informing all new arrivals to the school gates about the classrooms having been 'BURNT TO THE GROUND', and hence didn't notice her current squeeze walking off with his ex-wife. Accusations he was wearing Gemma's pants would have been the least of Nick's worries if she had.

'Morning, Nick. Having fun?' Grateful for once for the presence of Vivienne, who would ensure that the first-day-back playground headlines were centred around the burnt-out classrooms, as opposed to her own allegedly missing pants, Gemma was unable to resist a snide comment in respect of her ex's relationship with Vivienne, which was clearly going about as well as she could have hoped in her wildest dreams.

Rounding the corner of the school, out of view of his girlfriend, Nick shook his head in despair. 'Don't even go there.' He looked at Gemma. 'Babe, I'll be frank with you. I don't think it's going to work out.'

'I absolutely cannot imagine why,' Gemma told him, manfully keeping a straight face.

His face brightened. 'But I've got news, though! That job I got . . . they've told me they might have something permanent for me. Would mean me having to move out to Berlin, though.' He screwed up his face. 'That's in America, right?'

Fortunately for Nick, they had arrived in the KS2 playground before Gemma could tell him exactly what she thought of his geography knowledge. Instead, she turned her attention to the children. This was the first time they'd both been on the same side of the school together since Ava had started there. 'Won't it be nice, you'll be able to play together at break times now?'

Sam looked at his mum like she was a total moron and shook his head in disbelief and despair, as Ava responded in delight, 'Yes, and unless you are very very nice to me, Sam, I will tell everyone about that time that you did a wee in the bin in your bedroom because you couldn't be bothered to go to the toilet.'

Gemma kissed them both goodbye – Sam squirming out of her grasp with an 'Urrrrggghhhh, Muuuuuuum, you're so EMBARRASSING' – there was a glowing review for you – and left them squabbling over the relative consequences of Sam not being nice to Ava versus Ava telling everyone Sam had weed in a bin. She waved to a still bemused-looking Nick ('or is it in Spain?'), and left to drive to the office.

It was funny how your expectations changed once you became a parent: these days, the twenty minutes or so she had in the car by herself each morning and evening – with her own choice of music on the stereo and no one asking her questions about who she thought would win if Donald Trump and a giant squid were to wrestle each other – felt like a spa day.

Work had recently been even more full-on than usual. She'd had to juggle the school holidays with frantic preparation for the launch of her new venture, where she would be transitioning from her role as Operations Director at Zero, the fashion software business where she had worked since she left school, to Managing Director of Pert. Pert was the new subsidiary business her boss – and owner of Zero – Leroy had come up with. At the time, Zero had been on the brink of collapse, but thanks to Tom's incredible generosity and his offer of investment into the business – using the money he'd made when he'd been working in the banking industry – they'd not only been able to save Zero, but to set up Pert too. She'd been flat out brainstorming their new products – bras that actually fit, and didn't lacerate your nipple in the process of keeping your breasts above knee level – and couldn't wait to make the new business the success she knew it had the potential to be.

Zero was as busy and frenetic as ever; she parked her car outside and walked through a cacophony of office noise. Siobhan, her assistant for more years than either of them could remember, was involved in a full-blown argument with Mark, one of the sales guys, over the destiny of her office chair.

'It's coming with me.' Siobhan, arms crossed, was absolutely adamant.

'It bloody isn't.' Mark shook his head. 'That's property of Zero, and as of next week, you won't be working as part of Zero, will you? So that chair doesn't belong to you.'

'It *does* belong to me, I *will* be working for Zero, and you can shut the fuck up before I remove your testicles with a spoon and crush them underneath my stiletto heel. I've worked hard for that chair; perhaps when you start bringing in some new business instead of wasting time arguing with me you might end up with enough on your commission statement to mean you can afford to buy one of your own.'

Game, set and match to Siobhan. Gemma looked on in amusement as her assistant stuck about twenty labels with her name onto the back of her leather, high-back office chair and left Mark to slink back to his own chair – fabric, missing one arm, clearly inferior – on the other side of the room.

If Gemma was honest, she had completely underestimated how much time and effort it would take to set up Pert. In her head, she was just going to come into the office on her first day in post and start phoning up bra manufacturers to partner with.

In reality, of course, there was so much more to it than that. The registration of the new company, the liaising with their legal team and accountants, the branding, the discussions with Leroy about new hires and bringing across existing key members of staff . . . it had been endless. And then some space had become available in the purpose-built building in which Zero leased their offices, and Gemma and her new team were now about to move into an office of their very own.

Leaving Siobhan boxing up everything they were going to need in their new space – probably including Mark's testicles, if he made any more moves to acquire her chair – Gemma dumped her laptop on her desk and wandered over to see Leroy. Dressed as flamboyantly as ever – today in chrome PVC jogging bottoms and a hot-pink T-shirt – he looked delighted to see her.

'Gem! How are you doing? How was your break?'

She looked at him sternly. 'Leroy, what have I told you about things you don't say to people with children? Annual leave when you spend it looking after anyone under the age of twelve is never, ever a "break". Coming back here and having a wee without having to pause mid-flow – though it does wonders for your pelvic floor muscles, I'm not going to lie – to stop your youngest child causing grievous bodily harm to your oldest child, on account of the fact that he "looked at me" . . . now that's a break!'

Leroy looked suitably chastened. 'Sorry, Gem. I do think of you, you know, when I'm sat with Jeremy in some high-end bar drinking obscenely priced cocktails until four in the morning, safe in the knowledge that I can lie in until midday the next dayaaaaaarrrgghhh. I'm sorry, I'm sorry!' He held his hands up in mock surrender as Gemma picked up his treasured phone and made to snap it in half. 'Not the iPhone!'

Gemma's face grew serious as she thought about the task she had ahead of her. Not for the first time, imposter syndrome threatened to overwhelm her. 'Leroy, are you sure I can do this? Are you sure I'm the right person to head up Pert?' They both sniggered; the name they'd come up with for the new company had caused them untold amounts of amusement, something Gemma hoped would appeal to prospective customers. 'I just . . . I don't know.' She looked down at the floor. 'Some days I feel like I can do anything I put my mind to . . . and then there are other days when just getting everyone out of the house on time feels like an impossibility. I mean . . . are you sure?'

Leroy looked at her sternly. 'Gem, how often have we had this conversation? You're my right-hand woman, yes? There's no one in the business who I would trust more to make Pert a success. Now shut up with your self-indulgent whinging and go find me a bra that will simultaneously stop one's breasts from hanging round one's knees while also not slicing one's nipple with an underwire, or whatever the fuck you tell me bras do.' He looked appalled. 'The things you women put yourselves through.'

Gemma laughed grimly. 'Tell me about it.'

Mrs Goldman might have said the same at that point in time. In fact, she'd arguably have snapped at Gemma that she had it easy, compared to the baptism of fire the Head was currently putting herself through.

Mrs Goldman had never really intended to go into teaching. Small children had always horrified her, with the mess and disorder and chaos they appeared to create wherever they went. Nevertheless, she had found herself at teaching college after her father had suggested teaching would be a suitable career for her. Without any other real aspirations, she duly picked up her teaching qualification and spent her first few years of employment in the trenches of KS1 – or 'primary school', as it was simply known then, before the Department for Education went on a single-minded mission to ruin education for parents, pupils and teachers alike.

The sheer quantity of bodily fluids she had to deal with – really, she should have gone into farming, or midwifery: neither could be any worse than this – meant that Mrs Goldman soon found herself with one goal: to get the hell out of a classroom. She had every confidence that education could actually suit her rather well ... just so long as she didn't have to have anything to do with the children.

Before too long she had got her wish, climbing the career ladder to be deputy head and then finally achieving her first role as headmistress in a school of her own. A natural leader, she had proved to be impressively successful, working in two other schools before joining Redcoats fifteen years previously.

And now, for the first time, she found herself with no alternative but to go back into the classroom. She shuddered at the very thought. This wasn't just any classroom either: this was the Year 3 classroom, filled with the feral classmates of Ava, Rosie and Satin. Simon Barnes. Noah Hardcastle. The stuff of school legends. And not the good ones, either.

Bracing herself that morning, Mrs Goldman had buttoned up her starched linen shirt before walking decisively into the temporary classroom that had been allocated to Year 3. She would source a new supply teacher; until then, she would teach. After all, how bad could it be?

'Mrs Goldman, do you know how babies are made?' Ava stood wide eyed, the very picture of innocence, in front of her teacher, who was physically holding apart two of the boys in the class: Noah and Simon (who else). Simon had been threatening to bite off Noah's little toe.

'Ava, I am busy right now.' Mrs Goldman gave the little girl one of her sternest looks. 'Kindly return to your desk and complete the worksheet I gave you.'

'But *do* you?' Ava was unmoving. 'Because if you don't, I can help you. It's a while since you have done any teaching, isn't it, and so I thought I might be able to help. And I know that sex education is one of the bits that teachers dread having to talk to children about the most. Mr Jones told me. So what happens is, there is a sperm and there is an egg. The egg is in the mummy and the sperm is in the daddy. The sperm has to get to the egg, and do you know how that happens?'

'AVA, kindly return to your desk. I don't expect to have to ask you again.'

For a moment, the two of them stared each other out. Mrs Goldman had no confidence in who was going to break first.

'Or I will have to cancel football practice at lunch time.'

'FINE.' It was the only thing that could have persuaded Ava to capitulate. 'But you will be sorry you didn't find out the answer when it turns out you're going to have a BABY.'

Dear God, no wonder Miss Collins hadn't turned up.

The rest of the morning continued in a similar vein. One of the quieter boys in the class, George Lancaster, was found in a corner of the room showing an enthralled selection of the class the series of condoms he'd taken from his dad's bedside drawer, not knowing what they were. 'Look at all of the different colours, and they smell like strawberries,' said one of the girls in wonder as Mrs Goldman walked over to see what was going on. 'Wouldn't you love one of these lovely things, Mrs Goldman? They are like swimming costumes for your fingers.'

At break time there was a brief – and very welcome – hiatus as the class streamed out into the playground, Ava marshalling half of them over to a makeshift goal at the side of the field 'to practise taking penalties, because we don't want to be as rubbish as England usually are when we get to play in the World Cup'. Mrs Goldman exhaled, and was about to escape to the sanctity of her office, when Noah raced over to her from where he'd been playing football.

'Mrs Goldman, Mrs Goldman,' he groaned, clutching his groin. 'Simon's just kicked me in the BALL SACK.'

Mrs Goldman let out an internal silent scream. Now she understood the rumours that Miss Thompson used to keep an emergency bottle of crème de menthe in her handbag at school. This couldn't go on. Either she needed to find a substitute teacher – and fast – or she was going to have to seriously consider feigning her own death.

CHAPTER THREE

Making an extra effort on account of it being the first day
of term, Gemma managed to amaze both herself and her
children by not being late to collect them from after-school
club. 'We didn't even have to sit outside in Mr Cook's car
and wait for you after he locked the school up,' said Ava in
tones of surprise and wonder. The incident she was referring
to had happened once – *once* – after Gemma had been stuck
getting back from a meeting in London. Following his regi-
mented timetable to the letter, Mr Cook had indeed locked
up the school buildings, showing an unusual consideration
for duty of care by not actually abandoning the children on
the pavement but instead sitting with them in his car, while
Ava lectured him on the dangers of smoking, and how 'you
need to stop this very soon, Mr Cook, or otherwise you will
die a horrible death and your lungs will go all black and
mouldy. You are a very silly man.' The dressing-down Mr
Cook had given Gemma after she'd finally arrived, almost

thirty minutes late, had ensured that such an occurrence never happened again, but that didn't stop Ava reminding her mum about it approximately every second day.

Having exchanged the usual pleasantries – 'How was your day?' 'S'alright.' 'What did you do at school today?' 'Don't know.' 'What did you have for lunch?' 'Can't remember.' – anyone who ever said that you should treasure the precious early years with your children had clearly never experienced the joy of an attempt at an after-school conversation – Gemma announced to the children that she would be going out that night.

'You're leaving us ON OUR OWN?' Ava was wide-eyed in wonder, no doubt already thinking about the Childline call she would get to make.

'No, Ava, funnily enough I will not be leaving you on your own. Primarily on the grounds that I would rather not come back to find the house destroyed. Jon has offered to look after the two of you as well as Rosie and Ella, so Becky and I can go for a quick drink together.'

'Good.' Ava nodded approvingly. 'I like Jon. He does not make me do stuff that I don't want to do.'

Knowing Jon – and Ava – he probably didn't stand a fighting chance of getting Ava to do anything that she didn't want to do.

'Can Dad not look after us?' Sam asked.

Gemma inhaled. Nick had actually called her at work that day to tell her he'd definitely been offered the job in Berlin. 'Which is in Germany, not America, did you know that?' he'd said in tones of amazement. 'It's a fixed-term, twelve-month contract, so I'm not really going to be gone for all that long, not in the grand scheme of things.'

'And the kids?' Gemma had asked tersely. 'Your agreement that you would see them regularly?' She felt her anger rising. 'They're not toys, Nick. You can't drop in and out of their lives whenever you want to. It's not fair on them ... and it's not fair on me, either.'

Nick had been full of platitudes, promising her that he'd talk to the kids about it, that it would all be okay. Gemma didn't believe him, not for a moment, but she was damned if she was going to do his dirty work for him yet again.

'Not tonight,' she settled on for the time being, and both Sam and Ava seemed quite content with that.

The three of them duly knocked on Jon and Becky's front door shortly after seven that evening. Becky answered; in contrast to her usual sprightly and perfectly groomed appearance, she looked absolutely exhausted, dressed in skinny jeans paired with an oversized checked shirt and with her thick black hair scraped back into a bun.

'Come on in, guys.' She gestured to the children, who needed no encouragement; already Gemma could see Sam making a beeline for the TV (Becky and Jon had Sky, which in Sam's eyes made them officially the Coolest Parents In The World) and Ava hassling Jon to come out in the back garden with them 'because we need to practise our tackling, and you are really good to practise on, Jon, because you don't complain when I kick you too hard or about that time when I accidentally knocked you over and you fell into Becky's flowerbed'.

'Your husband's a hero, you know?'

'Tell me about it.' Becky smiled at long-suffering Jon,

already being marshalled through the back door by Rosie and Ava, Ella on his hip and Boris, their absolute fucking liability of a golden retriever, bounding outside with them. 'Come on, let's get out of here before he realises quite what he's let himself in for and changes his mind.'

It was a beautiful evening, the sky glowing a perfect shade of blue as the two friends walked down their tree-lined street to the pub just a few roads along. Gemma was excited to hear how Becky's new job was going.

'So come on, then.' They had settled themselves in a booth at the back of the pub with two large glasses of Sauvignon Blanc and packets of salt-and-vinegar crisps. 'Are you absolutely loving it? I want to hear all about it.'

Becky smiled. 'I really am. The people I'm working with are so lovely, and what we're trying to do is so important. I genuinely feel this is my chance to help to change the world.' She crunched down on a crisp. 'I'm not going to lie, though, Gem: it's an uphill struggle. I don't think I realised quite how tough it would be until I properly started making calls to companies. You only have to go and look at Companies House and search for the owner or CEO of a business. Nine times out of ten, they're going to be a white, able-bodied man. They're not interested in what we've got to say. And why? Because they're happy with the status quo. Of course they are. The status quo suits them quite nicely, with their fat salaries and obscene bonuses. They've got to where they are partly because they've closed off the opportunities open to anyone who has a different skin colour or disability or set of genitals to them. I can hammer on those doors as loudly as I like,

Gem, but until they decide they're willing to at least unlock them, it's going to be fucking tough.'

Becky took a sip of her wine, and screwed up her face. 'Urrrgghh. This is horrible. What sort of wine did you order?'

Gemma looked perplexed. 'It's just Sauvignon Blanc. It's what we usually drink in here. Mine tastes fine. Here, have a sip.' She pushed her glass over to Becky, who lifted it to her lips.

'No, that's fucking awful too. Can't you taste it? It's like the bottle's been corked.' Becky stood up. 'I'm going to take them back; that's outrageous, that they'd expect us to drink something that tastes like that.'

Gemma tasted Becky's wine. It was absolutely fine, exactly the same as hers. What on earth was her friend going on about?

Becky reached her hands out for the glasses, but as she did so, a light bulb went off in Gemma's head.

'No. Don't take the wine back.'

Becky looked askance. 'What do you mean? I'm not drinking that shit. Honestly, Gem, you have to learn to stand up for yourself and stop being so politely British all the time.'

Gemma took a deep breath. 'No, I mean don't take the wine back ... because I don't think there's anything wrong with it.'

Becky looked confused. 'Then what ... ?'

'Becky,' Gemma looked her friend straight in the eyes. 'Is there any possible chance, that you might just be ... pregnant?'

*

It took a good forty minutes and a strong cup of (decaf) coffee to calm Becky down. She sat there, compulsively folding her crisp packet over and over while staring at Gemma in a slightly histrionic fashion. 'I can't be ... I can't be ...' she kept muttering to herself.

Gemma – who had finished her own wine and started on Becky's – sought to bring her back to reality. 'Listen, Becks, calm down. Let's run through the facts again. Your last period was six, maybe seven weeks ago, you're not totally sure but whenever it was, it was a period for sure and not just spotting, because when you pulled out your tampon in the toilet cubicle in Tesco' – she winced – 'a clot shot out with it and stuck to the back of the cubicle door. God, the things we share with each other.'

Becky managed a weak smile. 'Could have been worse. It could have skidded out underneath the toilet door, straight into the queue of waiting pensioners. Not that that has ever happened to me, nope, absolutely not.'

Gemma shook her head to get images of blood clots and startled pensioners out of it. 'Okay, so you definitely had a period then ... but nothing since?'

Becky shook her head. 'Nope, definitely nothing since then.'

'And you didn't think to take a test?'

Becky looked sheepish. 'I'd kind of optimistically convinced myself that maybe it was just the early menopause.'

'In other words, you buried your head in the sand and hoped it would all go away?' Gemma looked stern.

'Well ... there is that too. I've just been busy, Gem, with

my new job and everything . . . And anyway, we don't *know* that I'm pregnant. Maybe it is the early menopause!'

Gemma took another sip of her wine. 'Maybe it is. But I guess there's one way to find out for sure.' She took out her purse. 'You stay here. I'm popping to the late-night chemist and buying you a pregnancy test.'

Twenty minutes later, she was back, brandishing a cardboard box. 'Right, here you go. Get on with it.'

Becky looked appalled. 'What do you mean, get on with it? I don't have to do it right now, surely. There's no rush.'

It was rare for Gemma to take control in their relationship; the naturally extroverted Becky defaulted to the position of leader, which suited Gemma down to the ground. Today, however, would be a notable exception.

Gemma grabbed Becky by the shoulders and frog-marched her to the toilets. 'No. Here. Now. Piss. On. The. Bastarding. Stick.'

The test was positive. Of course it was positive; even Becky herself, in her happy state of complete and utter denial, hadn't for one moment considered that it would be anything other than positive, from the second Gemma had raised the possibility. That was what happened when you didn't bother to sort out your contraceptive affairs and then had wild and insatiable Making-up Sex in the middle of the kitchen floor with your husband after you'd thought you were on the brink of divorce and had then realised you'd got it all totally wrong. A wry smile formed on Becky's face as she remembered that night. She should just have given him a blowjob: they might be about as exciting as watching paint dry and leave you convinced that at any moment your jaw was going to dislocate, but at least they didn't get you up the duff.

Perhaps they might have got away with it if it had been just that one night, but with Jon now no longer in the office 24/7, and their relationship newly rekindled, the entire summer had been something of a honeymoon period for the two of them. And yes, they had used condoms, but hadn't Becky known since she'd been a teenager how relatively unreliable they were as a form of contraception? She had always prided herself in being the exception to the rule. It was a shame that also seemed to be the case when it came to the percentage chances of her getting pregnant while using contraception.

'Okay.' Gemma had led a shell-shocked Becky back into the bar, once she had washed urine off her hands (both women agreed it was a physical impossibility to take a pregnancy test without weeing on your hand and halfway up your arm) and they were sitting back down in their booth. 'So what are you going to do?'

Becky looked at Gemma. 'What do you mean, what am I going to do? We're going to finish our drinks, we're going to go home, and then I'm going to bed, because I'm absolutely bloody exhausted, which is—'

'Another major symptom of early pregnancy! I thought you looked tired when you opened the door earlier – now I know why!'

'Shit, you mean,' said Becky flatly. 'I look shit. My skin's gone to pot, my mouth is absolutely covered with fucking ulcers … I now know why my skinny jeans wouldn't do

34

up – and it's only going to get fucking worse. Fuck, Gem, what *am* I going to do? Am I really going to put myself through all that again?'

It wasn't a question Gemma could answer for her friend. She'd surprised herself by actually rather enjoying both of her pregnancies; celebrating the feeling of the growing life inside of her while using being pregnant as an excuse to sit on her arse and eat as much cake as she wanted to.

Becky, she knew, though, had found things very different, hating her swelling stomach, the restrictions of pregnancy and the way everyone around her kept telling her to rest up and be careful. She'd had long, difficult, back-to-back labours – with pre labours lasting for the best part of a week – and delighted in telling her dramatic and gruesome birth stories to anyone who would listen, swearing on everything she held dear to her that hell would freeze over before she would consider putting herself through that again.

Such thoughts were clearly also running through Becky's head: she was visibly wincing as she looked down at the pregnancy test she still held in her hand.

'Becks?' Becky looked up. 'Why don't we head back? I think it's probably time for you and Jon to have a bit of a chat.'

The house was surprisingly quiet when they let themselves in with Becky's key. Ella was in bed; Ava, Rosie, Sam and Jon were gathered around the TV with Boris; Ava had taken charge of the remote control and was now talking them through a blow-by-blow account of the latest

Eden Hazard goal. 'And you see, Sam, THAT is how you kick a football,' she said scathingly. 'I think that if you were in the Olympics doing sport you would get no points at all.' Sam looked wounded, and Ava, unusually, took pity on him. 'Well, maybe you might manage to get one point. Because I do think, if you properly tried, that you might actually be quite good at roly-polys.' Sam looked pleadingly at his mum and Becky. Jon was valiantly keeping a straight face.

'Okay, come on, kids, time we got back. It's a school night, and we know what you're like to try and get out of bed in the morning, Ava. You do like your sleep.' Thanking Jon, Gemma took Ava by the hand and ushered both children down the path to their own house. Becky closed the door to the sounds of Ava telling her mum, 'I do not like to sleep; it's just that I like to be difficult.'

Jon had taken Rosie upstairs to bed and so Becky busied herself with straightening the cushions on the sofa and tidying the few bits that had been left out. Friends always commented on how immaculate their home was; it was a source of pride to Becky, who struggled to stomach disorder (Gemma's house frequently tested her nerves). God, the chaos a small baby would cause. Becky winced at the very thought.

'Cup of tea, love?' Jon came back downstairs and kissed Becky on the top of her head. 'Or do you fancy a glass of wine?'

She shook her head emphatically. 'No, tea, definitely. I've got work again in the morning, don't forget.' She was absolutely exhausted; the thought of having to get up in less than twelve short hours and head off to the office practically reduced her to tears.

Jon boiled the kettle and Becky pondered how to break the news of her pregnancy to him. Given her flair for planning, her pregnancy with Rosie had been announced with aplomb: she'd taken out a series of adverts in the local paper, the first word of each collectively spelling out: 'We Are Going To Have A Baby!' (It had arguably been a bit much for Jon, who struggled to remember the simple, four-digit code for their burglar alarm and was unable to find his cycling jacket even when it was literally hanging right in front of his face, owing to his infamous ability to look for things without actually using his eyes. He would have completely missed what his wife was trying to tell him if it hadn't been for Becky sitting down next to him with the paper and physically spelling it out for him.)

With Ella, Jon had been on hand while she'd done the pregnancy test and they'd discovered to their shared delight that they had a second child on the way.

And now, here she was again. She couldn't entirely decide how Jon was likely to react. On the one hand, he was Mr Laid Back – so much so that their combined friends and family collectively referred to him as Lovely Jon. On the other hand, their relationship had been through quite the upheaval in the last year. There were times when Becky genuinely hadn't been sure if they would make it through. Would Jon fear – just as she did – that an unplanned pregnancy might be the straw that broke the camel's back?

She couldn't quite bring herself to say the words 'I'm pregnant'. Maybe she would just hint her way around it and hope that he worked it out without her ever actually having to tell him.

Jon came and sat down at the table with their tea. Boris was lying under it, chewing happily on his favourite toy, a well-masticated dildo that he'd once stolen from an Ann Summers party a friend of Becky's had thrown at hers. Becky had convinced herself that over the years Boris had slobbered and gnawed at it so much that its true nature as an object was no longer recognisable. Friends of hers frequently reminded her that she was kidding herself.

'Here you go, love. So, how was your evening? Gemma okay?'

She sipped at her tea. 'It was fine, but I tell you something, I am *so* tired.' She added a large yawn for dramatic effect. 'Absolutely *exhausted*.'

He looked concerned. 'Maybe it's the new job. I guess the first few weeks were always going to be tough, while you get used to the rhythm of it all.' He winked. 'Early night?'

God, that was the last thing she needed, Jon thinking she was angling for a shag. It was bloody shagging that had got them into this mess in the first place! She sought to bring him back on track. 'I don't think it's the job. Actually, the last time I felt this tired ... was when I was first pregnant with Ella.' She looked at him meaningfully.

Jon looked thoughtful. 'Goodness. I wonder ... do you think we should see about finding a nursery for Ella?' He ran one hand over his stubbled chin. 'It's not that I'm trying to get out of looking after her – she could go on one of the days when I'm in the office and you're at home. It's just, spending more time with her, I really think she could do with a bit more social interaction and stimulation. What do you think?'

What did she think? Actually – Ella starting nursery wasn't the worst idea in the world, not if she was going to have a new baby to contend with soon. Becky caught herself. She hadn't decided yet if she was actually going to have this baby. It was something she needed to properly talk through with her husband.

If he ever caught on, that was. Okay, so her subtle hints hadn't worked. Standing up, Becky pushed her stomach out as far as it would go and looked at Jon. 'Do I look different to you, darling?'

He looked at her and shook his head. 'No, not at all. Are you worried about looking tired? Because you don't, you know. You look as utterly beautiful as you always have done, every single day since the moment we first met.'

At any other time she might have welcomed the compliment, but this was not that time. Fuck's sake. Becky sat back down. Her husband had never been one for subtlety: that much had been clear from the years she'd spent trying to seduce him, prior to them getting together, when he'd once looked over, as she was giving him her very best 'come to bed' eyes, and asked her if she had heartburn, he suffered terribly from it himself, and would she like a Rennie?

She was clearly going to have to make this more obvious.

Reaching into her handbag, which was hanging on the chair behind her, she located the pregnancy test and took it out, placing it on the table between them as Jon babbled on about nurseries and how he was going to commit to researching what was available in the local area, that Becky shouldn't think he would leave it to her, that he was really serious about wanting them to be a genuine partnership.

'Okay, great.' Becky gestured at the pregnancy test, lying on the table roughly two feet away from Jon. 'Do you know what this is?'

He looked at it dismissively. 'Oh, probably something that Ava and Rosie were playing with. The way those two girls were going on about football. It wouldn't surprise me in the slightest if one of them made the England ladies' team one day, although actually Ava was telling me that we shouldn't refer to it as the England ladies' team, it's just one of the England football teams, and she's right, when you think about it; the moment you refer to it as women's football then it suggests it's inferior to men's football, which is simply known as "football"—'

'I AM FUCKING PREGNANT!' roared Becky, standing up and brandishing the piss-soaked plastic stick in Jon's face. 'I really could not give a shit about the ins and outs of men's or women's football right at this moment, and this is not something that Ava and Rosie were playing with, it is a fucking pregnancy test, that I pissed on this evening in the toilets of the pub, after my wine tasted funny and Gemma suggested that I might be pregnant and she bought me a test and I pissed on it and also all over my hand and now I am pregnant only you were too stupid to realise and WHAT THE ACTUAL FUCK ARE WE GOING TO DO?'

There was a stunned pause.

In his early twenties, still slightly mystified by women,

Jon had read a series of articles that advised unwitting males on the best way to respond to some of the extremes of emotions they might see their partner or girlfriend experience. Jon had treated such articles like his personal bible, and had never forgotten their cast-iron, catch-all recommendation in the case of extreme crisis.

'Would you like some chocolate?' he tentatively suggested.

At the very moment that Jon was buying up all the chocolate in south London, Mrs Goldman was sitting alone in her living room, Radio 4 playing softly in the background, as she wondered quite what to do. This could not go on. She was not a teacher, and the children knew it. Her usual command and composure had been tested to the limit as Ava persisted in her attempts to find out if she knew how babies were made –'And you need to make sure you find the right hole, it's the front bottom, Mrs Goldman, not the back bottom' – and Noah Hardcastle told Mrs Goldman that he 'don't give a shit about ignorant rocks' – 'It's *igneous*, Noah, and we don't have that kind of language in this school' – 'or whatever they're called, Miss'.

Her phone calls to the supply agencies had been in vain. With teachers continuing to leave the profession in droves – Mrs Goldman composing yet another strongly worded letter to the Department for Education in her head as she worked her way through her list of agencies – there were simply no supply teachers available. The soonest the agencies would be able to get anyone to her would be at the end of the month. There was no way Mrs Goldman could take a whole month of Year 3. The way she felt now, she doubted she could take another hour of Year 3.

All out of ideas, she was staring blankly at the flocked wallpaper on her chimney breast when, to her surprise, the doorbell rang. At – she checked the clock on the mantelpiece – almost quarter to nine on a Tuesday evening! Who in the world would be turning up at her house at that time of night?

Expecting a case of mistaken identity, or perhaps Derek from number eighty-four, come to ask if he could borrow a drop of milk (his wife had recently died, poor Derek, and he was yet to grasp the necessity of actually going out shopping in order to procure the household basics), you could have knocked Mrs Goldman down with a feather when, to her surprise, she saw standing on her doorstep not Derek, nor a confused delivery driver . . . but Miss Thompson.

Angela Thompson had taught in Mrs Goldman's school up until the start of the previous school year when, without warning, she had suddenly upped and left, running off with the man she declared to be the love of her life to the South of France, to join his touring theatre company as Artistic Director. To say she had left Mrs Goldman in the lurch would be something of an understatement: she had been fortunate beyond belief to find Tom Jones (whose parents had clearly been having a laugh when they'd named him), a fresh-faced NQT whose previous school had had their funding cut, and who had therefore been available at very short notice to step into the breach.

'I'm so sorry, Sharon darling,' Angela had written, on the

back of a postcard depicting Romeo and Juliet, those two great Shakespearean lovers, 'but one doesn't meet the great love of their life every day now, do they, and I felt honour bound to give in to my wildest desires and follow him back to France. To the theatre! My every dream come true! I know that you will be furious with me, deserting you like this, but know that you and Redcoats will never be far from my thoughts. Who knows: you could bring the children out here on a school trip next year! With fondest love and greatest affection, Ange xxx.'

Mrs Goldman had torn the postcard up, stamped on it, and used it to line the litter tray of her large grey tom, Smokey. Never, she declared, did she want to see that ridiculous woman again.

But now, it seemed, such a declaration had been in vain, as here was Miss Thompson, larger than life, still clad in her ridiculous combination of sensible Hush Puppies ('it's my knees, darling, they're not what they used to be, not since I danced that cancan on the stage at the Moulin Rouge') and tweed, accessorised with clouds of brightly coloured chiffon scarves and what appeared to be half of the stock inventory of Accessorize.

Mrs Goldman, well-practised from her years of headship, recovered her composure rapidly. 'Angela,' she said, in a voice that was about as welcoming as the Grim Reaper. 'Can I help you?'

To her utter surprise, Miss Thompson burst into tears.

Twenty minutes later and the wretched woman was sat in Mrs Goldman's favourite armchair, steaming cup of tea in her hand, and Smokey – the absolute traitor – settled

43

comfortably on her knees. 'Such a lovely pussy,' cooed Miss Thompson, who seemed to have made a dramatic recovery from her outburst at the front door.

Mrs Goldman sat opposite her, back ramrod straight. 'Let's not beat around the bush, Angela. You left me in a shockingly difficult position when you disappeared at the start of last year, I don't mind telling you. I was incredibly fortunate to be able to find a replacement, and we had no end of trouble with Year 2 before things finally sorted themselves out. So, assuming you're here to offer me tickets to your latest production, I'm afraid it's with no regret whatsoever that I am going to have to decline.'

Miss Thompson shook her head emphatically. 'No, no, no. That's absolutely not the case. Sharon, darling' – Mrs Goldman gritted her teeth at the endearment – 'please, hear me out. I know things have been strained between us since I disappeared with Jean-Claude, but I'm actually here to help you.'

With little alternative, Mrs Goldman sat back as Miss Thompson launched, in her usual dramatic style, into an epic tale of everything that had befallen her since she'd left Redcoats. At first, it had all seemed to be going so well. Jean-Claude was a charming and attentive lover – a mental image Mrs Goldman was now going to have to scour her brain with bleach in order to remove – and his theatre company was thriving. Miss Thompson had been given free rein to create and rehearse new performances – '*Trolley Follies;* just imagine it, Sharon: an entire stage filled with bright young things dancing a specially choreographed routine that I based around my experience with a particularly difficult trolley in the car park of Aldi one day' – and life had indeed appeared to be wonderful.

All, however, had not been as it seemed. Jean-Claude had grown increasingly distant, spending more and more of his time away from the house he and Miss Thompson had been sharing, 'not even returning for my special treacle suet pudding! Imagine that, Sharon!' Mrs Goldman, uncertain as to whether the 'special treacle suet pudding' she was referring to was a literal pudding or some horrific metaphor, shuddered darkly.

Eventually, things had come to a head. Jean-Claude had approached Miss Thompson after curtain-down on the opening night of his latest production (*Man. Bat. Ball.* – featuring a naked man, a cricket bat and a giant inflatable beach ball, all of which sat silent and motionless on the stage for forty-six minutes before the curtain fell, to rapturous applause and talks of a potential Molière Award) and told her he could live a lie no longer. While he still felt genuine affection for her, their relationship was not to be. He was, in fact, romantically entwined with the lead actor of *Man. Bat. Ball.*, a dashing young Frenchman named Gabriel. 'I don't even want to think where that cricket bat had been during rehearsals,' sobbed Miss Thompson, wiping her eyes on Smokey's fur.

Furious at her lover's betrayal, Miss Thompson had stormed out into the night, and had hitchhiked her way up the country, before arriving at Calais and boarding a ferry back to England. During the journey, she had happened to meet up with a school party from the local area, just returning from a late-summer exchange visit. Miss Thompson and the Head had got chatting, Miss Thompson had mentioned that she had previously worked at Redcoats and the Head in turn had told her of the arson attack, which had made the local news.

'And that's when I knew, Sharon darling. This has all happened for a reason. Jean-Claude's betrayal was designed to lead me back to you. Redcoats needs me. So here I am, ready to do whatever you want in order to make amends for my previous misdemeanours. Just tell me, Sharon. Whatever you need. I will do it.'

Mrs Goldman had never been a particularly religious woman, but right there and then she genuinely considered dropping to her knees in grateful thanks. She was saved! Never would she have to step foot in a classroom with Year 3 again!

'Angela,' said Mrs Goldman in measured tones, 'how would you like to take on Year 3, effective from nine a.m. tomorrow morning.'

'Wonderful,' breathed Miss Thompson, tears of happiness misting behind her glasses.

'I quite agree,' said Mrs Goldman, exhaling for what felt like the first time in about three days. 'I feel this calls for a little celebratory sherry. What do you reckon?'

CHAPTER FOUR

Filled with renewed optimism, Mrs Goldman arrived at the school early the next morning, passing Mr Cook, who was already in situ at the school gates with what appeared to be a selection of homemade security screening equipment. 'Morning, Mrs Goldman.' He nodded his head. 'Right, can I just ask you to put your bag in here' – he gestured to a small metal cabinet – 'and then step through the screening device?'

Mrs Goldman took a closer look at the equipment. 'Cyril ... is this a microwave? And a wardrobe with the back missing?'

Mr Cook looked askance – 'How did you know that?' – before recovering his composure and tapping his finger meaningfully on the side of his nose. 'Ask me no questions and I'll tell you no lies. Those little buggers might have burnt down part of our school, but they're not getting past me again. I'm telling you, ma'am. Every visitor to the site will be personally screened by me. And if they even consider any funny business, I'll ... I'll ... I'll have their guts for garters!'

She couldn't doubt his commitment to the cause. Hiding her smile, the headmistress removed her handbag from the microwave and sidestepped the wardrobe. 'Thank you, Cyril,' she said. 'I appreciate the work you've put in here. But I think we can be confident that the person who attempted to burn down the school wasn't me.'

He let her go, but she could see from the look on his face that he was far from convinced. 'You say that, ma'am,' he called after her, 'but on them detective shows, it's always the ones you least expect who did it. Inside insurance job, you see.'

God, she really needed to get him to shut up before her visitors from the LEA arrived.

By LEA standards, they had moved surprisingly quickly, presumably because while it was quite possible to ignore multiple buckets catching the drips from multiple leaks around the school due to the roof being entirely unfit for purpose, an Actual Fire was somewhat more dramatic and therefore worthy of their interest. Having requested an emergency meeting, they had informed Mrs Goldman that they would honour Redcoats with a personal visit – no doubt so they could gawp ghoulishly over the burnt-out classrooms, just as every single parent and pupil had done since they'd arrived back at the start of term. Mrs Goldman had actually had to stop Vivienne's son Tartan from selling tickets.

Rachel, the stalwart school secretary, showed the two

men who arrived promptly for their 10 a.m. meeting into Mrs Goldman's office, setting out an array of chocolate biscuits on one of the plates from the kitchen in front of them. Mrs Goldman frowned: she had told Rachel to hold the biscuits. Getting additional funding out of the LEA was hard enough without them thinking you had money to burn on luxury chocolate biscuits.

'Good morning, Sharon,' said the slightly grimmer looking one of the two, although that wasn't saying much, with the less grim-looking one also looking as though someone had simultaneously stolen his last Rolo, let down his tyres and taken a dump in his briefcase. 'Thanks very much for allowing us to visit you this morning. It's obviously a terrible thing, what has happened to the school. Have there been any further updates with the police inquiries?'

Mrs Goldman shook her head. They had of course immediately handed over all CCTV footage to the police but, with the culprits professionally kitted out in black jackets and balaclavas, a positive ID seemed unlikely.

'It's a pity.' Grimmest shook his head. 'Appalling behaviour. One has to hope that it wasn't anyone connected to the school. I appreciate that, despite your Ofsted grading, some of your pupils are ... challenging.'

'I can assure you,' Mrs Goldman retorted, ignoring the veiled dig at her student population, 'that none of the students at Redcoats will have been responsible for this horrendous crime.' She held back from adding that half of them couldn't get themselves sufficiently coordinated to get their coats on the right way around, let alone instigate a major arson attack.

'Yes. Well. That's as may be.' The slightly less grim one dismissed her assertions, biting down into the thick chocolate surrounding the Mint Club he'd picked out from Rachel's selection. 'Either way, it doesn't change what we're here to discuss today, which is the future of Redcoats.'

Outside the headmistress's office, Ava was lurking. Surprised by the appearance of Miss Thompson in her classroom that morning, who she remembered without enthusiasm from when she'd taught them for the first term of Year 2, she'd asked where Mrs Goldman was and was told that she had a meeting with two very important visitors from the LEA.

Ava had heard about LEAs: they were the people who decided when schools could have more money. Ava quite liked Redcoats, but it was seriously lacking in one area, which was its absence of football provision. Honestly, thought Ava to herself, they couldn't even get organised to paint some white lines on the school field so that they had a pitch marked out. Instead all they had was a stupid running track, and some makeshift goals that Mr Jones had fashioned for them out of some pipe lagging, which fell over the moment the wind blew or Ava did a perfect first touch in their general direction.

Ava had long felt that the time was ripe for Redcoats to build its own football stadium, and now here, as if handed to her on a plate, was the perfect opportunity. The men from the LEA were bound to like football, and if Ava went in and demonstrated her skills they would be able to see how good she was and that she would definitely end up playing for England – the men's team, Ava didn't believe in being restricted to playing for the ladies, 'because the men get more money, and it's not fair that I shouldn't get as much money, just because I don't have a penis' – if only she had a football stadium at school to practise in. Ava wasn't sure how much football stadiums cost to build, but it couldn't be that much.

Telling Miss Thompson – who was heavily distracted pleading with Simon Barnes, who was currently standing on one of the tables, claiming he was allergic to carpets, and refusing to get down – that she needed to go to the medical room, Ava instead made a beeline for Mrs Goldman's office. To her delight, the door had been left open a crack, and she could hear the conversation taking place inside.

Mrs Goldman felt like she was caught in the middle of a nightmare. Even teaching Year 3 again would have been a positive pleasure compared to this. She couldn't entirely believe what she was hearing.

'So, let me get this straight.' She held herself together to keep her voice from quavering. She could have killed for another glass of that sherry she had drunk with Miss Thompson last night. A pint-sized glass.

'You're telling me, that what you propose ... is not to rebuild the classrooms, but instead, at the end of this academic year ... to close Redcoats down. That you don't believe the age of the building justifies the cost of the work required, and that you intend to merge this school – my school – with St Catherine's, which is on a purpose-built site with space for expansion.'

Grimmest nodded, his expression becoming microscopically less grim in his clear approval that she had understood.

'That's right. It simply doesn't make financial sense to do anything else. We've had the building surveyors out, they've estimated a minimum cost of seventy thousand pounds. Given this whole site will likely be bulldozed and given over for property development at some point, there's no way we can justify that level of spend. You understand, I'm sure.'

There was a short silence.

'No,' said Mrs Goldman. 'No, I truly don't understand. I know David Haines, the Head at St Catherine's. I'm sure you both do, too. You will know, therefore, how he manages that school, the way in which he encourages a culture of blame and fear, the way St Catherine's has haemorrhaged staff as they desperately look for somewhere – anywhere – else to work. I will not submit my staff and my students to that kind of environment. I'm sorry, gentlemen, but I refuse to accept.'

The less grim of the two turned to her, his face frozen in a grimace that perhaps, in the world of the LEA, counted as pity. 'I'm afraid you don't understand, Sharon. The LEA are not going to put up the money. The site has been secured, but we can't permit it to remain in this condition past the end of the academic year. It's already a major health and safety risk. Unless you can magically summon up seventy thousand pounds by July ... then I'm afraid you will have no choice. Redcoats *will* close.'

It was small consolation, Mrs Goldman thought afterwards, that at least Rachel had held back the Tunnock's teacakes.

Outside in the corridor, Ava was equally as appalled as

Mrs Goldman. Darting back to her classroom at the sound of chairs moving within the office, her mind was racing. Redcoats, *closing*? And she'd have to go to that stupid school down the road, St Catherine's, with their *red* uniform. Ava was a Chelsea fan! She couldn't wear red, for goodness' sake, people might think she was a Manchester United supporter and then where would she be? Not to mention that at St Catherine's you weren't even allowed to play football, their school sport was rugby and you couldn't even bring a football on to the premises. Noah in their class had a cousin who went there and he'd told Noah all about it, a tale Noah had brought back to the gang of them who played football together at break times, who had gasped in collective horror.

No, thought Ava to herself. This wasn't going to happen. But it was okay. Redcoats could still stay open. All she needed to do was to find seventy thousand pounds.

Break time couldn't have come soon enough for Ava, who had wriggled and jiggled so much through Miss Thompson's attempts to get the class to recite their four times table – 'NO!' Stanley Morris had screamed, after being told for the twelfth time by Miss Thompson that four times four equalled sixteen, not the twenty-two thousand he was convinced was correct, before going and lying, face down on the floor – that Miss Thompson had asked her if she had ants in her pants. 'I have NOT got ants in my pants, I change my pants every single day and I have NEVER seen any ants in them,' retorted Ava, appalled. The moment the bell rang she raced outside, delighted to find Tom on playground duty.

'Mr Jones, Mr Jones!' Ava was breathless with her excitement at being the first to break the news. 'The LEA are going to close our school down! They've said that unless we get seventy thousand pounds to rebuild the classrooms they're going to knock the school down and we all have to go to stupid St Catherine's and play *rugby*. So what I thought, Mr Jones, is that because you had all that money that you gave to Mum's work, could you find a bit more and give it to Mrs Goldman, and then we could stay here and keep on playing football, and maybe you could build us a football stadium as well. What do you reckon?'

Slightly shell-shocked, having successfully calmed Ava down and promised her that he would find out what was going on, Tom left his teaching assistant on duty and made his way to Mrs Goldman's office after break had ended. He found her on the phone, frantically calling building firms to find one who was prepared to tell her that the LEA's estimate of what the work would cost to complete was wrong.

'Tom, come in. What can I do for you?' Tom had to admire his boss's composure: she was the kind of person who was always impeccably calm, even in the midst of an absolute crisis.

'Um.' He didn't want to get Ava into trouble, but as one of the TAs had overheard their conversation it was no doubt halfway around the school by now. 'I've heard ... that the meeting with the LEA didn't go so well.'

'Oh really?' Mrs Goldman raised one eyebrow. 'And how, might I ask, have you heard this?'

'Um. You know what schools are like, Sharon ... Bad news travels fast, and all that.'

'Indeed.' She inclined her head. 'Take a seat, Tom. I'm afraid you are correct. The meeting with the LEA did not go at all as planned.' Briefly, she recounted the news that Tom already knew.

'So what are we going to do? Will we fundraise the money?' In a surprisingly short space of time, Tom had grown truly fond of Redcoats. He couldn't imagine having to move to another school, particularly St Catherine's, whose reputation preceded it.

'Tom,' Mrs Goldman looked at him over the rim of her glasses. 'You and I both know the implausibility of fundraising seventy thousand pounds, especially in the timescales required. I am in no way a quitter, but I think we need to consider the reality of the situation, which is that Redcoats really might close.'

As he walked over to his girlfriend's house later that evening, Tom found himself lost in thought. The previous year had been such a high for him. Having escaped from his high-pressure job at the bank, which had taken his mental health to the very brink, he'd found his way into teaching and had never looked back. Not only had he been successful at being appointed at Redcoats, to his complete astonishment he'd found a brand-new relationship too, and had fallen head over heels in love.

Already, with the news Ava had brought him that day, it felt like the rose-tinted haze of the previous year had started to wear off. His mind racing, he barely noticed he'd arrived at Gemma's front door, until Ava shot out and asked him if he thought that God was real, and if God was real, then did Tom think God would be a striker or a defender when he played football – 'Or maybe he would be a goalkeeper, because he must have really really big hands,' mused the little girl – and thoughts of the funding crisis Redcoats was now facing temporarily faded into the background.

Later that evening, over dinner, Tom brought Gemma up to speed on the news, filling in the gaps left by a thoroughly overwrought Ava, who had convinced herself that Redcoats closing would be the end of her football career. Reassuring her daughter that Redcoats wasn't at the top of the list of places the Chelsea talent scouts looked for potential players, Gemma sent Ava off to watch back episodes of *Match of the Day* while she and Tom talked.

'I feel horribly guilty.' Gemma looked down at her lasagne and salad; neither of them had much of an appetite. 'If it wasn't for me then you'd still have all of that money you ploughed into Zero. Then you'd be able to spend it on saving Redcoats instead.'

The thought had also occurred to Tom, but he didn't regret his investment into Zero for a moment. 'It is what it is. No ifs and buts. If I hadn't put that money into Zero then you might not still have a job. Everything happens for a reason, right?'

'And you don't happen to have another spare seventy thousand wasting away in a bank account somewhere?' asked Gemma, teasing him.

'If only,' said Tom. 'Although if I did, I doubt it would have been there for long. Teachers' wages are truly shit.'

Gemma's phone buzzed on the kitchen side where

she'd left it; it had been vibrating pretty much non-stop all evening.

'Sorry. I'll put it on silent. It'll be the class Facebook groups.' After the debacle of Sam's summer homework, Gemma had bitten the bullet and turned the Facebook notifications back on again, a move that had severely tested her sanity.

'What's the latest?'

Gemma shrugged, scrolling through the hundred or so notifications that had come in since she'd left the office earlier that afternoon. 'God, it's never-ending. Basically, the news is out there, and Vivienne is taking it upon herself to save the school. She's got an emergency fundraising meeting planned for tomorrow night, attendance mandatory. Apparently she's been officially appointed to the – unpaid, she's keen to point out – position of Head of Fundraising. Fucking hell. Our lives aren't going to be worth living if we don't turn up for that.'

'To be fair,' mused Tom, 'it's the impetus of Vivienne we need right now. Her sheer . . . *Vivienneness* . . . might just get us that money raised, you know. I wouldn't put it past her.'

'Hmmmm,' said Gemma. 'I hear what you're saying . . . but seventy thousand pounds? It seems a total impossibility.'

From Becky's perspective, raising seventy thousand pounds seemed less of an impossibility right now than keeping down the contents of her stomach. Morning sickness had hit her with an absolute vengeance. 'And I could sue whoever came up with that phrase through the bloody Trade Descriptions Act,' muttered Becky, regurgitating the plain water she'd attempted to drink into the basin. Morning, Afternoon, Evening and Middle of the Fucking Night Sickness would be a damn sight more accurate.

Becky and Jon had talked long into the night after Becky had broken the news of her pregnancy – and eaten the proffered chocolate – on a roller-coaster of emotional highs and lows. Jon, attempting a neutral stance, had tentatively asked her how she felt, and Becky had attempted a smile between her tears.

'I just don't know. On the one hand, this is *so* not what we planned. So, so, *so* not what we planned. I was just getting my life back together, Jon. I was just getting through the hell of the early months with a small baby, just starting to find my identity again. Just remembering who I was – me, Becky – as opposed to Rosie-and-Ella's-mum. You have no idea what it's like. I mean, you do, in so much as you became their dad at the same time, but it's just not the same for guys. It really isn't. You kind of get to go back to life as normal – albeit one where you're chronically sleep deprived and constantly defending yourself against the furious and grumpy witch your wife has turned into.

'But as a woman, who's just had a baby ... it's like nothing I can even describe. You've gone from being a normal functioning person with thoughts and opinions and interests of your own to someone who gets used as an incubator for nine months, and whose entire life then has to revolve around another, totally helpless, human being. It literally fries your brain. And I know I was frequently a dick when you came home from work and I flung the baby at you, but I was just so fucking jealous of you getting to go off and

58

wear proper clothes that weren't coated in baby sick and have proper adult conversations while drinking a hot cup of tea about something, anything, that wasn't nappy contents and weaning schedules.

And my job, oh God, my job.' Her stomach had lurched at the very thought. 'Alison has gone out of her way to take a chance on me and to offer me this position. It took me months – *months* – to find a job that would fit around our family circumstances and that actually enabled me to use my skillset. You've reduced your hours at work, just so that we could make it work. We'd just got our relationship back on track. What kind of *stupid idiot* throws all of that away?' She let out another panicked sob and covered her face with her hands, wishing that she was one of those women who looked attractive when they cried, as opposed to one who went bright red and blew snot bubbles out of her nose.

Tentatively, Jon reached out and held her hand, squeezing it reassuringly. 'You're not a stupid idiot. Even if there was a stupid idiot in this situation, it would be both of us – it takes two to tango, after all. But it was an accident. Nobody's fault. And now we have options, and we just need to decide which one of those we want to take. I'll back you, no matter what. You know that.'

She did know that. Jon had his faults – no matter how many times she reminded him, he still appeared convinced that the very best place to dry wet towels was on the floor of the bathroom, for example – but he was unceasingly supportive as a husband.

'What about you?' She looked at him, eyes still damp. 'What do you want?'

He paused, his expression grave. 'What I want is whatever the right outcome is for you. Because I can pretty much guarantee that the right outcome for you is going to be the right outcome for us. And that's not me dodging the decision, it really isn't. But it's your body. It's you who's got to go through the pregnancy. It's you who's got to push another human being out of you.' (Becky resisted the urge to press her hands over her ears and sing 'LALALALALA' at this.) 'So ultimately, it's your call. What do *you* want to do?'

Becky thought for a moment. What did she want to do? God, she didn't know. There were a million and one reasons why having another baby would be a really really bad idea, and almost no good reasons to go through with the pregnancy whatsoever. And yet ...

Just for a moment, she allowed the scene to play out. Allowed herself to imagine their little family, no longer just the four of them, but five of them. Both Jon and Becky were only children; secretly, she had always loved the idea of a large family. How lovely to have the unconditional love and friendship of your siblings. Or – Becky considered the scenes at bathtime last night, when Rosie had threatened to 'divorce' Ella if she did another poo in the bath they were sharing – the unconditional rivalry and veiled threats of your siblings. Either way.

Looking at her husband, she attempted to work out how she really felt. This pregnancy couldn't have been more unplanned if it tried. And yet. And yet ...

Slowly, ever so slowly, the corners of her mouth upturned, and, tears still sparkling in her eyes, she broke into a broad grin.

Jon raised one eyebrow. 'Well?'

She squeezed his hand. 'I think . . . that only an absolute lunatic would decide to go ahead and have a baby in our position.'

'So you've decided . . . ?'

There was a pause, before she took a deep breath. 'And I've always liked to think we live our lives on just the right side of insanity.'

His eyes opened wide as he took in what she'd just told him, an uncontrollable smile breaking out on his face. 'So we're having the baby?'

She returned his smile. 'We're having the baby! Oh my God, we've fucking lost it. Yes, we're having the baby!'

He jumped up from the table and kissed her with so much passion that she responded in the only way she possibly could . . . by throwing up in the kitchen sink. And she had not really stopped vomiting since.

That particular morning, it was Jon's day in the office, and so she had both girls to get dressed and out of the house in time for the start of school. Briefly, she contemplated asking Gemma if she'd take Rosie to school, before dismissing the idea. She wasn't ill; she wasn't an invalid. She was just pregnant, something that happened to thousands of women every single year and yet they still went around their business as usual. Morning sickness was not going to beat her.

Becky had been so unwell that they'd had to tell Rosie, earlier than they had planned as Becky was yet to get to the doctors' to find out how far along in her pregnancy she actually was. Hopefully not too far along: the jugs of

Pimm's and frosted glasses of ice-cold rosé she and Gemma had drunk in the back garden over the summer weighed heavily on her mind.

Rosie, with her sunny, happy disposition, was delighted. Not for the first time, Becky thanked her lucky stars she had been blessed with a child as placid and amenable as Rosie. They had given her permission to tell her best friend Ava, who had responded with an appalled, 'If I was you, and my dad had done that to my mum, I would tell him to cut off his willy and never to come back ever again.' Becky, laughing, had duly reported this anecdote back to Jon, who had clutched his genitals and begged her not to let Ava in the house with any sharp knives if he was in the vicinity.

Back to the morning routine, and they had been doing okay. Yes, Becky had had to pause three times while changing Ella's pooey nappy to vomit noisily and copiously into the specially purchased Vomit Bin next to the changing station, and no, she could tell from one glance in the hall mirror that with her complexion the colour of off milk and eyes that looked like they'd been excavated from her face, she was hardly looking her best . . . but with a considerable amount of help from Rosie they were eventually in the car and on their way.

Determined not to embarrass herself in front of the school mums, Becky choked back the bile she felt rising as they waited for Mr Cook to unlock the gates and clear them all for entry via his microwave/wardrobe screening equipment. They made polite small talk about how the children were finding Year 3 so far and Becky waved as she saw Gemma approaching, cutting it fine as usual, Ava and Sam in tow.

'Morning.' Becky managed a weak wave. 'You guys okay?'

'Better than you, by the looks of things.' Gemma looked at her friend in concern. 'Why don't you let me take Rosie in and you can go home and vomit?'

The very mention of the 'v' word took Becky beyond the point of no return. Face aflame with embarrassment, she turned away from her daughter and puked dramatically and profusely on to the pavement, splashing the edges of Mr Cook's wardrobe with regurgitated dry toast.

Appalled, the collected parents took a step back, while their children craned their necks in delight to get a better view. 'I think I saw a MINCE PIE in there,' Tartan announced to his friend.

Becky straightened up, wiping her mouth on the tissue Gemma proffered. The usual Becky would have attempted to brazen it out, but she felt so exhausted she didn't even have the energy for that. 'Dear oh dear,' she heard Vivienne stage whisper nearby. 'These mums who let themselves go. I do think I might sit Rebecca down and have a little chat to her about AA. It did wonders for my ex-husband, it really did.'

That did it. Carefully avoiding the puddle of her own vomit, Becky tentatively walked across to Vivienne on legs that threatened to collapse beneath her. All she could say was that all of that propaganda claiming pregnancy made you 'glow' was written by lying fucking bastards.

'Vivienne.' She deliberately exhaled, causing Vivienne to take a step backwards in her red satin Jimmy Choos to avoid the fumes of vomit that were heading in her direction. 'If it's all the same to you, I'd rather you didn't spread rumours around the playground that I was suffering with some kind of drinking problem. Particularly as it's completely untrue.'

A shark-like smile lit up Vivienne's face. 'Of course, Rebecca. I totally understand. It can be very difficult to accept one has a problem in the early stages. My ex-husband was the same, and it wasn't until he was able to stand up and say, "Yes, I am an alcoholic" that he was really able to start on the road to recovery. Have you considered contacting your local AA group?'

'I'M NOT AN ALCOHOLIC, YOU BINT, I'M PREGNANT!' yelled Becky, her temper stretched to breaking point by Vivienne. 'AND I'M NOT SURPRISED YOUR HUSBAND DRANK, BECAUSE I CERTAINLY WOULD IF I WAS MARRIED TO YOU!'

There was a frozen silence, only broken by Ava, entirely unperturbed by Becky's outburst. 'Mummy, what's a bint? Is it Satin's mummy?'

Almost as soon as the words were out of her mouth, Becky regretted them. 'Listen, Vivienne, I'm sorry. I've not been very well, as you can see, and I'm just struggling a bit at the moment. But yes. I'm not an alcoholic, but I am pregnant.'

'And clearly suffering from mood swings,' retorted Vivienne in caustic tones. 'I suppose congratulations are in order.' Rarely had anyone sounded less congratulatory.

From behind Vivienne there was a sudden commotion, and a pink-faced Andrea Barnes pushed her way through. Andrea was the mother of Simon, renowned Alpha

Hellbeast of Year 3, who had once memorably placed one of his own turds inside the lunchbox of another child who he had deemed to have wronged him. 'It was Actual Poo, in an Actual Lunchbox,' Ava had reported back to Gemma in tones of awe and wonder.

'Did I hear correctly?' Clad in her usual Laura Ashley and Boden combo, her well-maintained curls framing her perfectly made-up face, Andrea couldn't have formed more of a contrast to the pale, sweating and still slightly green Becky. 'You're pregnant?'

Becky nodded. 'That I am. Don't tell me. You've come to check if I know who the father is?'

Andrea shook her head. 'But this is wonderful! I've been waiting for the time to announce my news, and it seems this must be it. Because not only are you with child, Rebecca ... but I am too! Yes, little Simikins is going to be getting a baby brother or sister, aren't you, baby boy?' She chucked Simon under the chin and he made a growling noise and threatened to bite her fingers. 'Oh, he's so spirited!'

Becky was nonplussed. 'Um ... congratulations? What are the chances, eh? Two of us pregnant at the same time. Although I must say, you look substantially better on it than I do.'

'So when are you due?' Andrea came closer and pressed a conspiratorial hand on to Becky's arm. 'I'm late spring, just after the blossoms come out on the trees. Ooh!' She pulled a paisley-bound notepad out of her handbag and jotted something down. 'Blossom would be perfect for a girl! So? When will your precious bundle of joy be making its way into the world?'

'Um.' Becky had really had no desire to announce to half of the school – with increasing numbers of parents having gathered round, no doubt in response to her screaming at Vivienne that she was a bint (which Becky suspected most of them had probably wanted to tell her for years) – her lack of family planning, but it seemed Andrea wasn't going to leave her with much of an alternative. 'I'm not actually sure. I need to get a doctor's appointment and find out.'

'But you must know!' Andrea's voice was shrill with excitement. 'Here, I've got a little app on my phone that will work it all out for you. What's the date of your last period?'

'Mum, you do know that this means that Becky and Jon are still having sex, even though they are *really* old?' Ava looked utterly appalled.

'Oh, and I tell you what,' Andrea went on, now busy typing various numbers into the app on her phone, 'I'd been hoping to find someone who was pregnant at the same time as me, so this is absolutely perfect! I'll get you an invite to my antenatal group and we can do the classes together. I was thinking of signing up to some pregnancy yoga classes as well; I've heard of this one woman who's meant to be amazing, she encourages you to do her classes completely naked so you can really get in tune with your pregnant self. This is so exciting, I can't tell you! We'll be pregnancy BFFs, you and me! Won't that be marvellous?'

Becky vomited again.

CHAPTER FIVE

Ava sighed heavily. School had gone down rapidly in her estimation so far that term. Year 2 had been great. She'd had Mr Jones as a teacher for most of it, and he totally understood the importance of football as a fundamental part of her education, even if he did then turn up at their house and do sloppy kissing with her mum. Ava had managed to persuade him that she should take up some position of responsibility within the class, and so he'd created the position of Football Ambassador for her, and had even got her a blue and white enamelled badge (like Chelsea, yessssss!), which meant that at break times she got to go outside first and set up the goals and the pitch ready for anyone who wanted to play. Mr Jones would sometimes come and referee, and he was really pretty good, for an old person who was probably going to die quite soon.

But this year everything had changed. Mr Jones was stuck teaching the babies in Year 2, none of whom were interested in football even a little bit, even though it was very clearly the Best Game In The World, and meanwhile Ava was stuck with stupid Miss Thompson.

Ava and Miss Thompson could not have been more different if they'd tried, something which had been apparent from the moment Miss Thompson arrived on the second day of term and introduced herself to her new class.

'Good morning, Year 3! I'm sure you all remember me!' There were blank looks all round. 'I taught you last year, before I fell madly in love and had to run off and follow my heart to the South of France. Fortunately for all of you, though, love is a fickle beast, and now I have returned, minus my soulmate, but *avec* my great passion, *ma grande passion*, for teaching all of you, *pour mes enfants*.' She looked round at all of them with great affection. 'Isn't that wonderful?'

The class stared back blankly. 'Is Miss Thompson drunk?' Rosie whispered to Ava.

'Probably,' Ava whispered back.

'Now then.' Miss Thompson clapped her hands. 'Can you all say, "Good Morning, Miss Thompson"?'

'Good Morning, Miss Thompson,' the class chorused dutifully, apart from Simon Barnes, who was busy excavating the contents of his nostrils and sticking them down the neck of poor Laura Moon, who had the misfortune to be sat next to him.

'Now, come on, Year 3. You can do better than that. Let's all stand up. Come on, chop-chop. Up you get, standing nice and tall behind your desks. Now, I want you to breathe in through your nose, out through your mouth. In through your nose, out through your mouth. Let's really get those diaphragms working.'

'Definitely drunk,' Ava nodded at Rosie.

The class were made to repeat their greeting to their teacher twelve times, focusing on projection to the far wall of the classroom, before Miss Thompson deemed herself to be satisfied, and continued with her reintroduction.

'I will have responsibility for your education this year, and yes, there are a number of very important topics we must cover as part of the National Curriculum. Maths, English, Science, History, Geography, PSHE—'

'Touching yourself, she means,' Noah Hardcastle announced to his neighbour.

'But in addition to that,' Miss Thompson went on, ignoring Noah entirely, 'it is my intention to ensure a fully rounded education for you all. An education is not solely based on what you learn within the classroom, you know.'

Ava did a silent fist pump of delight underneath her desk. 'Yes!' she whispered to Rosie. 'She's going to tell us about all the football we're going to be doing.'

Miss Thompson did nothing of the sort. To the horror of Ava, Noah and Simon, she announced that the class would, wherever possible, be putting on a play to consolidate their learning. Acting, Miss Thompson told them, was one of the most important skills they could possibly acquire.

Ava could take it no longer. Putting up her hand, she waved it frantically until Miss Thompson paused in her dramatic reconstruction of the play she had produced with Jean-Claude's theatre company – *The Empty Milk Carton* – and looked up in Ava's direction.

'Yes, dear, what is it?'

'Please, Miss Thompson, when will we be doing football?'

Miss Thompson looked taken aback. 'What football?'

'The football; we play football every day in our class, and it's really important because I am going to be the captain of the England men's team one day, and probably lots of the others will be playing in the team too. So that's why we need to get lots of practice in, so we can get as good as we can possibly be. Mr Jones used to let us play every single break and lunchtime and also in most of our PE lessons too. He was the referee as well.' Ava paused for a moment. She couldn't entirely imagine Miss Thompson in football shorts and with a whistle around her neck. 'Will you be doing the refereeing as well, Miss Thompson, or would you like one of us to do it for you?' she asked nicely.

Miss Thompson was horrified. 'No, I will not be refereeing. And we will not be playing football this year. You will have your usual PE lessons, and I thought this year we would use them to focus on dance. Dance is a very good workout, you know. Perhaps some ballet or some period movement. We might even introduce a spot of rhythmic gymnastics; it would be ideal for use in some of our performances.'

If Miss Thompson had looked horrified, that was nothing compared to Ava's face at the thought that she might have to leap around in a leotard holding a ribbon on a stick. She tried again. 'But I don't like dancing, Miss Thompson. It's silly. And football isn't.' She held out her badge, pinned to her school blazer. 'Look, I'm a Football Ambassador. Mr

Jones told me so. And that means you have to let me play football.'

Miss Thompson had wasted enough time on this ridiculous child and her insistence that she run around on a muddy football pitch. What was wrong with the girl? Most children Miss Thompson had taught loved the idea of putting on a play. She could see that sweet girl Satin in the front row was already excited at the prospect of treading the boards. Her diction had been excellent in their morning vocal warm-up; she might consider casting her in a lead role at some point. Her face was stern as she looked back at Ava.

'No. Is it Ava?' Ava nodded mulishly. 'Well, Ava, it doesn't matter what Mr Jones told you last year. Mr Jones was in charge in Year 2, but this is Year 3. You are in Key Stage Two now, and that means there isn't time in the curriculum to waste on playing football.'

'But we can waste time on putting on plays?'

For a moment, there was silence. The class waited with bated breath, eager to see how Miss Thompson would react to Ava's deliberate defiance. Ava waited too, fired up with frustration. She would never usually have been so rude to a teacher, but when it was her beloved football that was at stake . . . that was a bit different.

Miss Thompson took a deep breath and flung one chiffon scarf defiantly over her shoulder. 'There will be no football this term, Ava. That is my final word on the subject. Now, let us start thinking about what we might like our first dramatic production to be.'

Shortly after, Ava excused herself and headed to the girls' toilets, absolutely furious.

She soon found herself in a minority gang of one. Even Simon and Noah had quickly got on board once they realised the potential for getting out of lessons, and Rosie, the traitor, whilst naturally introverted and therefore terrified of performing in front of an audience, had also been sucked in by Miss Thompson's enthusiasm. 'Come on, Ava. You'll like it. It's fun.'

But Ava shook her head. 'No. I don't want to.' And she sat there, a miserable little figure, covertly drawing out football pitches and squad line-ups on the back of the script she'd been given to learn, while the rest of the class hammed it up on stage and Miss Thompson applauded their attempts.

It was going to be a long year, Ava said to herself. A very long year.

It was Thursday evening and Becky knocked on the door for Gemma, whose parents were babysitting for Ava and Sam. Ava had got them sitting around the kitchen table and was forcing them to select their own fantasy football teams, ignoring Gemma's mum's pleas that the only football player she'd ever heard of was Bobby Charlton.

'God, is it that time already?' Gemma, disorganised as ever, came to the door with laptop in hand. 'Sorry, I just need you to give me five minutes. We moved into our new offices at work today and it's been absolute chaos. Not only that, but the main supply partner I'd lined up has been having wobbles and I'm desperately trying to get them back on track. Go and have a chat to my mum and dad and I'll be with you in ten, I promise.'

'It was five minutes a moment ago,' laughed Becky,

walking through to the kitchen where Gemma's parents greeted her warmly. Having finally made it to the doctor's, her pregnancy had been confirmed and the doctor had estimated her to be about six weeks along, meaning she'd be due in early May. He'd also recommended a number of methods to help control the morning sickness, so that while she was still puking regularly, with the help of a pair of Sea Bands worn around the clock and a never-ending supply of crystallised ginger, she could at least generally avoid the humiliation of throwing up in public places.

'You're positively glowing!' Gemma's mum proclaimed.

'You're very kind, but I'm not sure that's true,' Becky responded. 'If I am, I think it's mostly down to judiciously applied make-up and a load of sparkly jewellery to distract from the fact that my face resembles a kiwi fruit and I look like I've eaten everything bar the kitchen sink.'

Ava was staring closely at Becky's face. 'It is not very green, but it IS hairy,' she declared, as Gemma's mum attempted to shush her. 'What? It is and you said that we should always tell the truth, Granny. Do you know, Becky, a kiwi fruit is also very like a front bottom: it is smooth on the inside, and hairy on the outside.'

Every moment Becky spent with Ava, she couldn't help but marvel at how the little girl's mind worked.

Finally, Gemma having completed her emails – though still stealing nervous glances at her mobile phone – they made their way out of the house and jumped into Gemma's car to drive to the school in order to attend the inaugural meeting of the fundraising committee, which Vivienne had made very clear was mandatory for all parents at the school.

'Assuming, that is, that you actually care about the future of your children's education.' Which left them with very little choice but to attend.

'Bloody hell.' Becky had to wade through a sea of empty reusable plastic water bottles covering the floor of Gemma's car to the extent that in some places they were maybe two or three deep. 'What the hell's going on in here? It looks like you've bought up the entire contents of the Tesco packed-lunch container section.'

Gemma sighed. 'I pretty much have. Do you not have the same problem with Rosie? It feels like every single morning one of my children is absolutely baffled by the requirement to take a water bottle into school, despite me having reminded them of this fact EVERY SINGLE DAY since the moment they first started school. The water bottle is always lost, or missing, or they both deny all knowledge of ever having seen a water bottle at all, and so I end up buying more, because I can't bear the thought of increasing all of our plastic waste by using disposable ones, which they then leave in my car, and hence it looking like I'm setting up my own Tupperware party in here.'

Becky smiled. 'Say no more. Basically, you're saving the planet, is what you're saying?'

Gemma groaned as she started the engine. 'Something like that.'

'So . . . how do you think you're going to cope this time next year? When Sam starts secondary school. I mean . . . how do parents actually get their children to two completely separate locations at the same time? Where will Sam be going, anyway?'

Gemma groaned again. 'Don't even ask. Frankly, I don't have a clue. Since I turned those class Facebook notifications back on I've been inundated with comment threads from Vivienne and the coven, ranking all of the schools in the area on GCSE results versus Maths and English percentages at level 5 or above versus Progress 8 score versus Attainment 8 score, none of which I understand even slightly. All I want for Sam is a school where he's not going to totally flunk all of his exams, which is on a decent bus route, and where he won't get his head flushed down the toilet, but no one actually seems to be able to tell me if or where such a school exists.'

'And what does Sam want?'

'He's a ten-year-old boy. He's only interested in hanging out with his mates and staring at a computer screen. I've decided I'm going to drag him along to the open evenings to try to force him to have an opinion. Wish me luck.'

'Can you get Nick to talk to him?' Becky didn't have a huge amount of time for Gemma's ex, but it didn't feel entirely fair that Gemma had to deal with this all on her own.

'Oh my God, have I not told you?' Gemma pulled up at a set of lights and turned to look at her friend. 'Nick's off again!' Becky's jaw dropped open. 'It's true: he's been offered a twelve-month placement over in Berlin – which he thought was in America, and that right there tells you every single reason that I should never, ever have even contemplated marrying him.'

Becky was almost speechless. 'I can't believe it. After he promised you that he'd turned over a new leaf, that he was back for good.'

Gemma laughed. 'I know, and if you believed that, you'd believe anything.' Her face grew serious. 'I actually think it's a really good thing for him. He needs to grow up and work out what the hell he's going to do with his life; this should be the perfect opportunity.'

'And the kids? How have they reacted?'

'Do you know what? They've been absolutely fine. He actually kept his promise and came over to tell them; I thought we'd have tears and tantrums but Sam and him have already set up their Skype group so that they can chat online to each other about various inane computer games.'

'And Ava?'

Gemma smiled. 'Ava just told him that it wasn't a problem, because his football techniques were holding her back in training anyway.'

'Classic Ava. So when does he leave?'

'End of the week. I know, it's been a bit of a whirlwind really, and I was worried about how the kids were going to react, but they're not stupid. I think they'd been half expecting it.'

Becky sighed. 'God, parenting's complicated, isn't it? If anyone told you all of the stuff you have to deal with before you got pregnant, I swear the human race would die out within a generation.'

Gemma smiled. 'Yep, and you've got all of the really really fun bits just around the corner, all over again! You haven't lived until you've had someone regurgitate milk into your cleavage.'

Becky winced. 'Let's not be chatting about regurgitated milk unless you want me to pebbledash the inside of your car. Which, alongside Water Bottle Central, would probably give you an art installation in line for winning the next Turner Prize.'

Parking in the school playground, which Vivienne had arranged with Mrs Goldman would be opened for parking that evening – much to the horror of Mr Cook ('How can I possibly be expected to security screen all of those cars? There'll be enough petrol on site to burn down half the neighbourhood!') – the two friends made their way across to the school entrance. They were clearly some of the last to arrive; the car park was full, and Gemma thought she could already hear Vivienne's strident tones resonating out of the school hall.

To nobody's surprise, as they made their way into the hall, Vivienne was holding court in the centre of the stage, dressed in what looked to be a power suit she'd extracted from the 80s. 'She'll have somebody's eye out with one of those shoulder pads,' Becky whispered. The room was filled to bursting, with every last seat taken, leaving Becky and Gemma to stand at the back of the room, alongside Tom, who gave Gemma a covert kiss on the top of her head.

'Have we missed much?' she whispered as she leant into him, fighting as always her natural instinct to rip off all of his clothes and jump his bones. She still had to pinch herself on a regular basis to remind herself that this beautiful, beautiful man was actually dating her – dull, ordinary, Gemma – as opposed to any one of the model-like sylphs that made up Vivienne's coven, or, indeed, any other girl out there at all. He was constantly reassuring her that he didn't want any other girl out there, that he wanted her, that no, he wasn't in the slightest bit bothered by the fact that she had to pick up her stomach in the morning and physically pour it into her high-waisted pants, nor that her back fat bulged over the top of her bra, in fact, he didn't know what she was talking about, there was no back fat, and in any case, it really wasn't her back fat he was focused on when she was undressed and standing there in front of him in her bra.

One day, Gemma thought, she might just believe him.

Briefly, Tom filled them in: Vivienne had announced that she would be chairing the 'Fundraisers United Committee', and that she would be looking for a vice chair, a treasurer, and someone to take responsibility for all of the publicity and marketing. Kristin, Vivienne's BFF, had stepped up to take on the role of treasurer – 'Does she even know how to count?' Becky whispered, somewhat maliciously – but Vivienne's requests for a vice chair and someone to do marketing had been met with a room full of awkward silence, where ninety-five per cent of attendees were now staring down at their shoes, for fear that any kind of eye contact would be taken as them volunteering.

Vivienne's eyes swept the room, before landing on Gemma and Becky. 'This is perfect!' she announced brightly. 'Thank you for joining us, ladies, *so* pleased you could take time out of your busy schedules to attend such a critical meeting. It's just a shame you couldn't quite make it on time, isn't it?' A few veiled sniggers from the coven followed.

'Anyway,' she continued, 'no matter. Because you're here now, and I'm sure the two of you would be delighted to step up to take on the two vacant positions on the committee. Gemma, I've heard you've started running your own company' – from the look on her face she made it clear she had absolutely no idea who in the world would have entrusted Gemma with such a position of responsibility – 'so you must be good at telling people what to do, which means that you'll be the perfect person to step in and support me as my vice chair. And Rebecca ... isn't your background in marketing?'

Becky nodded reflexively, thereby sealing her own fate, as Vivienne announced that that was sorted then: Gemma would be the vice chair, Becky the marketing coordinator, Kristin the treasurer and she of course would be the chair. Their attempts to explain to her that they simply didn't have time to take on this additional responsibility, that their weeks were already filled to bursting with their jobs and with their children, fell on deaf ears.

'Of course,' said Vivienne, in saccharin tones, 'I would have thought that safeguarding the future of your children's education would have been just about the most important thing that any parent could possibly do. Should you feel differently ...' A roomful of heads swivelled around to stare at Gemma and Becky.

What else could they possibly do in the circumstances? 'No, that's fine,' said Gemma through gritted teeth. 'Becky and I will be very happy to join the committee.'

'Marvellous,' crowed Vivienne. 'Do come on up to the front of the room.'

Feeling rather as though they were on their way to their own execution, the two friends made their way through the crowds of parents and walked up the stairs on to the stage. There was a little spattering of applause and Gemma pulled out the chair next to Vivienne.

Under the cover of the relieved chatter of all of the other parents who were beyond grateful that they weren't in Gemma and Becky's shoes, Vivienne leant over to Gemma. Her eyes were like flint.

'I hear you've encouraged your ex-husband to move to Berlin. A bit dramatic, wasn't it, just because you were jealous of his relationship with me.' Vivienne's eyes narrowed even further. 'Not that it's any great loss. When I'd heard you referring to him as a "little prick", I didn't realise you were being literal.'

Completely lost for words, Gemma sat there with her mouth agape as Vivienne immediately recovered her composure and turned to her audience with a gracious smile. 'I have taken the liberty of having badges, T-shirts and hoodies made with the Fundraisers United branding on, all of which I will of course expect committee members to wear at all times in order to ensure maximum publicity for our fundraising efforts.'

'Oh, fuck my fucking life,' groaned Becky, who had slid into the chair next to Gemma. 'Pass me that wastepaper bin. I think I need to puke again.'

CHAPTER SIX

It was almost ten by the time Gemma and Becky finally managed to make their escape and wend their way back home. 'What just happened to us?' Becky blurted out as they got out of Gemma's car. 'Actually, don't answer that. I'm so fucking exhausted that I could fall asleep standing right here. I'm going to go to bed and pull the covers over my head and pretend none of tonight ever happened, and then when I wake up tomorrow morning it will all have been a bad dream. Right? Right!'

Kissing her friend goodnight, Gemma laughed and unlocked her front door. From the blissful silence that enveloped the house she could tell that Ava must be asleep, thank goodness. Her mum and dad, sat playing Scrabble, promised her that the children had been no trouble – 'Although Ava did ask me rather a lot of questions about what being transgender was, which, to be clear, dear, is not really my area of expertise, so you might want to follow up on that one in the morning' – and said their goodbyes before heading off home themselves.

Gemma switched off the downstairs lights and went upstairs. Ava was snoring loudly, having made herself a bed on the floor in the landing between Sam and Gemma's bedrooms, despite having a perfectly good bedroom, bed and mattress of her own, because who even knew why. Sam's room was dark and quiet, but when she popped in to check on him, to her surprise he was still wide awake.

'Hello, Mum. Did you have a nice time? Ava was asking Granny a lot of questions about being a transgender person.' He frowned. 'She keeps telling me that she is going to grow a willy, so that she can wee standing up, but that's not possible, is it?'

Laughing, Gemma tucked him in and assured him that no, Ava would not be growing a willy, and no, wanting to wee standing up was not a good enough reason to become transgender.

'What's that, Mum?' He pointed to the Fundraisers United badge that Vivienne had pinned to her top and had instructed her she was on no account to leave the house without.

She grimaced. 'Oh, it's a badge for the group that are going to be trying to raise money to rebuild the classrooms that got burnt. I somehow ended up getting voted in as vice chair. I just don't know how these things happen to me.'

Sam looked more closely at the badge. 'Of FUC?'

'Sam! Language, please.'

'But I'm not being rude, Mum. It's what your badge says.'

She pulled it round to face her. Sam wasn't wrong. The

design Vivienne had gone for inexplicably emphasised the F, U and C of 'Fundraisers United Committee'. Marvellous. Just ... marvellous.

'You're the vice chair of FUC, Mum.' Sam was proper belly laughing now. 'And you can't tell me off for swearing, because I'm not, that's just what your badge says. FUC. Brilliant.'

'Shush, before you wake Ava up. Right, come on, it's time to go to sleep. And this weekend, you and me need to sit down and work out which of the secondary schools we're going to go and have a look at. I haven't got long to get your application in, you know.'

Sam shrugged. 'I don't care, Mum. I just want to go where my friends go.' His eyes widened with horror. 'You won't be wearing that badge when you go round the schools, will you? I don't want everyone knowing that my mum's in charge of FUC.' He started laughing again.

'Oh, for goodness' sake.' Smiling, refusing to think about what she'd let herself in for as a result of that evening's meeting, Gemma went to bed.

Since their little interchange at the school gates, Becky had done everything possible to avoid Andrea Barnes, but with her still doing the school run two days a week, not to mention Andrea's persistence, it had been something of an impossibility. Having obtained Becky's phone number from the class list, Andrea had called, messaged, FaceTimed and contacted Becky through every single one of her social media channels. Finally, when she'd tracked down Becky's work phone number and called her at the office (leaving Becky crawling underneath her desk and begging Alison, her lovely colleague, to tell Andrea that Becky no longer worked there, that she'd unfortunately died), Becky realised she was going to have to give in and return the woman's calls before she called out the FBI. They had agreed to meet for a coffee – or, in Andrea's case, a camomile tea.

Becky had thought she was single-minded, but it was nothing compared to Andrea, who seemed to be on a one-woman mission to secure Becky as her new pregnancy BFF. 'Look, Becky! I've bought us matching pregnancy journals, and I thought we could do a joint pregnancy photoshoot! What do you reckon?'

'Um,' replied Becky. 'I'm not sure I'll have the time, what with my work, and the children, and now everything I'm going to be doing on the marketing side for Fundraisers United.' Andrea's face fell. 'But maybe we can see . . . nearer the time . . . maybe . . .'

'And of course, we'll have a full-on programme of ante-natal classes to be attending,' Andrea beamed. 'I've taken the liberty of writing them all into your pregnancy journal, so you know exactly what you'll be doing when.' She tittered. 'I know what pregnancy brain can do to a girl!'

Becky took the proffered journal, then inhaled. Andrea had indeed written down every single antenatal class she proposed she and Becky attend, along with a schedule of pregnancy yoga classes – God, how Becky hoped it wasn't the naked one. From the list, it seemed there were going to be more classes than Becky had days left in her pregnancy.

'Andrea, thank you, so much, for doing this . . . but listen, I can't commit to all of this. I have had two babies before, you know. From the looks of this you'd think we were training to run antenatal classes, not simply attending them.'

Andrea's face lit up. 'If it's something you'd like to do, I could arrange for the two of us to run a class together for first-time parents!'

'NO!' Becky's voice was sharper than she had intended, and Andrea's face fell again. 'Listen, Andrea, this is lovely of you . . . but I don't need to go along to antenatal classes. I know how childbirth and having a baby works.'

'But do you, Becky? Do you really?' Andrea, conspiratorially, leant closer. 'I've heard that your last two labours were really quite difficult.'

Becky started. How had she heard that? A split second later, she realised. Of course. Andrea had heard it from Becky herself. She had never held back from ghoulishly sharing her birth stories with anyone who would listen, or even anyone who wouldn't, smug in the knowledge that, having taken the decision to stop at two children, she'd never have to go through the whole hideous experience again. Now, it seemed, her oversharing was coming back to bite her.

Andrea was continuing. 'Wouldn't it be nice, Becky, if this time . . . it could be different? If this time, instead of the pain and the screaming and the agony . . . if you could breathe your baby out, feeling each contraction as a surge of pressure and power, not as the horrendous sensation of your body being ripped apart from the inside out as you let out a blood-curdling scream and contemplate your own

85

death? There is another way, you know, Becky. And I want to help you find that way.'

'Bullshit,' said Becky shortly. 'I'm having all the fucking drugs there are and getting my husband to slam me over the head repeatedly with a mallet to distract me from the fact I've got an object the size of a toaster attempting to emerge from my front bottom. There's no amount of breathing's going to help me with that.'

Andrea took a prim little sip from her cup of camomile tea. 'I really think that you're being terribly narrow-minded about all of this. I promise you, it works. My Simon veritably slid out, and he's hardly a slip of a lad, is he?'

That was the understatement of the year. Becky groaned as Andrea started bombarding her with yet another series of quite possibly completely fabricated facts and figures about how good hypnobirthing was as a pain-relief technique, how important a natural birth was, had Becky ever thought about the damage she could be causing to her unborn child with all the chemicals she was so insistent upon pumping into her bloodstream to alleviate her own pain, wasn't that a rather selfish choice to make—

'FINE!' Becky exploded, pushed beyond breaking point by the woman's sheer force of will. 'Fine, Andrea. You win. I'll come along to one of your antenatal classes, in the spirit of being open-minded, and I'll learn all about these so-called pain-relief techniques you've been telling me truly work, even when your body is being crushed into tiny fragments of pain and fear. So you just let me know when the first one is, and, provided it doesn't clash with work, I'll turn up.' In her head, she was thinking that she would still have weeks and weeks to come up with a suitable excuse not to attend, just so long as she didn't have to sit in this coffee shop and have Andrea talk at her for a moment longer.

'Oh, *wonderful*,' said Andrea, her eyes alight with pleasure. 'The first one's this Saturday, and don't worry, I already took the liberty of checking with your friend Gemma. She's available and she'll be more than happy to look after your two girls, so that both you and your husband will be able to attend.'

Oh, Jon was just going to LOVE this.

Saturday morning dawned, bright and clear, and Becky and Jon took the girls over to Gemma's in plenty of time for them to make the 9 a.m. start time for the class. Andrea had sent her the location: a church hall just a ten-minute drive away.

'Now, girls,' whispered Becky, 'if you want to make a real fuss and beg me not to leave, I really won't mind.'

'Why would we make a fuss?' asked Rosie in puzzlement. 'I love coming round to Gemma's. She never burns the dinner, not like you.'

'Yes, and come on, love,' said Jon as they waved goodbye to Rosie and Ella and climbed into the Range Rover, 'it's nice for you and me to have some time together to focus on the pregnancy. With everything going on, we've hardly had two moments together to let it all sink in.'

'It's only going to get worse,' said Becky, revving the engine and driving in her usual, slightly erratic fashion down their street and out on to the main road. 'You should have seen the schedule of classes Andrea's given me. If we attend all of those, the kids will have forgotten what I look like.'

'It's fine.' Jon's voice was soothing; he was well practised in dealing with Becky's emotions, which could be fairly . . . extreme . . . even when she wasn't two months' pregnant. 'Making time for you and the baby, that's what's important. You must get a scan date through soon, mustn't you?'

Becky tapped her hand fretfully on the steering wheel as they waited at a red light. 'And that's the other thing. We haven't even had a scan yet to confirm the baby's okay. It could not be viable, or have some horrendous disability, or have . . . two heads! Why am I wasting time on these stupid antenatal classes when I don't even know that my baby's okay?' She sniffed loudly. 'Can you pass me a tissue please. God, these stupid hormones. I'd forgotten that pregnancy turns me completely unhinged.'

Jon smiled as he passed her a tissue. 'And that's why I think it's important that you take these classes, to get some time for you.' Secretly he thought that anything that might get his beautiful, somewhat irrational wife on to a more stable emotional keel had to be worth a try.

Becky was not a fan of stereotyping. Far too many people, upon hearing that she was an only child who had attended private school followed by Oxford University, had built up a picture of her before she had even introduced herself. Nevertheless, she couldn't help herself describing what she imagined the other women in Andrea's antenatal group – who she'd apparently met at Pre-Conception Yoga ('when you're considering having a baby, and you want to ensure your body is perfectly in tune to accept the fertilis-ation of an egg,' Andrea had informed a bewildered-looking Becky) – to be like to Jon as they drove.

'They'll be fully graduated from the Earth Mother, happy-clappy school of parenting. They'll be dressed in cheesecloth, wearing sandals on their feet. The men will all have beards and will have not only cut the cord at any previous births, but will have followed it up by frying and eating the placenta. They'll use cloth nappies, feed their babies organic puréed vegetables that they've grown on their own allotments, and you and I are going to be like fish out of bloody water.

But to Becky's surprise, the group of parents already seated in the church hall seemed, at least on first appear-ance, to be surprisingly normal. Andrea was there, of course, with her husband Nigel, a diminutive man with a large ginger moustache, which he insisted upon stroking in a slightly disturbing manner the entire time.

There were two other couples in the group: Violet and her partner Genevieve ('do call me Geni') and Sophia, who looked like she'd walked straight off the catwalk of London Fashion Week, with her spiked black hair and piercing blue eyes, and her husband Jason. He was just as arresting looking and was clearly going to lead to Becky pulling in her stomach muscles the entire time she was there. Not that you'd notice, given they had almost completely given up the ghost after two previous pregnancies and Becky still looked like she was smuggling a hessian bag filled with porridge around underneath her top.

Also present was Daphne, the course leader, who had

four children and seven grandchildren of her own, and consequently considered herself to be something of the oracle when it came to childbirth.

'Becky! You came!' Pregnancy BFFs they might be, but it was clear Andrea had had no real faith that Becky was actually going to turn up. 'And this must be your lovely husband . . . James? Jack? Joseph?'

'Jon.' He held out a hand. 'You must be Andrea. It's lovely to finally meet you; Becky's told me so much about you.' Not for the first time, Becky blessed her husband's poker face and ability to charm even the most difficult of customers.

Andrea visibly melted in response to Jon's introduction, and as she introduced Becky and Jon to Nigel she told Jon how lucky it was that she and Becky had become such good friends. 'I know Becky doesn't know her exact due date yet, but just think, if the planets align, maybe the two of us could share a birthing suite! What do you think?'

Fortunately for everyone, at that moment Daphne clapped her hands and brought the group together. 'Welcome! Welcome, everybody! Do help yourself to some of the freshly brewed camomile tea I've made up on the side, there's obviously none of that nasty caffeine in it, so much better for mummy and baby. It might be a bit tepid, but don't let that stop you.'

Mmmm, tepid camomile tea. Becky rolled her eyes at Jon, who put his fingers to his lips and told her to listen. It was probably just as well Daphne wasn't aware of the steaming hot latte she'd been drinking just before she'd left to drop the children at Gemma's.

'So then, we've got two old-timers here' – she gestured at Becky and Andrea – 'and two ladies who will be going through the birthing experience for the first time' – smiling at Violet and Sophia. 'Why don't we start by going around the room and talking about what we're hoping to get from the course?'

Andrea – of course – went first. 'I'm Andrea, and this is Nigel, and little Pumpkin' – please, let this be a pet name Andrea had given her bump, and not what she was actually planning on calling it – 'will be our second child. We are already blessed with our angel, Simon, who is really a saint in human form, and is going to be the greatest big brother you could possibly imagine.' She beamed round at the room, while Becky attempted to equate the description she'd just given of Simon with the demon who had once handed Rosie her PE shirt, telling her he'd used it to wipe his arse.

Andrea carried on talking through her plans for the birth; it seemed she favoured the idea of 'free-birthing', a term Becky had never heard of, but which apparently involved giving birth without medical assistance, often outdoors, without any pain relief whatsoever. 'I just love the idea of being so in touch with my body,' Andrea gushed.

'Of course, I should point out at this point that, strictly speaking, free-birthing is not actually legal,' Daphne interjected. 'However, Andrea knows that I may have birthed one or two of my own children that way ... so who am I to deter anyone else from having a go?' She winked. 'And what are you hoping to get from the course, Andrea dear?'

Andrea beamed. 'Oh, really just to spend time with

like-minded people and for our babies to grow up being lifelong friends.' Good grief. If that was her objective, Becky sincerely hoped this baby was going to come out with very different personality traits to its sibling Simon.

Violet and Sophia went on to outline what they were hoping to get from the course – 'support, friendship, advice and companionship,' said Sophia, possibly confusing childbirth classes with a dating website – and then it was Becky's turn.

Daphne smiled at her encouragingly. 'Don't be shy, dear, tell us what you'd like to achieve over the next few weeks and months.'

'You should probably be aware that I don't know if I'm doing the full course just yet,' Becky confessed. 'I said to Andrea that Jon and I would come along and see if it was for us, but I'm not sure if I definitely want to attend all of the sessions. I obviously have two children already, so I'm not sure if there's a lot left that you can teach me.'

Daphne looked shocked. 'But you've already signed up to pay for all of the classes, dear. Why would you do that, if you weren't planning to attend them?'

'I've what?' Becky was nonplussed. 'When did I do that?'

Daphne rummaged in the folder that she had on the table in front of her. 'Here, dear. Your good friend Andrea passed it over to me.'

Becky took a closer look. Damn, she was right: there was no mistaking the flamboyant swirls of her signature (which she'd thought up as a teenager, convinced she was going to be the next Kylie Minogue). Andrea had handed her a load of pieces of paper, telling her that she needed to sign them in order to be able to attend the course, and Becky had done what Jon always warned her not to, and simply signed without reading what it was she was signing.

'Okay, so I might have signed that, but it still doesn't necessarily mean that I need to attend all of the classes. I mean, how much are we talking?' Daphne told her. 'Goodness.' She didn't dare meet Jon's eyes. 'That's quite ... sizeable.'

'But you do need to attend, dear. That's the whole point of how I run these sessions. I match one experienced mother with one first-time mother, and you work together. It's designed to increase the confidence of our new parents and open the minds of our old-time parents to different ways of doing things. I've arranged for you and your husband to be paired with Sophia and Jason. I don't really think that you can let them down, not at this stage.'

'Oh, please don't,' begged Sophia. 'Jase and I are so excited about taking this course, aren't we, Jase?'

'Jase' nodded, though he looked anything but excited. 'Thrilled, baby. Thrilled.'

'There you go, then,' said Daphne, as though it had all been decided. 'That's settled. So, tell us, Becky: what are you hoping for from this third-time birthing experience?'

'Drugs, drugs and more drugs,' said Becky succinctly.

Daphne let out a sigh. 'I can see we are going to have an awful lot of work to do with you.'

CHAPTER SEVEN

The leaves were starting to fall from the trees and the nights were drawing in as Becky went to collect Gemma for their latest Fundraisers United meeting. Despite the prospect of another evening with Vivienne, Becky was bubbling over with excitement. She'd had her twelve-week scan that morning and everything looked just fine with the baby.

'I mean, I could live without them referring to me as "geriatric" all the time,' she bemoaned to Gemma. 'Nothing makes you feel you're past it like being officially declared a "geriatric mother". Really, they could have picked a less extreme word. "Middle-aged". "Slightly past it". "Geriatric" is pretty fucking brutal.'

'But the baby's fine?' prompted Gemma.

'The baby's absolutely fine,' smiled Becky, protectively stroking her bump, which had suddenly popped out, and on Becky's tiny frame, made her look like she was already five months gone. 'Obviously, there was the ritual humiliation of having to drink just the right amount of water to enable them to see the baby, and not piss yourself while you wait for them to call your name.'

'And did you manage it?' Gemma remembered all too well that agonising sensation of two pints of water threatening to burst your bladder and the blessed relief when you were finally allowed to go and do a piss that would have befitted a carthorse.

Becky tapped the side of her nose knowingly. 'Tena Lady is a wondrous thing, that's all I'm saying.'

They got in the car, leaving the children with Jon, and drove off to the school. Neither of them were looking forward to the evening ahead. The last few Fundraisers United meetings had been fraught, with Vivienne increasingly berating them for their failure to come up with any brilliant fundraising ideas which were guaranteed to raise them the seventy thousand pounds that they needed.

'Rebecca, you're in marketing, for goodness' sake. You must be constantly coming up with ideas for that little charity of yours, whatever it is that it does.' Vivienne's eyes flashed black against her auburn hair as she stared Becky down.

'That "little charity" of mine, as you describe it, Vivienne, is slowly changing the world. Wouldn't it be nice if our daughters could go to get jobs one day and know that they'd be able to progress just as far as they wanted to in their careers, regardless of whether or not they chose at some point to pop a baby out of their vaginas.'

'Yes, yes.' Vivienne was dismissive. 'I'm sure it's all

terribly worthy. But what about your ideas? You must have some, surely. It's why I voted you on to the committee.'

Becky shrugged. 'I've told you all of my ideas. And while some of them are pretty fucking good – even if I do say so myself – none of them is going to raise seventy thousand pounds in such a short space of time.'

'You'd better keep thinking then, hadn't you?' Vivienne snapped. 'Gemma, what about you? What about that business of yours? They must have plenty of money, surely, that they'd like to invest in sponsoring the rebuilding of a school?'

Gemma laughed. Tom's investment into Zero had secured their futures – for the moment – but it had only just been sufficient to cover the payroll for the year, make a couple of crucial investments for growth and provide Gemma with the small amount of capital she needed to get Pert off the ground. As Dave the FD continued to remind both Gemma and Leroy, cashflow at Zero remained precarious. There certainly wasn't a magical seventy thousand pounds just wasting away in the company bank account that she was going to be able to commit.

'Nope, nothing doing, I'm afraid,' confirmed Gemma. 'I don't know about anyone else, but I'm starting to wonder if maybe this might be an impossible task. Seventy thousand pounds is a huge amount of money.'

'Oh, come ON, ladies,' barked Vivienne, slamming her fist on the trestle table they were seated around in the school library. 'What's with this defeatist attitude? There are a million and one things that we could be doing.'

'Go on then, Vivienne,' suggested Becky. 'If you're so certain that there are all these possibilities ... let's hear some of your ideas for a change.'

Vivienne's expression didn't falter, even for a moment. 'Of course.' She gave Becky a smile that didn't reach anywhere near her eyes. 'Let me just refer to my committee folder.' She opened the large, lever-arch file in front of her, which was neatly printed with FUNDRAISERS UNITED on the cover and sorted with alphabetical dividing tabs.

'Here we go. Ideas. So, how about a high-end auction? You know the kind of thing I mean. We get various parents and others connected to the school to offer up gifts or experiences that can be auctioned up. Imagine it! One night on Richard Branson's Necker Island should raise most of the money we need by itself!'

'Yes, but Vivienne? I mean, I hate to point out the obvious flaw in your plan ... but do any of us actually *know* Richard Branson? Let alone well enough to get him to donate a night on his private island to us.'

There was a sullen silence. 'I brushed past him at an airport, once,' Kristin offered up.

'Okay, so maybe we won't get a night on Necker Island,' Vivienne acknowledged petulantly. 'But there must be other things we could auction off. Someone must own a nice chateau in the South of France that we could auction a week's stay at, or a Maybach that they don't mind lending out for someone to drive around for the weekend.'

'Vivienne, you are fucking deluded,' burst out Becky, who was even less tolerant of Vivienne's nonsense than she would have been usually, on account of the fact that her bladder was stretched to capacity and she desperately needed a wee. 'None of the parents at this school have anything like that. And even if they did, who's going to bid on it? You know what house prices are like round here. I don't know about you, but most of my regular income goes on keeping a roof over our heads and food on the table. I haven't got a spare ten thousand pounds to bid for a night on Necker Island.'

'You wouldn't get a night on Necker Island for ten thousand pounds,' muttered Vivienne. 'Fine. So no one's got any ideas that are any use. In which case, I suggest that we disband Fundraisers United and accept that our children's time at Redcoats is over. I don't know why I care, really. Tartan will be off to secondary next year, and I can *easily* afford to put Satin into private school.' She said it in tones that suggested she was more than aware that she was the only one in the room who had anywhere near the amount of money needed for a private education.

At that moment the doors to the library opened, and in swept Miss Thompson, her usual cloud of chiffon scarves billowing around her, as though she might at any point break into the Dance of the Seven Veils. She approached the table where the four of them were sitting.

'This is the meeting of the fundraising committee, am I right? The one set up to save the school?'

Vivienne nodded suspiciously. She would usually hold no truck with someone who dressed as though she was auditioning to work in a haberdasher, but she knew the importance of staying on the right side of Miss Thompson if she wanted Satin and Tartan to be given the leads in any school productions that year.

'Wonderful.' Miss Thompson raised her hands to the air in delight and pulled up a chair, nestling in cosily between Becky and Gemma. 'I have come to offer you my idea. And it's an idea which, I genuinely believe, can by itself raise every single penny of the seventy thousand pounds that we need.' She paused dramatically; the committee members looked back at her. 'Shall I go on?'

Vivienne nodded. 'Please do.'

'Well,' continued Miss Thompson, 'it's quite simple really. You see, ever since I first heard the news of the arson attack, and then Sharon so generously offered to take me back on the teaching staff, I have really felt that I have wanted – no, that it is my calling – to give something back. And so I thought to myself, Angela, darling, what is it that you're good at? What is it that you could possibly deliver for the school? And then it came to me, in a blinding flash of inspiration, just as Elaine Paige on Sunday finished on Radio 2. Of course! I shall put on a production. A gala production, this spring, featuring all of the children in the school. It will be an original work, written by myself, with brand-new songs and choreography, and with the publicity that I know the four of you will be able to generate, I see no reason at all why we shouldn't meet, and most likely exceed, our seventy thousand pound target! Isn't it *brilliant*?'

There was a stunned silence. Kristin's mouth had fallen open slightly; even the usually impeccably composed Vivienne looked mildly shell-shocked.

'Well?' Miss Thompson prompted. 'I'm sure it goes without saying that I would waive my usual fee, and I'm fairly confident I will be able to source an orchestra who will play for minimal cost, given this is a charity event. Of course, I will require a small budget – just for the essentials, you understand: costumes, lighting, venue hire.'

'Venue hire? But you can use the school hall, surely?' Vivienne asked.

'Let's not worry about little details like that for the time being, shall we?' Miss Thompson smiled. 'So, are we agreed? That I will write, direct and choreograph the production that will save the school from closure?'

Gemma looked around at the others, whose faces were frozen into various expressions. 'Um … could you give us five minutes? We just need to … formally sign off the project,' she improvised.

'Of course,' agreed Miss Thompson. 'I'll just be waiting outside.' And she bustled off to the corridor, humming 'Do You Hear the People Sing' to herself.

The doors closed behind her, and Vivienne turned to the rest of the committee. 'Clearly, this is absolutely preposterous. A single production, raise seventy thousand pounds? The woman's out of her mind. Gemma, as vice chair, you'll have to be the one to tell her so.'

'Hang on a minute,' Becky interjected. 'Okay, so it does seem like a tall order, to raise all of the money we need by putting on a play. But have any of us had any better ideas? Most of the things we've come up with are okay, but at most are likely to raise us a few hundred quid. And there's nothing to stop us carrying on doing those things anyway:

I can source someone to print calendars and tea towels, and Gemma and Kristin will get a rota drawn up of cake sales and coffee mornings for the year. I don't doubt for a moment that Miss Thompson's production is unlikely to raise seventy thousand pounds. I can't imagine it'll clear seventy quid. But we're not exactly inundated with offers here. I say we let her get on with it.'

It was clear from the expression on Vivienne's face that she thought nothing of the sort, and was about to say so, when, unexpectedly, Kristin spoke up. 'I think we should have a vote.'

'A vote! Good idea!' said Gemma in relief. 'Okay, so all those in favour—'

Vivienne stopped her in her tracks. 'I think you'll find that *I* am chair of this committee, Gemma. Therefore *I* shall call the vote.'

They waited.

'All those in favour of allowing Miss Thompson to put on her ridiculous production, raise your hands.'

Gemma, Becky and, much to their mutual surprise, Kristin, all raised their hands. Vivienne looked at Kristin, aghast. 'What are you doing?'

'I think Becky's right,' replied Kristin, somewhat mutinously. 'We haven't got any better ideas. And besides, I thought you'd be pleased at the idea of a school production. Surely that gives Satin and Tartan the perfect opportunity to take the lead roles. If we invite the local papers to review it, maybe put a section up on YouTube, it could even kick start their professional acting careers!'

Ooh, now there was something she hadn't considered.

Her resistance to the production forgotten in an instant, Vivienne strode over to the library door and invited a delighted Miss Thompson to come and sit back down with them, announcing that she personally had approved the production and that she couldn't wait to see her little darlings, Satin and Tartan, starring in the lead roles, in fact how would Miss Thompson like to arrange to come round one evening to give them some audition practice ahead of time so that they were in the best possible positions to lead the cast.

'Oh, how wonderful!' Miss Thompson clapped her hands. 'You won't regret this, I promise you. I'll get working on the script and musical numbers just as soon as I get home. Now, of course, I will need some assistance from yourselves. Producing a large-scale production such as this takes a lot of work. I will direct, of course, but I will need a stage manager, a producer, hair and make-up, a children's chaperone . . .'

'I'm regretting it already,' Becky whispered to Gemma.

Since she'd taken on her new role as MD of Pert, Gemma had agreed with Leroy that she would work Fridays from home. She'd wanted to ensure there was at least one day each week when she could be there in the playground to pick the children up after school, rather than sending them to after-school club as she did on the other days; she also found a day each week away from the hustle and bustle of the open-plan office invaluable when it actually came to getting work done.

Things were progressing rapidly with her new project;

she'd identified a bra manufacturer who had been working with a new and interesting kind of natural fibre, which had built-in rigidity designed to support even the heaviest of mammaries without needing to add a metal wire which would dig maliciously into the side of your tit. Gemma had been incredibly impressed by the prototype she'd been given to try on. Not only did it keep her boobs well above knee height, it was also comfortable to wear and didn't seem to curse her with Double Boob, Armpit Swell or Overhanging Back Fat. Now she was working with the developers to produce the app that would be available to prospective customers to enable them to remotely identify the right bra size for them, ensuring that the perfect product could be posted out.

That Friday night, having sent her final emails of the day, Gemma summoned the children into the kitchen. Ava paused in her keepy-uppy practice and Sam reluctantly unplugged himself from his headphones and shuffled downstairs.

'Right, you two, it's time for tea. Tom's coming over in a bit, and so I thought you could help me get dinner ready. And while we eat, Sam, I need you and me to decide which of these secondary schools we're going to go and have a look around.

Sam shrugged. 'Don't know, don't care.'

Gemma inhaled. 'Yes, I appreciate that you don't care; you've done nothing but tell me that you don't care ever since I first broached the topic of secondary schools with you; nevertheless, you have to go to a secondary school, and while I can go and choose one without your assistance, it would be really great if you could provide at least some kind of input, even if only to tell me that that one's absolutely awful and you wouldn't go there in a million years.'

'Yes, Sam.' Ava sat down at the table and began writing on a pad of paper. 'Your secondary school is very important, because if you don't choose the right one then you will get bullied and want to kill yourself and fail all your exams and never get a job, ever.'

'Thank you, Ava. I would suggest you probably don't need to take up a role as a motivational speaker any time soon,' Gemma told her daughter.

Ava looked surprised. 'What? But it's true, Mummy. I mean, people are already going to bully him because he supports West Ham.' She shook her head in despair and exhaled heavily, presumably at the thought of having a West Ham supporter as a brother. 'It's not even like they're really a proper football team.'

'They are a proper football team,' Sam growled at his sister. 'We'll beat you when we next play you.'

Ava held up one hand. 'Please. *I* could beat West Ham, playing all by myself, with my eyes shut and one of my legs chopped off. Let *alone* if it was Chelsea playing them.'

'Okay, kids, I feel like we're getting somewhat off topic here. Back to secondary schools.' Gemma tapped the table with her pen. 'I've had a look, and here are my suggested three that we should go and look around.'

Sam shrugged. 'Fine. Whatever. I don't really care. You can go and look at them if you want.'

Gemma sighed. 'Sam, we need to talk properly about

this. It's all very well you telling me that you don't care, but I don't want it getting to March and you then suddenly revealing some kind of hidden agenda.'

Ava's mouth fell open. 'Sam's really a girl?'

By the time she'd finished explaining to her daughter the differences between agendas and gender, Sam was back on his feet, jiggling from side to side.

'Can I go now?' He looked as though he would rather be anywhere else than right there, discussing his educational future.

Gemma gave in. 'Go on, then. Off you go.' He was out of the room and back upstairs on his computer before she'd even finished the sentence.

Vivienne kept inundating the class Facebook group with messages about how critical their children's secondary education was, and how the choices they as parents made were going to affect the rest of their children's *lives*. Gemma was certainly feeling the pressure. She didn't know whether it was a blessing or a curse that Sam was so remarkably untroubled by it all.

Ava shook her head and looked at Gemma in mock despair. 'I know, Mummy. *BOYS*. Don't worry. I will come with you and look at the schools. It's important that I start planning for my future; you still need to have a good education behind you, even if you are going to be a professional footballer. And I also need to come and work out which one has the best football pitches.'

A thought occurred to the little girl, and she looked up from the pad she was writing on. 'Mummy, maybe you should do home schooling for Sam. I think you would be very good at it. You're very good at being strict and shouting.'

Gemma thought back to the dream she'd had and shuddered. There wasn't enough gin in the world for that kind of scenario.

CHAPTER EIGHT

Becky threw herself down on the sofa, absolutely exhausted. It was 8 p.m. and she had just got Rosie into bed, Ella having already been passed out in a sleep of milky dreams for an hour or so.

'Dinner's ready, love.' Jon called her in from the kitchen but she felt almost too shattered to move.

'Can you bring it in here and we can just eat on our laps? I'm ready to drop.'

He didn't reply, but did bring through her bowl of homemade chow mein on a tray, dragging Boris – who had exceeded even his usual fucking liability status that day by running amok on the common and rolling in fox shit – by the collar and locking him into the utility room to prevent him from inhaling the chow mein, bowl and tray whole. He went back through to collect his own and sat down on the sofa opposite Becky. She meant to thank him for making the meal, but her eyes were closing of their own accord;

just staying awake until they'd finished eating was going to be a challenge.

'How's work going?' He forked up his noodles and started eating.

Becky attempted to rouse herself sufficiently to at least be able to have a conversation. 'It's really good. The girls have been so supportive with my pregnancy – although at least the worst of the morning sickness is over now.' She winced. 'Narrowly avoiding splashing a client's foot with vomit was a real low point. And it does feel like we're making progress. Every time we go in to talk to an organisation, they're listening to us and they are genuinely taking on board our recommended toolkit of the changes – the real changes that they need to make to make all roles in all organisations accessible to everyone, as opposed to just running a couple of seminars entitled "Women in Business" and then patting themselves on the back for having closed the gender pay gap.

'The trouble is we're not even shaving off the tip of the iceberg. Yes, these companies are receptive, but that's mainly because they've agreed to let us come in to talk to them in the first place.' She named a series of huge, global corporations. 'Those are the guys we really need to be speaking with, if we want to elicit true change, but getting to the man – and it is always a man – at the top is a seemingly impossible challenge. So we've got that, and we're looking at how we can get the Government to bring in legislation that would enforce some of what we're recommending. But they're also ignoring us, at least for the time being. I guess what we're doing seems pretty low down on their list of priorities.' She sighed. 'Sometimes I feel like I'm changing the world ... and sometimes I feel like it's a struggle just to change one person's opinion.'

Jon looked her straight in the eyes. 'Do you think you're doing too much?'

'What do you mean?' Becky was immediately on the defensive, as she always was when anyone suggested she had stretched herself beyond what was feasible for one person to achieve. She hated the idea of failure.

'Well, your job ... the kids ... the pregnancy ... all the work you're doing at the school on the fundraising side of things ... the house ... me.' He said the last word in such a way that suggested he felt like he was pretty low down her priority list. 'Do you think you've got the balance quite right?'

Jon was either feeling particularly brave or stupid. It didn't take much to get Becky to flare up, and that was without the additional hormonal cocktail which was pregnancy. She put her tray of food down sharply on the coffee table and stared back at him.

'Yes, Jon, I *do* think I've got the balance right. I suppose you're referring to the fact that one of the cushions on the chaise longue is a couple of centimetres out of place, or that the kitchen's still recovering from Boris deciding to try and take on the overflowing bin. But guess what? There's two of us living here, two of us in an allegedly *equal* partnership, and so if you've got a problem with the way the house is looking, then may I suggest that you make it *your* problem, not mine. You're perfectly aware of where the J-cloths and the disinfectant are kept, and are just as capable as I am of moving that rogue cushion' – she stood up and straightened it – 'into the correct place. We can't live in a show home the whole time, you know? And, if you were shortly going to be having to squeeze something the size of this dinner tray out of the hole in the end of your cock' – Jon winced – 'then cushion positioning might not be top of your list of priorities either.'

'Becky.' Gently, he stood up, crossing to her sofa and putting his arm around her. 'I didn't say anything about the state of the house. I just pointed out that you've got a lot going on right now. I want you to make sure you're looking after you, as well as worrying about all the rest of us.'

Becky attempted a laugh. It turned into more of a shaky sob. 'Oh, there'll be plenty of time for looking after me once the baby is here. You know, in between the three hundred night feeds, and the championship finals of Competitive Sleep Deprivation, which you know we're going to imme-diately be throwing ourselves back into, and the sweating thirty-eight gallons of water out of your body in a single night, and the after-pains that feel like you're shitting out another three babies, and the sensation of your nipples being dissolved in hydrochloric acid, and, and, and . . .' Jon cradled her protectively as she wept.

'It might not be that bad, you know,' he tried. 'I mean, this is your third time around. You've probably got nothing to worry about.'

Becky lifted her head and stared him down through teary eyes. 'Tea tray coming out the end of your penis. I'm just saying. Would you be telling me it was nothing to worry about if our roles were reversed?'

'I love you, you know,' said Jon, kissing the top of her head. 'Let's go to bed.'

Tom had his head in his hands. It had been agreed by Mrs Goldman that this year the classes would be putting on joint productions for Christmas, in the hope of raising additional money for the fundraising efforts, meaning Year 2 and Year 3 had been paired together. Ava had been delighted. 'Yes, Mr Jones!' she'd declared over breakfast that morning. 'You can tell Miss Thompson that we're not going to put on a stupid Nativity play. We'll play an exhibition match of football instead!'

Gently, Tom had reminded her that not everyone in the class was able to play football as well as she could. Ava shrugged her shoulders. 'So? They can learn. We'll just tell them that's what we're going to do.' Tom looked unconvinced, and so she followed up with: 'It's a *democracy* you know, Mr Jones.'

How to explain to Ava that a democracy didn't mean always doing what Ava wanted, Tom mused, as he returned to his classroom. That was the question.

Despite her protestations, it turned out that Ava was out of luck. Distracted though she was with thoughts of the spring gala performance, Miss Thompson was still putting her heart and soul into this year's Nativity. The Nativity play had always been what she'd been renowned for prior to leaving Redcoats; the critics' reviews of the year she'd got her Year 4 class to tell the story of Jesus' birth using cooked pasta, formed into words and images on the stage by dancers dressed as Herod, were something Miss Thompson would take with her to her grave. As would those members of the audience who had been unfortunate enough to sit through that particular performance, only maybe for slightly different reasons.

'So this year,' Miss Thompson announced to the combined audience of Year 2 and Year 3 who sat in front of her in the school hall, 'I thought we could put on the Nativity from the point of view of the straw.'

The children stared at her, their mouths wide open. Tom had a feeling his mouth might be wide open too.

'Pardon?' he asked.

Miss Thompson clapped her hands together. 'I know! It's inspired, isn't it? There have been several attempts to portray the Nativity story from a different perspective, but never from that of the straw.'

'That's because it's the most batshit fucking crazy thing I have ever heard of in my life,' said Tom, fortunately inside his head.

'Please, Miss Thompson,' said Satin, who had her hand raised and waving violently over her head. 'I want to be Mary.'

'I want to be Mary too,' came a chorus of voices from what seemed like every other girl in the room, and also Noah Hardcastle.

'I want to be dead,' muttered Ava, staring furiously at Miss Thompson. Tom bit back his laughter.

'No, Satin, no.' Miss Thompson clapped her hands again. 'Children, in this particular telling of the Nativity we won't be having a Mary, or a Joseph, or shepherds, or wise men. They'll be off stage, out of sight. You'll all be playing pieces of straw – matching costumes all round, you can wear your yellow PE shirts and a pair of yellow tights' ('I'm not wearing pissing tights,' Simon Barnes muttered) – 'and you'll be lying down on the stage and talking about how excited you are to have the baby Jesus sleeping on top of you.'

'I hope he's going to be wearing a nappy,' said Noah.

'What do you think, children? Doesn't that sound wonderful?' Miss Thompson looked expectantly at her audience.

There was an appalled silence.

Despite Tom's protestations that could they not, please, just do a traditional Nativity – 'Even if we rang the changes and did let Noah play Mary, which would stop all the girls arguing over who's going to get the part' – Miss Thompson was insistent. 'I hardly need to tell you, Tom, that my experience in the dramatic arts is far greater than yours. No: *STRAW! – The Musical*, it is. I've already started working on the musical numbers.'

Tom shook his head, baffled. 'Can they not just sing carols – "See Him Lying on a Bed of Straw", for example?' He was quite proud of having come up with that one. 'Surely that's loads easier and will save us a huge amount of time?'

Miss Thompson looked at him in disbelief. 'I hope you don't mind me saying, Mr Jones, but are you sure you're cut out for this?'

No. No he fucking wasn't.

Rehearsals took up a surprisingly large amount of the academic week; Tom dreaded to think what he'd be left with to squeeze the National Curriculum into and also somehow get all of his classes through their utterly-pointless-and-completely-stupid SATs once rehearsals for the gala production got underway. He decided to put his head in the sand and refuse to even think about it.

The children had been allocated their parts, which had caused predictable consternation. Vivienne had actually made an appointment to come in and see Miss Thompson and him, such was her horror at the casting.

'But this can't be right, Miss Thompson. Satin tells me she's been cast as Straw 48.'

Miss Thompson nodded. 'Yes, that's right.'

'But Satin's Mary! She's always been Mary, ever since she was old enough to totter on to the stage with my home-made headdress on her head.' Vivienne pulled out a series of professionally shot photographs featuring Satin in her Mary costume. 'See, here she is aged two ... and three ... and four ... and—'

'Yes, thank you. I get the idea.' Miss Thompson, who could be just as bloody-minded as Vivienne in her own way, closed the portfolio of photographs. 'But Satin will not be Mary this year, because there is no Mary. She is Straw 48.'

'Out of how many straws?'

'Sixty,' said Miss Thompson.

Vivienne made a noise rather like a howl, and clutched her chest, as though physically wounded. 'That cannot be right. Satin is NOT Straw 48 ... out of SIXTY! She is Straw 1. Straw 2, at the very least.'

Tom sighed. 'Vivienne, the straws aren't weighted.' He couldn't entirely believe he was even having this conversation. 'Being Straw 48 doesn't mean you are any less important than Straw 1. It's just a way of identifying which child speaks where.'

'That's right,' nodded Miss Thompson. 'There are no lead parts in my Nativity. Every child will be treated the same.'

It was too much for Vivienne, who stood up in absolute horror, snatching up her bag and her portfolio and staring at both of them in a dark fury. 'No lead parts? Then what's the point in doing a performance at all? Really, Miss Thompson, I thought you were supposed to understand the theatre.' And turning on her heel, to their shared relief, she left.

It was just after six on Wednesday evening, and, not for the first time, Gemma really wished that at least one of her children could have been blessed with some kind of a sense of urgency. She'd raced back from work to collect them from after-school club and get them home, fed, and back out in time to visit the extremely prestigious secondary school across the other side of town, St Luke's, which was holding its open evening. With Sam as reluctant as ever to offer up a view on which secondary school he would like to attend, Gemma had been swayed by the hyperbole flying around on the Year 6 Facebook page, and had dutifully put it in her calendar for them all to go along and visit.

Her parents had kindly offered to have Ava for her, which she had been poised to accept, until Ava had intervened, telling her in no uncertain terms that she was *not* going to be left behind, that it was critical that she started to think about this next stage in her education, and that it was clear without her there that her mum and Sam didn't have a hope of making the right decision. Gemma had rapidly lost the will to live and had decided that this was one argument she was unlikely ever to win.

As a result, Gemma now stood in the doorway, brandishing her car keys, begging her children to just, please, hurry the fuck up and get in the car. Sam's disembodied voice floated down the stairs to her. 'I'm coming, Mum. I just need to find some socks.'

'But you were wearing socks when you came home from school. Just wear those ones.'

'Yeah ... I don't know where they've gone.'

'What do you mean you don't know where they've gone? They were on your feet!' Gemma had never known getting dressed could be such a complex process until she'd had children.

'Yeah, and now they're not. So I'm finding some. Chill, Mum.'

Chill? CHILL! It was perhaps fortunate for Sam that, before she could run up the stairs and tell him exactly what she thought of him telling her to 'chill', Ava materialised, dragging behind her an enormous bag that was filled to the brim and threatening to burst open at the zip.

'Ava! Come on, we need to go. We're going to miss the Head's speech if we don't get in the car five minutes ago.'

'Are you going to be the next Doctor Who?' Ava paused from where she was lacing up her studs and looked contemplatively at her mother.

'Am I ... what? What do you mean, am I going to be the next Doctor Who?'

'You said we needed to be in the car five minutes ago, and that wouldn't be possible unless you can bend time, like Doctor Who, so that was why I thought maybe you were going to be the next Doctor Who. Can I bring a football with me?'

Honestly, thought Gemma, corralling a sockless Sam and Ava, enormous bag in tow, into the car. How she hadn't had a complete and utter breakdown a long time ago was nothing short of a minor miracle.

The car park at St Luke's was already overflowing by the time they arrived, and Gemma settled for dumping her car on one of the nearby residential streets and walking briskly to the school gates. Ava, much to Sam's mortification, had spent the journey there transforming herself into the Incredible Hulk, the enormous bag she'd felt necessary to bring with her now explained. Not only had she teamed her football socks and studs with a Hulk costume, she'd also managed out of sight to paint her face green.

'Ava!' Sam looked like he might cry. 'WHY do you have to be so embarrassing? Mum, please don't let her come with us looking like that.'

'Sam! I am doing this for your good, you know.' Ava stood there, defiant. 'What? We need to make sure that this is a school that is accepting of people's differences. And so I thought, what could be more different than having green skin, and so I have decided to come as the Hulk and see if they are nice to me. If they are not nice to me, then Sam, they are definitely not going to be nice to West Ham supporters; but if they are kind to me when I am being the Hulk then you might just about be okay.'

It was going to be a long evening, Gemma thought to herself, as she dragged a protesting Sam and a delighted Ava along behind her. A long, long evening.

Inside, the school was packed. The Head's talk, which she'd hoped to make it in time for, had just finished, and a stream of parents was filing out of the hall. With her typical luck and sense of timing, she walked straight into Vivienne.

'Gemma!' Vivienne looked as appalled as she did, rather as though she'd found something unpleasant-smelling on the sole of her shoe. 'Fancy seeing you here. I didn't think ... I mean, this is quite an exclusive school, you know? They don't just take anyone.' She smirked and chucked Tartan under the chin, who had the good grace to look mortified. 'Not that it really matters to me. Tartan will of course be privately educated; the state system simply isn't up to supporting such genius.'

Gemma would have simply walked away, but she felt a responsibility to Sam, so stood her ground. 'You're right, Vivienne: they don't just take anyone. In fact, I believe from reading their admissions policy, they don't take anyone who isn't allocated a place under that.'

'Oh, Gemma,' Vivienne laughed bitchily, 'I'm only messing with you. You really must learn to take a joke.'

At that point the Head emerged from the assembly hall and Vivienne – who it became rapidly obvious was considering him as a candidate for Husband Number Two, now that Nick was out of the picture – threw herself in his general direction. 'Oh, Mr Fitzpatrick,' she could be heard to gush, 'I'm Vivienne; you might remember me. What an utterly inspiring speech. It's no wonder St Luke's is thriving under your tender care.'

Mr Fitzpatrick looked horrified as she cosied up next to him in her cropped leather bralette and figure-hugging pencil skirt; give him dealing with hundreds of recalcitrant teenagers over managing their mothers, any day. 'Um ... very good. I'm, um, very pleased you enjoyed it.'

Vivienne ran a hand down the Head's tweed-jacketed arm, much to his distress. 'I just really feel so at home here; of course, it's not the first time my darling Tartan and I have paid you a visit. Do you remember the time I came to see you alone and you were kind enough to receive me in your office ...?' She gave a girlie peal of laughter. 'Goodness, that was a memorable experience, wasn't it?'

With a start, Mr Fitzpatrick realised exactly who this woman was: the same one he'd had to practically barricade away from his person with the judicious use of a filing cabinet and the tray he'd had his eleven-o'clock coffee and digestive biscuits on. He shuddered at the very thought.

'Ah ... um ... yes, I'm sure it was very memorable, but as you can see, I have rather a lot of parents to see this evening. So if you don't mind ...' His eyes alighted upon Gemma, Sam and the Hulk, watching on in amusement. 'I tell you what would be an enormous help. As you're so familiar with our school site, why don't you give this family here a guided tour?' He nodded at Gemma. 'Would that be okay with you?'

Gemma could think of a million reasons why that was very not okay with her, none of which she managed to artic-ulate before Vivienne had walked over to her, disgusted at the prospect, yet keen not to do anything that might put off her prospective husband. 'But of course, Mr Fitzpatrick, I'd be happy to help,' she said, in a voice which Gemma could hear only too clearly was laced with fury. 'Come on, Gemma. Let me take you and Sam and' – she cast an appalled look at Ava – '*that* ... round with Tartan and me. Chop-chop, off we go.'

Did she have a choice? Sighing heavily, Gemma followed Vivienne and Tartan, Sam and Ava trailing in her wake, as Ava told her brother in furious tones that 'I am NOT a "that"' ... and Mr Fitzpatrick raced for the sanctity of his office, where he poured himself a stiff whisky and told himself that he really must think about taking early retirement.

The school was enormous; Gemma felt she should have dressed less to impress and more like she was going for a workout at the gym. Panting slightly, she made it to the top of the third flight of stairs and found herself in a hallway. She'd somehow fallen behind Vivienne and the children and peered round a series of classroom doors in an attempt to locate them.

Gemma's complete bemusement as to why Vivienne would lower herself to visit a state school, given her mind was made up to educate Tartan privately, was suddenly cleared up when she happened upon the two of them: Vivienne was in the middle of what seemed to be a fully prepared monologue to the Head of Year 7 about Tartan's obvious genius. Of course. Vivienne was never going to miss out on an opportunity to subject a captive audience to the many and varied plaudits of her prodigal son … even if they were employed by the state sector. To be fair to Tartan, he looked mortified about the whole situation; even more so when Vivienne asked if she could use the classroom projector 'as I just have a short PowerPoint presentation to run through with you which highlights some of Tartan's greatest achievements to date.'

Leaving Tartan to his fate, it took Gemma a couple more classrooms before she found Ava and Sam, who were in the modern languages section. Sam, looking as mortified as Tartan had, was slumped on a chair, while Ava/The Hulk was at the front of the classroom, talking to the really rather beautiful French teacher whose nametag declared him to be Mr Michel.

'So I just don't think Sam is ever going to be very good at French,' Ava told Mr Michel sadly, 'because all he is ever interested in is looking up the rude words. Did you know, his teacher at school once said to him "*Ca va?*", which I know means how are you, and instead of saying that he was good, Sam said, "*Merde*!" Do you know what that means?'

'AVA!' Stopping her daughter before she could reel off any more swear words, Gemma marched to the front of the room and over to the amused-looking Mr Michel. 'I'm so sorry, she doesn't know what she's talking about.'

'Yes I do!' Ava was having none of it. 'I know exactly what I'm talking about, because that word that Sam was saying, it means sh—'

'YES, Ava.' Gemma stopped her in her tracks, gently holding one hand over her mouth. 'We all know exactly what that means, and there's no need for you to repeat it, thank you very much.' She smiled at Mr Michel, who with any luck was going to be so impressed by her decisive parenting that he was going to forget all about a seven-year-old reeling off French swear words in his classroom.

Hauling Ava out of the classroom, Sam dragging his feet behind them, Gemma's humiliation reached new levels as she heard the little girl announce, clear as a bell: 'He was very good-looking, Mummy. Do you think that when you finish doing sloppy kissing with Mr Jones you might want to do sloppy kissing with him instead?'

'AVA,' Gemma fury-whispered at her daughter, 'come on, let's go and see the rest of the school.'

On the plus side, they had at least managed to lose Vivienne. Systematically, they worked their way through the rest of the school: Sam, slumped and muttering an 'it's fine' whenever Gemma attempted to ask him what he thought of it all; Ava, at her most Ava-ish, marching up to every teacher she saw and grilling them on anything from the football provision at the school to what the evacuation plan was if Donald Trump tried to blow up the building. Credit to the teaching staff; for the most part they engaged with the little girl delightfully, and Gemma felt herself warming to this as a genuine option for Sam. Redcoats would be a hard act to follow, and yet Gemma felt like St Luke's might be somewhere Sam could truly thrive.

Finally, with even Ava/The Hulk starting to flag, they wandered across the courtyard to the sixth-form centre. Here, students studied for their A levels in a far more relaxed environment. Gemma engaged the Head of Sixth Form in conversation while Sam looked down at his feet.

Meanwhile, Ava had made a beeline for the common-room area and was walking in circles round the many armchairs that were laid out in order for students to relax with their friends.

A strident voice behind them alerted them to the fact that Vivienne had arrived; she had managed to track down the long-suffering Mr Fitzpatrick and had insisted that he personally introduce her to the Head of Sixth Form, 'because Tartan really is so tremendously advanced, and I wouldn't wonder if it might perhaps suit him to start studying for A levels on the side, so to speak, while he takes his GCSEs'.

'THERE you are!' Vivienne proclaimed when she saw Gemma, annoyance clear in her voice. 'Really, Gemma, Mr Fitzpatrick asks me personally to take you around the school ... and then you just disappear on me. I do think you might have made more of an effort to keep up ... but I suppose we can't all be blessed with my level of athletic prowess.' She looked meaningfully at Gemma's muffin top, taking delight in stretching up and revealing even more of her own taut midriff as she did so.

Gemma was about to smile beatifically while writing 'WANKPOODLE' on the roof of her mouth with her tongue – her usual method of dealing with Vivienne – when a little voice piped up.

'Mummy, Sam, did you know that lots of these chairs have writing on them?' Ava had been fascinated by the way students over the years had graffitied the common-room armchairs, and had been studying them intently. 'Mr Fitzpatrick, here is one about you. Let me read it to you.'

It was a little bit like when you knew a terrible disaster was about to occur, but were powerless to stop it, Gemma reflected afterwards. Her mouth was already opening to tell Ava to keep quiet, that whatever was written on the chair about Mr Fitzpatrick, he almost certainly didn't want to hear it, and even Sam had emerged from his self-induced stupor to raise his head, aware that something awful might just be about to happen, equally unable to do anything about it.

In a voice that echoed around the silent space, her green facepaint smeared all over her face and on to her blonde curls, Ava precisely articulated. 'This chair, Mr Fitzpatrick, says, "Mr Fitzpatrick is a cunty twat."' Her face screwed up in confusion at the unfamiliar words, before she smiled reassuringly at the Head. 'I have never heard of a "cunty twat", Mr Fitzpatrick, but whatever it is, I am sure it is something absolutely *lovely*.'

If she never saw Mr Fitzpatrick again, Gemma concluded, as she dragged a protesting Ava back to the car ('But what did I do?'), a mortified Sam following . . . it would still be far too soon.

CHAPTER NINE

It took quite some time for them all to recover from their trip to St Luke's. During that period, Gemma and Sam tentatively visited three other schools; Ava was told in no uncertain terms that she would not be joining them. 'They are just upset because I told that headmaster what that chair said,' she told Becky sadly, who was looking after her during one such school visit. 'I don't know what they were so upset about. Mummy says that you shouldn't call people things like that, but it was not me saying that, it was the writing.' She looked at Becky. 'Is calling someone a cunty twat a really really bad thing, Becky?'

Stifling her laughter, Becky agreed that yes, calling anyone a cunty twat was a pretty bad thing, that she understood that Ava hadn't actually called Mr Fitzpatrick that, that she had just been reading it out, but it still wasn't the kind of thing you should be shouting out in public.

'So you could write it in a story?' Ava mused, thinking about the homework she had to do. Becky would have paid good money to have seen Miss Thompson's face when Ava handed in her creative-writing book to be marked the next week.

Sam had continued to appear completely uninterested in any of the schools they went around, and so Gemma nearly fell off her chair when, a couple of weeks before the school places had to be submitted, he suddenly announced at dinner that he had decided where he would like to go. 'I liked Catswells, Mum.'

'Pardon?' They'd been chatting about football – what else? – and Sam's comment had come completely out of the blue.

'I liked Catswells.' He shrugged. 'What? It felt really nice, and I think I would do well there.'

As this was the only opinion Sam had offered up at any point during the secondary school selection process, Gemma jumped on it. 'Fantastic! I really liked Catswells too.' A smaller school than many of the others they had looked at, she had been really impressed by the attitudes of the staff and the range of extra-curricular activities that were open to the students. 'It's not easy to get into, mind, but it's definitely worth a try, right?'

'Sam,' Ava was stern, 'are you sure you want to go to Catswells? None of your friends will be going there, and then you will be all alone and everyone will flush your head down the toilet, and—'

'AVA.' In a firm but not unpleasant voice, Sam for once shut his little sister down. 'My friends will be going there, and anyway, it's my choice, and Catswells is where I want to go. Is that okay, Mum?'

Smiling, Gemma opened her laptop. 'That is definitely okay. Here, why don't we sit together and fill in the application form so we can submit it in plenty of time?'

Ava looked furious as her mum and Sam pulled their chairs together and started typing on the laptop. 'WELL. I do not think it is okay for you to speak to me like that, Sam. I know why you are being like this. It must be because you are having your PUBERTY.' And she stormed out, as Gemma and Sam looked in bemusement at each other for a moment and then burst out laughing.

School application submitted, it seemed like no time at all before preparations for Christmas were in full swing, and Gemma found herself trapped in a never-ending cycle of buying presents, losing presents somewhere in the house, panicking that she'd failed to buy presents, buying replacement presents, and then feeling her soul dissipate into tiny pieces as Ava brightly announced to her that, in fact, everything she'd written down on her list for Father Christmas wasn't what she really wanted at all, and she'd just decided that the only thing she actually wanted in the entire world was the much advertised self-proclaimed Toy of the Year, which of course was completely out of stock and entirely unobtainable.

'Ava, you can't just change your mind like that,' Gemma gently berated her daughter. 'Everyone will have already bought your presents. It's too late, I'm afraid.'

Ava looked at her as though she was stupid. 'No they

won't have done. It's only the middle of December. Father Christmas won't put all of our presents on to his sleigh until Christmas Eve, that's what you always tell us. So there's still plenty of time for him to get it for us.'

Gemma sighed. Ava had something of a laissez-faire approach to Father Christmas, choosing to believe in him when it suited her, and to completely deny it when it didn't. Gemma still shuddered when she thought of the time that a four-year-old Ava had announced to the rest of her nursery class that 'Father Christmas has died, you know. It was on the news', and Gemma had spent the rest of Ava's time at nursery issuing grovelling apologies to the parents of the other children in the class, emotionally scarred as they were by Ava's declaration.

Sam, who Gemma had been convinced had worked out that Father Christmas was actually a fictional creation, designed to bring the magic of Christmas to children everywhere, had announced to her in September, apropos of nothing, that it was okay, he had had his doubts, but now he had worked out with absolute certainty that Father Christmas really did exist.

'Really?' Gemma scratched her head. 'How come?'

'So,' continued Sam, 'I thought that it was actually the mums and the dads, but then last year you showed me and Ava that video, the one that showed him arriving in that boy's house and leaving all the presents' – Gemma remembered it well, a wonderful CGI-ed YouTube creation, by a US dad who worked for a film company, made for his son – 'and then I realised that I'd got it totally wrong. He does exist. So now I know that, and when anyone tells me at school that he's not real, I just call them a massive hairy git.' He looked very proud of himself.

'Um.' Gemma wasn't entirely sure what to be most concerned about: the fact that the video she'd put on for Ava's benefit – assuming that Sam (who spent half his life playing computer games and looking at CGI graphics that clearly weren't real) would see it for what it was – had had the unexpected effect of causing her son to suddenly believe in Father Christmas all over again ... or the fact that he was calling his classmates massive hairy gits. Good, that would be another nice thing for her to have to unpick before he went to secondary school. She couldn't wait for that conversation.

Rehearsals for *STRAW! The Musical* had ramped up considerably over the last few weeks, leaving both Tom and Ava close to breaking point. Mutinously, Ava had capitulated, reluctantly agreeing to participate and take on the role of Straw 10.

'I got you that part because I thought you would like it, having the same number as Eden Hazard,' Tom had whispered to her during one particular rehearsal.

Ava had given him a withering look. 'I know you're not supposed to say this to teachers, but if you think having the number 10 would make me like having to be in this play, then you really are stupid.'

Now, at last, the evening of the performance was here, and mums, dads and grandparents filed into the packed hall and took their seats.

Backstage, chaos was raging. Simon Barnes, in particular, was refusing to put on his yellow tights.

'I'm not putting them on,' he told a pleading Miss Thompson. 'So that's that.'

'But Simon, darling, they're an integral part of your costume,' she begged.

'Yeah, well, they're squashing my ball sack, and so I'm not putting them on,' Simon announced decisively, to sniggers from the rest of the class.

'Simon! We don't use language like this, do we? Come on, now.'

Simon was unrepentant. 'You might not, Miss, but I do, especially when you're trying to make me put on a stupid pair of tights that squash my ball sack.'

'SIMON! Just stop this now and put the tights on. It can't be that bad.'

Simon looked her square in the face. 'How would you know? You haven't got a ball sack.'

It was at this point Tom took over, taking Simon to one side, helping him into his yellow tights, and reminding him of all the reasons why it wasn't really okay to start yelling about your ball sack in the classroom, however squashed it might be.

Finally, the children were ready, lying in their places on the stage behind the curtain, ready to sing their opening number. Simon Barnes was next to Ava and was writhing around, more like he was being a snake than a straw, Ava thought to herself.

'Sssshhhh,' Ava whispered sternly. Simon ignored her, groaning louder and clutching at himself.

'What's the matter?' she tried.

And thus it was that, as the curtain rose on the scene,

the audience were greeted not by the sight of sixty perfectly drilled children singing 'We're Yellow and We're Waiting for a Very Special Baby' ... but of Simon Barnes, leaping up in the middle of the stage and shouting, 'MY BALL SACK, MY BLOODY BALL SACK', while all around him, the cast descended into absolute mayhem.

It was certainly, Gemma and Becky declared afterwards, as they stood around the table serving mulled wine and mince pies at the back of the hall, one of the most memorable Nativities they'd ever attended.

'It's not often I find myself lost for words,' Becky said, 'but I genuinely think this might be one such moment. I mean ... where do you even begin?'

Gemma shook her head, half laughing, half afraid of quite what kind of carnage Tom must be involved with clearing up backstage. 'I actually don't know. One thing's for certain, though: I think in her next production Miss Thompson might go for a costume colour that does a slightly better job of hiding bodily fluids.'

Becky agreed. 'Although I've never seen a piece of straw vomit before; nor punch another piece of straw in the nose. Always good to experience firsts.'

'And the red blood was very festive,' quipped Gemma, taking another sip of mulled wine. 'Poor teachers, though, having to deal with all that. And they've got the gala performance to come. I wonder if they realised just what they were letting themselves in for.'

Tom had been wondering the same thing. His face was sombre when he finally finished at the school and stopped by at Gemma's, his girlfriend having long since returned and sent both children up to bed following Ava's threat to bite off both of Sam's ears. ('But he told me I looked like a singing yellow penis!' 'And you DID look like a singing yellow penis.' 'I was a STRAW!' 'A penis-shaped straw.')

'Hello, love. Sorry I'm so late. I got called into an emergency meeting.' She raised her eyebrows. 'Sharon wanted to see both myself and Angela. She was obviously furious with what happened tonight, said that it simply wasn't the kind of behaviour we could tolerate at Redcoats. I explained that most of it was just the kids in high spirits, that they were messing around, that we'd speak to them tomorrow. She thinks Simon was the root cause – she's probably not wrong – and she's banned him from performing in any future productions.'

Gemma bit back a smile at the thought of what Andrea would have to say at her 'precious angel' being banned from the gala performance. She didn't envy Mrs Goldman that particular showdown.

Ava hurtled back down the stairs, before stopping short at the sight of Tom. 'Oh. Hello, Mr Jones. You took a long time. Where have you been?'

'Hello, Ava.' He tousled the little girl's curls. 'I've been at a meeting at school. I had to go and see Mrs Goldman. She was very cross, you know, about everything that happened tonight.'

Ava looked defiant and crossed her arms, staring at him with those piercing blue eyes. 'It wasn't my fault. It was Simon. I don't even have a ball sack.' Gemma and

Tom both hid their smiles. 'So I don't know what you're blaming me for.'

Tom shook his head. 'Whoa whoa whoa. I'm not blaming you for anything. I'm just saying, tonight was a bit of a disaster, and Mrs Goldman is probably going to want to speak to you all tomorrow.'

'Fine.' Ava stood her ground. 'I hope that Mrs Goldman *does* want to speak to us tomorrow, because I want to speak to her, too. About why she needs to think about the consequences of making us stand on a stage and sing songs dressed as straws.' She sighed. 'Really, it's no wonder that it all went wrong.'

Tom was watching Ava closely. 'Ava ... are you trying to tell me that this was planned? That you all meant to spoil tonight's performance?'

'No!' Fire flashed in Ava's eyes; there was nothing she hated so much as someone blaming her for something she didn't do. Well, that and not being allowed to play football.

'Okay, okay.' Tom took a step backwards. 'I believe you. Listen, you must be exhausted. Isn't it time for you to get to bed?' He looked at Gemma for affirmation, but before she could say anything, as if from nowhere, Ava exploded.

'It is NOT time for me to get to bed, Mr Jones, and you are NOT in charge of me. You are NOT my dad, and so I do not know WHY you think you can tell me it is time for bed.'

'AVA!' Gemma was horrified; she took her daughter gently by both arms and knelt down until she was at her height. 'What on earth do you think you're doing? Where did that come from? You don't talk to Mr Jones like that. You don't talk to anyone like that!'

Ava was unrepentant. 'He's trying to tell me what to do, Mum, and I don't like that. I don't like that at all.'

'You need to apologise.' Gemma held her gaze.

'FINE.' In the most unapologetic tones possible, Ava responded: 'I'm SORRY, Mr Jones, that you were so rude and told me that I had to go to bed when you're not even in charge of me. When you're not part of my FAMILY.' And then she ran upstairs and slammed her bedroom door.

The house was silent. Inexplicably, Gemma found herself close to tears. 'I'm so sorry. I can't believe she spoke to you like that. I'll get her to apologise properly in the morning.' Harassed, she ran her hand through her curls.

'Don't worry.' Tom pulled her into his arms and kissed her lightly on top of her head. 'She'll be exhausted; she's had quite the day. Now, do you want me to stay, or shall I head off?'

Gemma hardly heard what he said; a million different thoughts were suddenly racing around her head. Distracted, she looked up at him. 'What did you say?'

He smiled. 'Looks like Ava's not the only one who's exhausted. I said, did you want me to stay or shall I head off?'

Gemma needed to think. 'I think ... probably better that you go back to yours tonight.' She deliberately kept her tone light.

'No problem. Although I'm not going to pretend I don't

miss you like crazy when I haven't got you by my side.' He kissed her deeply, a long, lingering kiss that at any other time would have made her knees go weak, but tonight she was deep in thought.

He picked up his bag, and turned at the front door to say goodnight to her. 'I love you, you know.'

For the first time, distracted by thoughts of Ava, she didn't say it back.

CHAPTER TEN

It had been an unusually sedate end to the term at Redcoats, thanks to the disastrous performance of *STRAW! The Musical*. Despite that, there was clear excitement in the air as the children brought out of school plastic bags filled with crap.

'Not literal crap, I hope,' Becky had said when Gemma had first forewarned her of this end-of-term tradition. 'Although, to be fair, if I look at some of the stuff that Rosie comes home with, it would be quite hard to distinguish it from an Actual Turd.'

The two friends had agreed to convene at Gemma's for a celebratory end-of-term get-together that night. 'All the Schloer you can possibly drink!' Gemma cheerfully told Becky, who groaned, and announced that if she never drank a glass of Schloer again, it would probably be too soon.

Ava was having a sleepover round at Rosie's. Having left Jon in charge next door, Sam upstairs glued to his computer, Gemma and Becky settled down on the sofa, ordering enough takeaway food for twenty people and raising their glasses of Pinot Noir and Schloer respectively.

'Cheers! We made it to the end of term!' Gemma clinked her glass against Becky's, who drank with considerably less enthusiasm, grimacing as the painfully sweet Schloer made contact with her taste buds.

'I keep thinking they're going to come up with a non-alcoholic drink that doesn't taste like the love child of a bottle of Lucozade and a hefty dose of cough medicine.' She winced. 'Seems like I'm going to be a long time waiting. I might just have a glass of water instead, if it's all the same to you.'

They relived the horrendous Nativity performance; Gemma filled Becky in on the scene Tom had played out to her, when an outraged Andrea Barnes had accosted Mrs Goldman in the playground and asked her what in the world she was playing at, that of course it hadn't been her precious Simon's fault that he had kicked off, that he was quite right to speak up if his most delicate parts were at risk, that did Mrs Goldman really want it on her conscience if little Simikins was never to have children of his own as a result of his testicles being compressed in a pair of yellow tights.

'I imagine Mrs Goldman probably thought she was doing a service to humankind, suppressing the chance of future generations of Simon Barnes,' quipped Becky, easing herself into a more comfortable position on the sofa. 'That child is something else. I pity any teacher who has to contend with him.

'Speaking of which … how *is* the delectable Tom?' She was expecting Gemma's eyes to go all soppy, as they always did at any mention of her boyfriend, but to her surprise, her friend shifted in her seat and looked distinctly uncomfortable.

'Fine. He's fine.'

There was a short pause. 'Fine? Really, Gem? The great love of your life, and you've just described him to me as "fine"? Come on now: even Sam could do better than that. What's up? You guys had a row, or something?'

No. No, they hadn't had a row. In some ways, it would have been better if they had. A row at least would have got things over and done with, and they could have gone back to normal again. Instead, Gemma's thoughts and concerns had been going round and round, eating her up inside, as she pretended to Tom that everything was completely fine, whilst at the same time increasingly keeping him at arm's length. It had not been a happy few days.

'We're just … it's difficult,' she settled for. 'You know what it's like. Relationships. Never exactly straightforward, are they?'

Becky laughed. 'Oh, c'mon, do you think I was born yesterday? No, you're absolutely right: relationships are very much not straightforward. But that's when you get to the same jaded point that Jon and I are at, where you've seen each other at your absolute worst, when you've let all social niceties go by the wayside, when you barely remember to say hello to each other any more and your idea of a romantic gesture is taking the bins out or remembering to put the toilet seat down. You and Tom are still in the first throes of lust, when you're reduced to a panting, quivering wreck just by the mention of each other's name. So don't try and pull the wool over my eyes. What's going on?'

Gemma didn't need to be asked again. Willingly, she unburdened herself; telling Becky how the exchange between Tom and Ava the other night had meant that, for the first time, the situation had properly hit her. Because what she had with Tom wasn't – could never be – just a normal relationship. Ava's uncharacteristic behaviour towards her mum's boyfriend had meant it had hit her like a ton of bricks. It wasn't just her and Tom in this relationship. Ava and Sam were irretrievably mixed up in it as well. For it to work, all four of them needed to be happy with it. And, right now, it really didn't seem like Ava was happy.

Becky shook her head. 'But Ava's fine! I've seen her a couple of times since then when I've gone to do pick-up at school, she's been running around at after-school club with a football begging Tom to sack off doing his marking and come and referee for her. It doesn't look like there're any problems between them. She was probably just overtired that night.'

Momentarily, Gemma felt reassured, until all her previous doubts came crashing back. 'But how can I be sure, Becks? That's the problem. I'd never even considered how my relationship with Tom would affect them, until I saw that little scene play out the other night, and I realised how completely stupid and naïve I've been, crashing into this and thinking only about myself, only about what I want. I'm a selfish arse, is what I am.' Crossly, she took another swig of her wine.

'Now, I know I'm not the authority on much, but I can say with some confidence that you are really not a selfish arse,' Becky responded. 'For a start off, a selfish arse wouldn't even be having this conversation: they'd be off shacked up with their other half leaving their kids to fend for themselves. You'd move heaven and earth to make sure Sam and Ava are okay; I've seen that with my own eyes. Their feckless father's fucked off once again to a city that he couldn't even point to on a map, leaving you holding the fort, and you've given everything you have to make sure it doesn't negatively impact on the kids, that they're happy and settled and generally A-OK. Please, please don't put yourself down and pretend to be something that you're not. You're bloody superwoman, Gem, is what you are.'

Gemma shook her head sadly. 'I'm not. I only wish I was. I spend pretty much morning to night feeling like I'm failing. Failing the kids. Failing Tom. Failing my job. Failing you, for not being a better friend, for not being around more.' She sighed heavily. 'I look at all the other mums out there and I just don't know how they do it.'

'But they don't do it!' Becky was up off the sofa now, her eyes bright. 'That's the whole point! *Everyone* feels like you do: it's the Great Parent Conspiracy. The Great Life Conspiracy, in fact, because I don't think it's just parents who suffer from this. We convince ourselves that everyone else is having it all, that everyone else is winning at life while we fail miserably, careering from one crisis to the next and never quite feeling like we're good enough. But we are good enough, Gem! All of us. Being a great parent, a great friend, a great person ... it's not about being perfect. It's just about being good enough. And you are.' Her face was serious. 'You really are.'

Gemma attempted a smile. 'Nice try. You almost had me believing that there.'

'It's true!' Becky sat back down, looking closely at her friend. 'And the one thing I worry about with you, Gem, is that you very rarely seem to think about what you need. You're always prioritising everyone – everything – else. For the first time in your life, you've met someone who makes you truly happy. And I think you owe it to yourself to throw everything you can at that.'

'My kids come first. You know that.'

'Of course I know that! But I don't think you being with Tom and the kids coming first need to be mutually exclusive, that's all I'm saying,' Becky concluded.

At that point the doorbell rang, and they were distracted by enough Chinese food to feed the street. Sam joined them for dinner, hoovering up noodles as though he was auditioning for a role as the next Dyson model, and by the time the last prawn crackers had been crunched and Sam had come up with three hundred reasons why the concept that he should be asked to load the dishwasher was the most unfair suggestion in the known universe, bordering on child cruelty . . . the opportunity for Becky to press Gemma any more on the subject was gone.

Gemma and Tom were perfect for each other! She knew it, and she had every confidence that things would work out just fine, she thought to herself as she walked back home, to find Jon decamped to the spare room after Rosie and Ava had taken over the master bedroom – 'Because we want to know what it would be like if we were lesbians, and we thought that if we slept in the same bed that would be a good start,' Ava had told him seriously.

Gemma, lying awake, an over-consumption of sweet-and-sour chicken sitting uncomfortably in her stomach, only wished she had Becky's confidence that everything was going to work out.

'And a Merry Fucking Christmas to me.' It was Boxing Day, and Tom was sitting alone in his flat, the forlorn party popper his nephew Isaac had pressed into his hand as he'd left his parents' that morning, and which he'd just set off in an attempt to create some much needed festivity in his life right now, his only companion.

He'd had such high hopes for this Christmas. For the first time since he'd left the bank, he was in a happy, secure relationship, with the woman he loved more than anyone else in the world. Christmas, however anyone tried to spin it, was an utterly shitty time for singles.

But then had come the school Nativity and the aftermath back at Gemma's, when, out of nowhere, Ava had exploded at him. At the time, Tom had taken it with a pinch of salt. Ava was overtired and overexcited, she'd had a long day, and Tom knew enough about children to know that the very worst of their behaviour was saved for when they were with those adults they felt most secure with.

Since then, though, Gemma seemed to have gone out of her way to avoid him. They'd always known that they'd spend Christmas Day separately, with their respective sets of parents; but Tom had imagined cosy evenings together, as the kids played around them with their presents, Tom and Gemma sat together on the sofa, and his home was filled with love and laughter.

Instead, his flat sat as silent as his mobile phone. Gemma had texted him to wish him Happy Christmas, of course; to thank him for the beautiful presents he'd so carefully curated for her, and to tell him how much she loved him. There'd been no answer, though, when he'd tried to call her, and the text he'd sent earlier that day to ask if she and Sam and Ava would like to come over that evening had thus far gone unresponded to.

His sister Georgina, emboldened by one too many glasses of Asti Spumante, had not held back her opinions on the situation, when she'd asked Tom on Christmas Day night how things were going with his girlfriend.

'Um.' He had shrugged. 'If you'd asked me a couple of weeks ago, I would have told you everything was perfect. But now . . .' He sighed. 'If I'm really honest, I'm not entirely sure.' He filled Georgina in on what had happened on the night of the Nativity, and Gemma's subsequent disappearing act.

'She's not going to hurt you, is she?' Georgina's eyes flashed fire; she remembered all too well the state Tom's ex had left him in, just before he'd departed the bank. 'Because if she is, then I'm telling you now, you need to tell her to fuck off and find yourself someone who isn't going to fuck you around.' Her tone softened. 'Look, I know that you love her. I just don't want to see you get hurt again.'

'Thanks, sis.' He put a brotherly arm around her and

squeezed her tightly. 'But Gemma's not like that. Honestly; she wouldn't hurt a fly. I'm sure it's just a blip; I'm sure everything will be fine.'

How he hoped he was right.

After two weeks of what felt like almost continuous eating, drinking and celebrating, before they knew it, the Christmas holidays were over, it was the start of January and the beginning of a new term. At Vivienne's insistence, Fundraisers United had met up the previous week, to review performance against their fundraising goals for the term.

'Okay.' Kristin had opened up a spreadsheet on her MacBook. 'We raised £150 at the November coffee morning; £207 from the cake sale; £368 from selling mulled wine and mince pies at the Nativity performances, and a further £514 from ticket sales, although £150 of that had to be held back to pay for the additional sound and lighting equipment Miss Thompson had hired in. So that leaves us having raised a grand total of . . .'

'One thousand and eighty-nine pounds,' said Becky dully. 'A thousand measly pounds. Basically, we're already a third of the year through, and we've raised one seventieth of our total. Absolutely fucking pathetic. I don't know why we're bothering. We might as well bulldoze the school ourselves and have done with it.'

None of the rest of the committee said anything, but it was all too clear that they were thinking exactly the same thing.

At the first staff meeting of the term, Mrs Goldman gave

Miss Thompson a full third of the agenda to outline her plans for the gala performance, which had been scheduled for the end of April, just after the school had returned from their Easter break. She had prepared a PowerPoint presentation to take them through the proposed timeline between now and then.

'But this is ridiculous,' said Mrs Willoughby, who taught Year 5. 'Angela, this rehearsal schedule suggests you're putting together a West End production, not marshalling a few kids to stand on stage and trot out a couple of lines. We just can't have this amount of class time given over to rehearsals. And as for auditions! You don't need the school hall booked out for three whole weeks to hold auditions! There're only two hundred children in the school.'

Miss Thompson was having none of it. 'Of course I do.' She laughed throatily. 'Really, anyone would think that the rest of you don't want this production to be a success.'

The teaching staff stared back at her, their expressions mutinous. It was Mrs Goldman who spoke first. 'Angela, of course we want the production to be a success. But the staff are right; we also have a National Curriculum to deliver. We're well overdue for an Ofsted inspection; the last thing we want is the inspectors turning up and discovering we've replaced SPAG with turning ourselves into the school from *Fame*.'

'I hardly think that Ofsted are going to bother turning up to inspect a school they've been told is on the brink of closure,' Miss Thompson retorted, before her eyes lit up. 'Ooh, the children singing on top of a car, though; wouldn't that be marvellous?' she trilled. 'I wonder if we could persuade the local garage to loan us one. I could speak to Mr Cook about widening the hall doors in order to get it in there.'

Tom sighed. It was going to be a long, long term.

Back in the Year 3 classroom, Ava was thinking the same. Having secretly hoped that this term might be an improvement on the last, now that that stupid Nativity play was over, she realised that that was very much not going to be the case. Here they were, supposedly meant to be getting on with learning their times tables, but in reality, having various members of the class constantly asking ridiculous questions about the play – they had very quickly worked out that the easiest way to distract Miss Thompson from doing Actual Work was to get her on to the subject of the gala performance. Ava growled under her breath as Satin primped and preened herself in front of Miss Thompson's desk.

'And what will you be looking for the stars of your show to do, Miss Thompson?' asked Satin breathily.

Miss Thompson smiled indulgently. 'Sit down, please, Satin dear. There won't be any stars of the show. It's an ensemble production.'

'A what?' Simon Barnes paused from where he was surreptitiously kneeing his neighbour in the testicles, underneath the table. 'What's a Womble Production, Miss?'

'An ensemble production, Simon.' Her eyes narrowed, remembering the previous term's debacle. 'Not that you'll be involved, of course. Anyway, an ensemble production is where you don't have any lead roles, but everyone joins together to create a beautiful outpouring of creativity.' Her eyes were misty as she spoke, reminiscing. 'I remember a production we toured down to Nice. *Womb!* Every member of the cast played an egg, moving down the fallopian tubes, ready to be fertilised by ...' She trailed off, remembering that she wasn't supposed to be covering sex education with Year 3.

'PENISES!' shouted out Noah Hardcastle, who, thanks to a multitude of elder brothers and sisters, was well schooled on exactly what went on in wombs. The rest of the class let out shrieks of laughter, except for Satin, who was still staring at Miss Thompson crossly.

'At least we only had to be pieces of straw,' Rosie whispered to Ava.

'I just don't understand what the point is, Miss Thompson,' Satin continued. 'If you're not going to be a star, then why would anyone bother doing a play?' She exhaled dramatically. 'If I ended up in the chorus, then I'd probably DIE.'

'We can but hope,' Ava whispered.

'Satin, what have I told you before?' Miss Thompson remonstrated with her. 'Actors don't go into the theatre because they want to be stars. They go into the theatre because it's their calling; their passion.'

'Then they're stupid, aren't they?' Satin folded her little arms and stamped her foot. 'I want to be a star, and I'm *going* to be a star, and my mummy's in charge of Fundraisers United, so I'm going to tell her to tell you to make me be a star, and then you won't have any choice in the matter.' She turned on her heel and stormed back to her desk, leaving a speechless Miss Thompson staring after her.

'If she was my daughter, I'd lock her in the airing cupboard,' Ava told Miss Thompson sternly.

It was break time, and Ava and Rosie were kicking a football between themselves, well out of view of Miss Thompson, who was on playground duty that day. Ava was fuming; Satin had wasted almost all of that morning's lessons talking about the stupid play, which had meant Miss Thompson hadn't had time to test them on their times tables, which had meant that Ava hadn't got the five house points she had been absolutely convinced she was going to get, because she was the best in the class at her four times table, she even knew four times eight which almost *no one* else did, even Sam still got that wrong, although Sam was extremely stupid, so that was probably why.

'I just don't see what the point is of this play.' Ava grumpily retrieved the ball from the bushes and expertly controlled it with her feet before kicking it towards Rosie. 'It's not going to raise all of the money we need. Plays are stupid, no one is going to want to come and see it. Why couldn't we have played a football match instead? People like watching football.'

Rosie's eyes were bright. 'Maybe we could do a football match as well.'

Ava shook her head. 'We can't. I asked Mr Jones. He said that the teachers were going to be too busy with the play. More like he's going to be too busy doing sloppy kissing with my mum. Urrrgggghhhhh.' Both children looked appalled at the very thought, and Ava booted the ball violently, as though to physically express her disgust.

'Stop it, Ava.' Rosie jogged to retrieve the ball before Miss Thompson caught sight of what they were up to and confiscated it.

Ava, unusually, looked contrite. 'Sorry, Rosie. I didn't mean to.'

'Do you think the play is going to raise all of the money we need?' Rosie asked.

Ava shook her head emphatically. 'No way. Seventy thousand pounds is *loads* of money. We'd probably have to ... rob a bank to get that much money!'

'Should we rob a bank?' Rosie suggested tentatively.

'NO. No, we would get into a *lot* of trouble if we did that. But we do need to find a way of raising the money. It's obvious that none of the grown-ups know what they are doing. Come on, we have to think. If we needed to get seventy thousand pounds, where would be the best place to go?'

CHAPTER ELEVEN

As their daughter was, that very moment, plotting with her friend to save their school, Becky and Jon climbed out of their car in front of the church hall where they were due to meet Andrea and the rest of the antenatal group.

'This is ridiculous.' Becky squeezed herself out from behind the wheel of the Range Rover. Her morning sickness had passed, to be replaced with an appetite like nothing she'd ever experienced before. Frankly, she'd have eaten anything that wasn't nailed down. As a result, while she might have only been five and a bit months' pregnant, her bump had expanded to a size that had elderly gentlemen moving to avoid her in the street, lest her waters suddenly explode all over them, and seemingly every second person she met telling her that she must be due 'any day now'.

'What's ridiculous, love?' Jon held her hand as she locked the car and they walked across the road together.

'This! Having to come to these classes is bad enough, but to have to do them on a working day as well. It's a bloody good job my job's as flexible as it is.'

Jon raised one eyebrow at her. 'It would be a bit bloody hypocritical if it wasn't.'

Becky hit him with her handbag. 'Oh, shush.'

Daphne, Andrea and the rest of the class were already in situ when Becky and Jon walked in. Today, they appeared to have eschewed chairs for reclining on yoga mats. Becky looked at them, askance. 'Um . . . okay if I get a chair?'

Daphne shook her head. 'No, no, no. You won't want a chair today. We're going to be sharing our previous birth stories, to help Violet, Geni, Sophia and Jason when it comes to writing their birth plans. But before we do so, Andrea has offered to give us a practical demonstration of some of the birthing positions we might want to consider.

Becky sighed heavily as Andrea took centre stage and beamed round at the group. 'I firmly believe that the birthing position you choose can make or break how well you're able to birth your baby. Nigel and I had religiously studied the possibilities available to us when I was pregnant with our little angel Simon – who, let me tell you now, was not a small baby, weighing in at just over ten pounds.' The women in the room collectively winced. 'But I suffered not a single tear, or even a graze, and I firmly believe that my choice of birthing position was the reason why.' She clapped her hands together to ensure she had their attention. 'Nigel's kindly offered to be my model today – not that he'll be having the baby, of course – so that I can manipulate him into the correct positions, and you can really see how they work in practice.'

Becky lowered herself on to the yoga mat next to her husband, muttering 'You are fucking kidding me', as Nigel nipped behind the curtain at one end of the hall and returned wearing a pair of cycling leggings.

'Ooh, I wonder what kind of bike he's got?' mused Jon, a keen cyclist himself. 'Maybe we could invite them round for dinner.' Becky gave him A Look.

'Now then,' announced Andrea, as Nigel reclined next to her, in a position disturbingly reminiscent of a page out of *The Joy of Sex*. 'Let's start with the obvious. Lying flat on your back, like you see in all the movies. Nigel.' She gestured towards him and he immediately flopped flat on his back, his legs splayed out towards his wife. To her horror, Becky realised Nigel's cycling leggings were going to leave absolutely nothing to the imagination; despite doing her very best to avoid it, her eyes were so inextricably drawn to the bulge in his groin that she thought she would likely be able to identify his scrotum in a line-up.

Over the next twenty minutes, Andrea and Nigel worked their way through a series of positions that seemed less like they would be suited for giving birth in and more like they were auditioning for an illustrated version of the *Kama Sutra*. Andrea looked approvingly at her husband as he obediently rolled over into yet another birthing position in response to her direction.

'Now this,' she trilled, 'is an excellent position, which really encourages your perineum to stretch and relax, streeeeetch and relax. This will prove to be invaluable as your baby's head moves down, and should minimise the possibility of an episiotomy being needed.'

'Excuse me.' Geni, partner of Violet, had been taking notes on a white A4 lined notebook. 'What's an episiotomy?'

'We'll come on to that later in the course,' announced Daphne, at the same time as Becky told her bluntly, 'It's when they cut you. Down there. With scissors. Sounds like they're cutting bacon.'

Geni turned the colour of her notebook.

'Right then!' Daphne took back control of the class, before Geni literally keeled over. 'Thank you very much, Andrea and Nigel, for that very practical demonstration.' Andrea preened; Nigel, red in the face and breathing heavily, looked like he was in danger of needing CPR. 'Let's move on to the next stage of today's class, which is sharing our birth stories with those mummies- and daddies-to-be who are yet to experience a bundle of joy of their own. I'll start.'

Becky had practically dozed off by the time Daphne had taken them through an extended dramatic reconstruction of her four children's births, all of whom she had apparently birthed au naturel, without the need to resort to any kind of pain relief other than her own 'mental self-belief and natal hypnotherapy breathing, which we'll be learning the basic techniques of later in this course'. After Daphne, it was the turn of Andrea, who talked about the 'loving and tender' experience that she and Nigel had shared, as she had pushed their perfect baby boy out 'from between my most private, intimate parts; such a very special thing for a husband to witness his wife do'. Even Nigel had the good grace to look abashed, and Becky decided that if she never had to make eye contact with Andrea again, it was still probably going to be too soon.

Finally, it was Becky's turn. The group turned to her expectantly. 'So then, Becky, you've got two lovely girls, is that right?' Daphne nodded at her encouragingly. 'Why don't you share with us all exactly what their births were like?'

Becky looked at the course leader. 'Are you sure?'

Daphne nodded her head. 'Quite sure. Don't worry, dear. This is a "safe space".'

'And you really want me to be completely honest?'

Daphne nodded again. 'Absolutely. One of the founding principles of these classes is empowering women by letting them know exactly what to expect. Please be as open as you possibly can and tell us exactly what happened.'

And so Becky did.

Forty minutes later, you could have heard a pin drop. Becky sat back happily on her haunches as Sophia and Violet looked like they might cry. Even the usually unmovable Jason looked shell-shocked.

'Of course,' said Daphne, in a voice most unlike her usual confident tones, 'not every birth is like that.'

'No.' Andrea shook her head fervently. 'It really isn't. It's very ... *kind* of you to share your birth experiences, Becky, but I would suggest that there was probably more than a little dramatic licence based on what you've told the group.'

'There bloody wasn't.' Becky shook her head, unmoving. 'Ooh' – turning to Jon – 'remember when, on the fourth

154

night of no sleep and screaming agony every four minutes I told you to go and get the shovel out of the shed and hit me over the head with it, because I'd rather be dead than go through a single solitary second more of feeling like I was living out that scene from *Alien* when it bursts out through John Hurt's stomach.'

Violet was turning a whiter shade of green. 'But you're not really in labour for a week, are you? Surely they'd perform a Caesarean section if you were.'

Daphne nodded. 'That's right, dear. It sounds to me like what Becky was experiencing was pre-labour, which is your body getting ready to birth your baby. A series of mild stretching sensations: a warm-up for the main event, if you like.'

'That wasn't a fucking warm-up.' Becky shook her head emphatically. 'It was the worst pain you can imagine, just continuously coming in waves and waves, making you throw up and shit yourself all at the same time. Oh, and did I mention the hallucinations?' She looked around at the group. 'By the time Rosie was born, I hadn't slept for four days. They weren't going to let me stay at the hospital, because they said I wasn't dilated enough, so I started smashing my head into the concrete wall and screaming, because I thought then they might take pity on me and kill me or something. Then they did let me stay, and they gave me something which they said was going to help with the pain, diamorphine, which was about as effective as giving you a paracetamol and a dinosaur plaster for an amputated leg would be, but combined with the sleep deprivation it did have the added bonus of making me hallucinate as though I'd been smoking a crack pipe all night. I thought the midwife was Carol Vorderman and she was pulling consonants and vowels out of my vadge.'

Daphne looked as though she was torn between wanting to hit Becky and running out of the room and never coming back.

'And so what did you use to cope with the pain once you started pushing?' asked Sophia, wild-eyed.

Becky thought for a moment. 'A metric fuck-ton of drugs ... oh, and I squeezed down so hard on Jon's hand that I broke it.'

From the other side of the room, there came a gentle 'thud'. Jason had fainted.

'It's not that I don't want you to come back to the classes,' Daphne emphasised to Becky and Jon, Andrea hovering by her side, as Nigel moved the yoga mats to the side of the room, the other two couples having left just as quickly as they could after Jason had revived himself. 'You are, of course, welcome. However, I just feel, perhaps ... that your approach to childbirth is not entirely in keeping with the ethos I try to ensure prevails during these classes.'

'Flat-out lies, you mean.' Becky looked her straight in the face. 'Daphne, I don't know why you don't just tell them the truth. It's going to fucking hurt. Really fucking hurt. And of course it's all totally worth it, eventually, but it doesn't necessarily feel like it when you've just squeezed a badger-sized object out of an exit channel that had previously objected to so much as a super-plus tampon being shoved up there.'

Daphne winced. 'I appreciate that your experience was particularly challenging—'

'No.' Becky cut her off in her stride. 'Sorry. I'm not having that. There is nothing magical about childbirth. I'm telling you now. I've spoken to extensive numbers of women on the subject, and pretty much every single one of them will tell you that it hurts like fuck and is damn well undignified to boot. We need to stop treating women like children and do what you told me these classes were meant to be doing: empower them. Tell them the reality, and then give them the tools that they need to tackle it. Which might be drugs, or it might be hypnobirthing, or it might be getting knocked over the head with a brick. But it's about having that choice. And you can't have the choice if you don't know the truth about what you're facing.'

Daphne stood there, her lips pursed. 'That's your view, Rebecca. It happens to be a very different one to mine, so I suggest this might be the point for us to part ways. While I appreciate that we don't usually agree to refund course fees, I'm sure this could be arranged, under such unique circumstances.'

Becky nodded her head. 'I wish you all the best, Daphne. I truly do.' She turned to Andrea and Nigel. 'And the same to the two of you. Thanks, Andrea, for thinking of me and inviting me on to the course.' To her surprise, she realised that she actually meant it; pregnancy could be a pretty lonely gig.

Andrea kissed her on both cheeks. 'Thank you, Becky. I appreciate the course might not be for you, but let's still meet up for coffees. After all, we'll be off on maternity leave at the same time. Ooh!' Her face lit up. 'Maybe we could find some nice baby sensory classes to attend together.'

Becky pushed Jon forwards. 'We've agreed that Jon will be taking the bulk of shared parental leave to look after the baby. I'm sure he'd be delighted to go along to baby sensory classes with you.' Going to the antenatal classes had almost been worth it, she decided, just to see the expression on Jon's face.

Leaving Daphne, Andrea and Nigel in the hall – no doubt to express their collective horror at Becky's behaviour – the two of them walked out together.

'So,' said Becky brightly, 'that went well, I thought.'

Jon turned to look at her and they collapsed into giggles.

To their surprise, next to their car was a small gathering of people. It turned out to be Violet, Sophia and their partners.

'Um . . . hi.' Becky was somewhat nonplussed.

'Hi.' Violet, clearly self-appointed spokesperson, spoke up. 'We were just wondering . . . well, we know that Daphne wasn't very happy when you told us your birth stories. But, actually' – she looked around at the others, who nodded in agreement – 'we found it really helpful. After all, it's good to know what the worst-case scenario might be. And so, even though we're going to carry on going to the classes . . . we wondered if, as well as that, you might be willing to meet up with us a couple of times and tell us how you found it all, I mean, not just having the baby, but also what it's like afterwards. Does breastfeeding really come naturally? Is it as simple as just getting your baby into a routine and sticking to it if you want them to sleep through the night?'

Becky looked around at their eager little faces, simultaneously remembering the first couple of weeks of breastfeeding Rosie, when it felt like half of her nipple was being sliced off with a scalpel, and the moment when, after surviving on three twenty-minute chunks of sleep per twenty-four-hour period, thanks to having given birth to the Incredible Non-Sleeping Baby, she had actually managed to briefly pass out in a stupor while standing up.

Her face broke into a broad smile. 'Of course I will. Let's make a date.'

Gemma was on to her second glass of wine already. It had been one hell of a day. Leroy had taken it upon himself to arrive, unannounced, at her desk that morning and demand a blow-by-blow update of performance and progress against her business plan.

To no one's surprise but Gemma's, Pert was thriving. Spring-boarding off the platform and reputation Zero had already built, and benefiting not only from the existing client base but also from some of the very best developers, product managers and salespeople that Zero had – whom Leroy had generously allowed her to transfer across to get Pert off the ground – there had been immediate interest almost from the get-go, and they already had a committed group of core corporate clients, along with a consumer panel of users who had helped them to select the first products for their portfolio. One of which Gemma was wearing herself, right now, and had been for the last week. It was the first bra ever she hadn't wanted to hurl, screaming, into a corner of the room the moment she got home from work: a pain-free, genuinely supportive experience. Incredible.

So, while Leroy's visit was not exactly unwelcome, it was still an inconvenience, in so much as it required her to cancel her planned meetings for the day and clear the time she needed to take him through her projected sales figures, product development and business strategy for the next twelve to eighteen months. Gemma had to pause briefly to remind herself of all the reasons she loved working for Leroy, despite his maverick tendencies to shift the goal-posts and suddenly require her full and undivided attention at any given moment.

He had sat back, impressed. 'Blimey, Gem. I mean, I'm no accountant, but even I know that looks good. You'll be doing me out of a job here.' He sighed. 'Although, good to know I've got a natural successor when I've finally had enough of it all and decide to sell the business and retire to a Caribbean island like Jeremy keeps telling me we should do. Only trouble with Jeremy is he doesn't just want a week on a Caribbean island, he wants us to buy the sodding island, up sticks and go and live there. Still!' He perked up again. 'Would make a bloody nice holiday destination for all of you lot, wouldn't it?!'

Exhausted though she was by Leroy's day of interrogation, Gemma allowed herself to feel a vague sense of satisfaction as she drove home, collecting the children on the way. When they'd finished running through the figures, Leroy had started chatting to her about a major trade show which was coming up. He wanted her to go along with him and Natalie – their Sales and Marketing Director – 'the perfect opportunity for us to showcase you and Pert and the amazing progress you're making,' as he told her. Perhaps she wasn't doing such a bad job after all.

That feeling soon dissipated when all hell broke loose in the car: Sam had chosen to goad Ava about the casting for the gala performance, which was being announced that week. 'You're definitely going to have to wear a pink dress, Ava. It will be pink and sparkly. I heard Miss Thompson saying so when she was chatting to one of the other teachers in the playground the other day. She said, "And Ava will be wearing the biggest, sparkliest dress of all, because she will be our Fairy Princess." So you'd better get ready, Ava. I bet it has PINK FLOWERS on it.'

Ava completely lost it. 'I will not be wearing a pink dress, it will not have pink flowers on it, I have told Miss Thompson I am not having anything to do with her stupid play, and if you go on any more about the pink dress that I will NOT be wearing, Sam, then I will get into your bed when I get home and I will crouch down on your pillow and I will pull down my pants and I will LAY A POO on your pillow, like I am laying an egg, DO YOU UNDERSTAND ME?'

From the volume of Ava's response, Gemma suspected that everyone in the street would have understood her intentions to lay a poo in Sam's bed, as she dragged the protesting pair inside and told them both to go to their respective bedrooms.

'But why am I being sent to my room?' Sam crossed his arms and looked mutinous. 'That's not fair. Ava's the one who said she was going to poo on my pillow. I didn't do anything.'

'Yes you did,' Ava practically hissed at him. 'You said that I was going to be wearing a pink dress, which is a LIE, a big fat lie, and you should not lie, Sam, because that's when Satan will come and get you' – Ava had a somewhat medieval view of religion – 'and drag you into his fiery pits of hell, and then I will have no one left to play with, I will just be all by myself, and that is NOT FAIR.'

Gemma stood between the two of them, holding them at arm's length. Her daughter's ability to turn a situation from the sublime to the ridiculous never ceased to simultaneously impress and infuriate her. 'I can tell you right now, that the only thing that is not fair here is that I am having to spend the few precious minutes I get not working or fundraising to save your school wanting to lock both of you in the airing cupboard so I can just get five minutes' peace.' She sighed. 'What's the matter with the two of you?'

'You can't lock us in the airing cupboard. It's illegal,' Ava announced, conveniently forgetting that she'd had exactly the same intentions towards Satin at the start of the term. 'And if you break the law, I will phone the police, and they will put you into prison and hold down your arms and put tape over your mouth so you cannot scream, and then they will pierce your ears, because that is what happens in prison.' She looked defiant. 'Which is why nobody is ever going to pierce my ears, ever ever ever.'

Gemma ran one hand across her face. As ever, quite what went on inside her daughter's head was an utter, utter mystery to her. 'Ava, just ... what?' She sighed. 'Right, go on, both of you. Up to your rooms for a bit. And, please, try not to be complete dicks about it while you're up there. I'll call you when dinner's ready.'

All of the official parenting guides told you that it wasn't appropriate to call your children dicks, but then Gemma was fairly certain that no one who wrote any of these guides had ever actually met a child or owned one of their own.

And now it was eight thirty, the children were, if not asleep, at least in their bedrooms, and Tom had poured her a second glass of wine, which she sat drinking at the kitchen table as he washed up the pans from dinner.

She and Tom had gradually rekindled their relationship since Christmas. She knew that she needed to be honest with him about what had led to her behaviour over the festive period, but she just hadn't found a way to articulate the thoughts that were whirling round and around in her head. 'You're the absolute love of my life and being without you is physically painful but I can't risk being in a relationship which damages my kids,' being quite hard to blurt out, all things considered.

Ava had not repeated her meltdown of the night of the Nativity, and had even gone so far as to ask why Tom hadn't been over, so Gemma had felt it safe to invite him over for dinner that night. Her daughter had been wildly distracted by the latest Chelsea signing ('But he's USELESS, even you could play football better than him, Mum, and the last time you tried to play with us you sounded like you were going to have a heart attack and fell into a bush') and Sam had been his usual monosyllabic self. They'd made polite yet comfortable conversation, Gemma secretly dreading the moment the kids ran off to their rooms and she was left alone with her boyfriend.

'So ... how's the production going?' Desperate to avoid the elephant in the room, the gala performance provided the perfect distraction.

Tom groaned. 'Don't even ask. It's been like trying to teach on the set of *The X Factor* for the last few weeks. Kids asking to miss lessons so they can audition, the hall being set up in a permanent Six Chair Challenge – I was asked to be a judge, but refused – dance routines being performed in the corridors, causing Mr Cook to totally lose his shit and demand to come into assembly so that he could inform everyone that 'it's not the ruddy Bolshoi Ballet'. Roll on May, when the whole thing will finally be over, that's what I say.'

Gemma couldn't have agreed more. She was running on empty right now, a combination of work, the children and bloody Fundraisers United meetings meaning there was almost no time in her day for anything else. Including poor Tom. But, God, it was wonderful having him back, it was like the missing puzzle piece to her life had suddenly been returned. If it hadn't been for the children she'd be perfectly happy to go to bed with him and not emerge until some time in the spring. Why did life have to be so complicated?

Aware of her gaze, he polished a pan with a tea towel until it was gleaming and placed it carefully into the rack, before turning to face her.

'Gemma?'

Her heart flip-flopped in her chest.

'Yes?' She took another sip of her wine and hoped it wasn't obvious that her hands were shaking.

'I feel like ... we need to chat. About what happened at Christmas. I know we've kind of glossed over it, but something happened, right? You went out of your way to avoid me. And that felt ... well, if I'm honest, that felt totally shit. So tell me. Are you planning to dump me? Have you got another guy – or girl? Did you decide to take vows of celibacy and couldn't risk being near me for fear of the inevitable happening?' He raised one eyebrow and smiled at her – belying the fear he felt that he might just have hit the nail on the head – and she wondered how it was possibly fair for one human being to be so disgustingly good-looking.

Gemma's face fell. 'I—' How could she possibly articulate everything that she was thinking? 'It's complicated.'

'So there is someone else?' Tom took a step back, devastated.

'No! Oh my goodness, no.' She got up and walked towards him, feeling her body melt as she pressed up against him. 'Tom, there could never be anyone else. Do you have any idea how much I love you?' She kissed him, and felt their shared tensions immediately dissipate. 'And I am so sorry, I am so, so sorry, if for a single moment you thought that I'd ... God. I would never, ever do that to you. I love you so much!'

'Thank goodness for that!' He exhaled in sheer relief, his lips grazing the top of her head. 'So the weirdness over Christmas? The crossing to the other side of the playground

165

to avoid me? Yes, don't think I didn't notice. What was that all about?'

She sighed, sitting back down at the table, where he joined her, holding her hand and stroking it gently.

'You're right. I was avoiding you, and I'm truly sorry. I never, ever meant to make you feel shit; it mortifies me that I did. It's just ... Tom ... do you feel like you get a bit of a raw deal?' He raised his eyebrows. 'Being with me ... it can't be much fun for you. You spend the whole day teaching other people's children, then you come home and still can't get rid of my two, Ava's usually got you out practising penalty shootouts until it gets dark, and then I'm more often than not working for half the evening. I mean, these are the early days of our relationship. We should be out wining and dining and ice-skating holding hands and wearing winsome fluffy hats. Whereas here you are, finishing my washing-up while I yawn at you and tell you that I'm so exhausted all I want to do is get to bed.'

He grinned. 'And I am *always* happy to get you into bed.'

She laughed. 'That's not what I meant, and you know it.'

He shrugged. 'It works for me. And I can't ice-skate, either.' He pulled her closer, putting one arm around her and holding her tightly.

'The thing is, Gemma, I'm not all that interested in the honeymoon period. And I mean that in the nicest possible way. Hearts and flowers and meals out in nice restaurants are all very well, but after that all fades, then what are you left with? I'm in this relationship because of you. And whether you're running around like a maniac obeying Vivienne's every fundraising command, or coming up with the latest bra-related product, or telling Ava that no, when you die, she can't "rip off your skin to see what bones look like" ... that's the you that I love. You don't need to pretend to me to be something you're not. It's the real you that I fell in love with, not some made-up fantasy of what features writers – usually male ones – seem to want to tell us that women in relationships are actually like.'

She looked at him suspiciously. 'Are you sure you're not gay?'

He responded by tickling her furiously, until she collapsed into giggles, and Ava came downstairs with her hands on her hips to announce, 'I am trying to get to SLEEP. And if I don't get to sleep then I will be very tired in the morning and then I will be extremely DIFFICULT.' She paused and looked contemplatively at Tom. 'Also, are you murdering Mummy? Because if you are, please can you check her will first to make sure that I am definitely getting all of her jewels and not Sam.' Which, if she'd wanted a definition of true love, was surely it.

Ava successfully returned to bed, Tom turned back to Gemma, inwardly bracing himself to ask the question he'd been plucking up the courage to voice. 'The thing is – before you'd started behaving like a mad person who would do anything in their power to avoid me – I was actually wondering about asking you how you would feel ... if we moved in together. The lease on my flat is up this summer and I need to decide whether to extend it. That absolutely shouldn't be the deciding factor but ... I miss you, Gem. I miss every single moment that I'm not with you, and so I suppose what I really wanted to know is ... do you feel the same? And do you reckon that living with me . . . might be something that you fancy giving a go?'

Oh God, the million-dollar question. Had it just been her to think about, Gemma would have said yes before the words were even out of Tom's mouth. To wake up every single morning with this beautiful, beautiful man by her side. Was it even really a question?

But, of course, it wasn't just her that she needed to consider. Sam and Ava had to come first, and she realised that, while she'd skirted around the issue, she still hadn't told Tom what she was really thinking.

She avoided the question by leaning forward and kissing him deeply. One thing led to another, and it was only much, much later, as Gemma lay by his side in her bed, snoring peacefully, that Tom, staring at the ceiling, realised she'd never actually answered him at all.

CHAPTER TWELVE

It was six thirty in the morning a couple of weeks later, and Gemma's alarm had just gone off when the little 'beep' from her phone told her that she had a new email. Groggily, she reached for it, suddenly snapping awake when she realised it was an email from the LEA admissions service. At the same time, her Facebook notifications started going into overdrive; presumably Vivienne and her coven wasting no time in gloating about which secondary school their offspring would be attending, and how utterly dismal everyone else's prospects would be by comparison.

On tenterhooks, she waited the agonising seconds for the email text to load, until ... YES! Sam had his first choice of school! He'd been offered a place at Catswells, the lovely, small secondary on the edge of town, which, while it had slightly poorer academic results than the others nearby, had such a lovely atmosphere and ethos.

Pulling on her dressing gown, she ran across the hallway and woke a sleeping Sam by thrusting her phone in his face. 'Sam! Look! It's here, and you've got into Catswells! Just like you wanted! Isn't that brilliant news?'

Groggily, he sat up, rubbing his eyes, then leant forwards and took her phone from her, reading the words on the screen for himself. A slow smile lit up his face. 'That's brilliant, Mum. Will some of my friends be going there as well, do you think?'

Wanting to avoid the class Facebook page, with Vivienne's comments inevitably taking the shine off the morning, Gemma shook her head. 'I'm not sure, sweetheart, but you can ask them at school this morning. Here, if you get yourself up and dressed now we'll have time for a special celebratory breakfast. How do you fancy some pancakes?'

As she dropped both children off at school, Gemma mentally congratulated herself. There were certain parenting milestones that it always seemed important to meet, however much you prided yourself on not getting caught up in the competitive parenting mindset. And finding the right school for your children was definitely one of them. It wasn't easy to get into Catswells, but Gemma happened to live on the right side of town and had also written what she supposed must have been a pretty compelling case as to why Sam would thrive there. Even Ava had been impressed, in her own inimitable way. 'I never thought you would get into there, Sam, because you are often quite smelly.' She shrugged her shoulders and then cackled uproariously. 'It is probably because they like boys to join their school who have VERY HAIRY BALLS.'

Regardless of Catswells' rationale (which Gemma suspected was simply their adherence to the strict admissions policy, which happened to place Sam over a number of other applicants, as opposed to the hairiness of his genitals), it didn't really matter. Sam had got his first choice of school. Things were going well at work. Her and Tom – while she still hadn't been entirely upfront with him, and the unanswered question of whether they were going to live together hung between them – seemed to be back on track. She had made her children sodding *pancakes* for breakfast, as though she was some kind of Betty Crocker style parent, as opposed to her usual approach of pointing at the cupboards and the fridge and informing them that they would find within them all of the ingredients they required to make themselves a filling and nutritious breakfast. Maybe Becky was right, and she actually was superwoman.

Ten hours later, it was a very different story. Sam's expression as she walked into after-school club – a mixture of fury and distress written all over his face – told her everything she needed to know. 'Sweetheart, what's up?' She went straight over to him to comfort him but he ducked out of her way, went to get his book bag and coat and stormed out into the playground.

'Hello, Mummy.' Ava had been busily writing something which she folded up and put into her book bag before Gemma could see it. 'Sam is being Very Mean, and Very Angry, and if I were you, Mummy, when we get home I would send him straight to his room and not let him out again for the rest of the week. Or maybe ground him until he is thirty.' She looked up, an idea having just occurred to her. 'Or we could phone up the police and see if they could find him a little space in prison, so that he doesn't cause us any more bother.'

Thanking the girls who ran the after-school club, Gemma helped Ava to get her belongings and then walked outside after Sam. His behaviour was very out of character. Ava regularly came out of after-school club furious with some perceived wrong that the universe had committed against her, but Gemma had never known Sam to behave like that.

Tom was just finishing at school as she collected the children; they'd planned to have dinner together that evening, so he jumped into the front seat of the car and she drove them all back to hers. Not wanting to embarrass Sam in front of Tom, she refrained from asking her son what was troubling him until she could get him on his own at home, despite Ava's many attempts to get her to do otherwise. 'But you need to ask him, Mummy. Maybe he has *killed* a person.'

Finally, after a strained drive home, they arrived. Sam immediately stormed upstairs, slamming the door to his bedroom, just as soon as Gemma had opened the front door.

She looked at Tom. 'Sorry, love. I need to sort this one out. Reckon you can handle Ava for me?'

Ava, who had slipped into earshot without them even noticing her, looked affronted. 'I do *not* need handling, thank you very much.'

Tom laughed and ruffled her hair. 'Come on, let's you

and me go into the back garden and practise some foot-work, before it gets too dark. You need to work on your ball placement.'

Gemma left them discussing a world she still, despite Ava's best efforts, knew relatively little about, and headed up the stairs, genuinely concerned about Sam. This was totally out-of-character behaviour for him. Thoughts ran through her mind, spiralling irrationally. He was being bullied. He'd got into trouble at school. He was ill. He was on drugs. By the time she knocked on his door and opened it she was almost convinced she'd find him sitting in there snorting up cans of aerosols, or whatever it was that the youth of today had as their drug of choice.

To her surprise – and relief – Sam was not snorting up aerosols. Nor, unusually, was he sitting glued to his computer; the omnipresent glow from the screen was absent, and he was simply lying on his bed, despondently staring at some of Ava's Match Attax cards that she must have deposited on there in her last failed attempt to tidy up her room (which usually just meant shifting belongings from her bedroom into Sam's). Turning on the overhead light, Gemma walked over and sat down on the bed next to him.

'Sam, sweetheart, what's up?' She felt his forehead. 'Are you poorly?'

He shook his head, no, and rolled away from her. 'I just want to be on my own. Can you go away, please?'

'But what's the matter?' Gemma persevered. 'Has something happened at school today? Come on, you can tell me.'

Sam shook his head again. 'I don't want to. Just go away.'

She looked at his face: had he been *crying*? Since his dad

had left, the first time around, Sam had very much seen his role as man of the house. However much she told him that he didn't need to, that she was quite man – and woman – enough to look after them all, Sam had taken his perceived responsibilities very seriously; she'd rarely seen him visibly upset since that day. Now, though, there was no mistaking the two tear tracks that snaked down his cheeks.

'Sam, baby, come on.' A cold finger of fear ran down her spine. 'Whatever it is, we'll sort it out. You can tell me anything, I promise, and I won't be angry. Come on. Spit it out. What's up?'

In response, he shoved his head into the duvet and muttered something unintelligible.

'What's that? Can you say that again, sweetheart? I couldn't quite hear you.' Gently, she stroked his back.

Suddenly, in a rush of motion, Sam sat up, throwing the covers from him as he did so. 'Schools, Mum. That's what's up. Schools. Which you'd know about, if you'd bothered to read any of the messages on that stupid Facebook group. Do you even know where all my friends are going?'

To her embarrassment, Gemma realised that she did not. She'd been so intent on avoiding Vivienne putting down the school she'd chosen for Sam that she hadn't thought to check on where his mates might have got into.

Her face said it all. Sam shook his head in disbelief. 'NONE of my friends are going to Catswells. Not a single one. They're all going to St Luke's, absolutely all of them, because it's a much better school with much better results, much better than Catswells, which is apparently rubbish, they've been telling me all day. Especially Tartan.'

'Tartan's going to St Luke's too?' Gemma couldn't hide her surprise; despite Vivienne's attendance at the St Luke's open evening, she'd been open in her disparaging of the state sector and her clear intention to educate her son privately from Year 7 onwards.

Sam shook his head again bitterly. 'No, of course Tartan's not going to St Luke's. He's going to some posh private school, I can't remember what it's called, except that it's twinned with Eton and all the students graduate and get jobs which earn them millions of pounds and the inside of it's apparently just like Hogwarts. And all day, *all* day, I've had nothing but people telling me how terrible my school is and how much I'm going to hate it and how my exam results will be dreadful and I'll never get a good job and that I'm basically completely screwed for the rest of my life.' Throwing himself back down on the bed, Sam began to cry in earnest.

Gemma rubbed his back, feeling impotent to make the situation better. 'Sam, sweetheart, that's horrendous. I'm so sorry you've had to deal with all of that. I'll come in and speak with your teacher, of course. Did you tell any of the teachers today what they were saying to you?'

Sam made a noise, which might have been 'there's no point', continuing to sob into his duvet.

There was a creak, and the door opened a crack. Ava's bright blue eyes stared in in wonder. 'Mummy, why's Sam crying? Are you actually sending him to boarding school?' She paused for a moment. 'If you do, can I have his bedroom? And his computer? And his football kit?'

Emphatically, Gemma gestured for Ava to go away. The

door closed; Gemma had no doubt whatsoever that Ava would still be just outside, furiously listening to find out what was going on.

'Sam, love.' She tried again. 'Come on. Your friends are just being stupid. They're probably jealous you've got into the school that they actually wanted to go to.'

Sam sat up, wiping his eyes. 'Jealous? Yeah, right. As if, Mum. Who would be jealous of anyone going to stupid Catswells? No, everyone else is quite happy, they're all going to go off to their good schools, and Tartan's going to get the best job of all, because his mum can afford to send him to private school, and so the rest of us might as well not bother.'

Gemma had never been a fan of private education, and this conversation was just demonstrating to her exactly why. She rubbed Sam's back in an attempt to calm him down, but he was on a roll now.

'And another thing, Mum. You keep going on all the time about how you've got this really good job, and that's why me and Ava have to go to after-school club, and that's why Tom takes Ava to her football practice a lot of the time when you're working, or Becky and Jon, or Granny and Granddad are looking after us. But if your job's so good, then how come I don't get to go to private school like Tartan? It can't be that good, can it, if you haven't got enough money to send me to private school. Oh, you don't mind spending money on shoes, or wine, or a new Chelsea football kit for Ava, but you're not going to pay for me to go to the best school, because you just don't care about me. Is that right, Mum? Maybe you should send me away to boarding school like Ava keeps telling you to, then at least you wouldn't have to put up with me. You clearly don't want to. Maybe I'll just go and live with Dad instead.'

He stood up and started furiously slamming around his room, pulling clothing out of cupboards and shoving it into a small rucksack. Shouting now, he told her, 'That's it! I'll pack, and then you can drive me to the airport, and I'll get on a plane and go and live with Dad, and you'll never have to see me again.'

As she wondered quite what the hell to do now, the door swung open again. Gemma braced herself to tell Ava to get lost, but to her surprise it was Tom who stood there, his face impassive.

'Sam, mate?' His voice was low. 'Come on. What's going on up here? You need to calm down.'

Sam ignored him, slamming around even more furiously, seemingly completely out of control.

'Sam?' Tom approached him, sitting down on Sam's computer chair so that his face was level with the boy's. 'Mate, seriously. You need to calm down. I heard what you were saying just now – I think the whole street might have heard – and that's not on. Your mum works really hard looking after the two of you. It's not fair for you to speak to her like that. I know you're upset, but I think you owe her an apology.'

Sam exploded, using language Gemma had never heard him use before, certainly never in the context of screaming at someone else, as he was now. 'Fuck off, Mr Jones. It's nothing to do with you. You're not my dad, I don't know why you're in my bedroom, I don't want anything to do with

you so FUCK OFF, I hate you, I hate you, I HATE YOU.'
Sobbing, he threw himself down on the bed.

Tom and Gemma exchanged glances, both of them
ashen. Briefly, the two of them stepped outside the bedroom door, Gemma holding it closed behind her.

'You go downstairs. Thank you, but I'll deal with this.
Could you make Ava some tea?' Ava, for once stunned
into silence, was peering out of her bedroom door, tears
in her eyes. 'Are Sam and Mr Jones having a fight? Did
Sam win? Was it a wrestling fight?' Her eyes brimmed and
overflowed. 'I don't want anyone to fight.'

'Neither do I, sweetheart,' said Gemma, holding her
daughter close, kissing her hair and feeling her breath
coming in short gulps. 'I'm going to go and sit with Sam
for a bit. Will it be okay if Tom takes you downstairs and
makes your tea?'

'Okay.' Ava nodded her head and reached for Tom's
hand, which he held out towards her. 'I'm feeling very
sad, Mr Jones,' Gemma could hear her saying as they went
down the stairs, 'and so I think I will probably need an
extra-specially nice tea to make me feel better again. Do
you know what usually makes me feel much *much* better?
It's if somebody makes me pancakes.'

A half-smile on her face at her daughter's attempts to
capitalise on the situation, and listening to Tom debate
with her over whether two lots of pancakes in one day was
really a healthy balanced diet (Gemma knew without even
needing to stay to listen who was going to win that argument), she went back into Sam's bedroom. In stark contrast
to the scene she'd left, the room was now quiet, and Sam

was undressed, in bed, and looking for all the world like he was fast asleep.

Gemma went over and sat down on the bed next to her son, laying one arm on his back. 'Sam?'

There was no answer, but the momentary pause in his breathing told her he'd heard her.

'We need to carry on our conversation, but I think, for tonight, it's best if you just get some sleep.' She stroked his hair. 'You must be exhausted. Would you like me to bring you up some dinner?'

He shook his head, no. 'Okay. I'll make you a sandwich and bring it up to you, that way if you get hungry later on you can have something to eat.' She kissed the side of his face. 'I love you, very very much, you know. And I'm sorry, truly sorry, that all of this has upset you so much. But we'll sort something out, Sam. I promise you that. And have I ever let you down?'

There was a silence, a silence which communicated all too clearly what Sam was thinking, that yes, she had let him down, probably on multiple occasions, not least the time last year when she'd spectacularly failed to remember yet another school trip, and had promised Sam she'd cut down her hours at work so that she could be there for him more, only to completely forget.

Sighing, she kissed him once more and left the room, turning out the light as she did so.

Downstairs, the kitchen was in disarray, with Ava consuming what she proudly announced was her 'fif-teenth pancake'.

'Good grief,' said Gemma faintly. 'You must have been

hungry. Finish that one off, and then I think it's probably time for a bath.'

Ava shook her head emphatically. 'No. No, I still feel very upset after all of that shouting, and so I think the worst thing for me right now would be to have a bath. It would be very' – she searched for the word – 'distressing.' She cast a sideways look at her mother. 'I think, really, what would be the best thing for me would be if I finished eating this pancake, and then I sat down in the living room and watched some of *Match of the Day* that I recorded from the weekend.' Her eyes twinkled. 'And, maybe, Mr Jones, if you brought me a mug of hot chocolate. Just to wash down my pancakes.'

Stunned, Ava found herself, twenty minutes later, unbathed and sitting in front of *Match of the Day* in her Chelsea onesie. Wow, she thought. This really is the best day ever.

Gemma would not have agreed. In fact, thought Gemma to herself, as days went, this was fast turning out to be one of her worst on record. And, with a full marriage to Nick the Dick behind her, that was saying something.

She cleared up the remainder of the pancake carnage as Tom took Ava her hot chocolate. By the time he returned she was sitting at the table, two mugs of tea in front of them. He sat down to join her.

'Fucking hell.' She shook her head. 'I'm so sorry about that.'

'Don't be,' he told her. 'It's fine. I mean, it's not fine, in so much as Sam's clearly really really upset, but I've been called far worse things in my time.'

'I still feel dreadful.' She sipped her tea. 'He should never have spoken to you like that.'

'He shouldn't,' Tom admitted. 'But you've heard the adage about kids playing up when they feel safest. It shows what a secure home environment you've given Sam, the way he feels like he can behave like that, and you'll still love him.'

She glanced at him. 'You're being serious, aren't you?'

He nodded. 'Genuinely. What's that saying: every cloud, and all that. You guys will get through this.'

She exhaled. Tom was right. They would get through this; of course they would get through this. She'd have a proper chat with Sam tomorrow, get to the bottom of all of this school stuff. Maybe arrange to have a chat with his teacher and find out if the situation was really as bad as it seemed. Surely it couldn't be the case that *no one* in the class was going to Catswells; Sam must have been mistaken. Her face set grimly as she thought about Tartan. She was certainly going to be sitting down with Vivienne for a little chat after tomorrow night's committee meeting.

Tom went over to the sink to rinse out their cups. 'Do you want another one, or shall we head up to bed when Ava does? Want me to go and check on Sam?'

Her mind flashed back to the scene that had played out in the bedroom earlier that evening: Sam screaming at Tom that he wasn't his dad. All the doubts and concerns that she'd had about the impact of their relationship on her children came racing back.

'Um. If it's okay, Tom . . . I think maybe, you should head back to yours tonight. I just think, with everything . . .' Her voice trailed off and she gestured at the ceiling helplessly. 'It might be best.'

There was a pause before he responded. 'Sure. I'll just get my stuff and say goodbye to Ava. Give me a second.' His face was unreadable.

She walked him to the door and he kissed her lightly on the lips. 'It will all be okay, you know?'

Maybe he was right, Gemma thought, as she closed the door behind him. Maybe he was right, and it would all be okay. The trouble was, she mused, as she checked on a sleeping Sam – ham sandwich uneaten – and gave in to Ava's demands that she be allowed to sleep with her in her bed ('because Sam said the F word, Mummy, and that is *really* distressing for me') … maybe he wasn't right at all.

Tom, walking home in the lightly drizzling rain, was thinking exactly the same.

CHAPTER THIRTEEN

It was six o'clock on Friday night by the time Mrs Goldman had finally managed to get through the mound of paperwork Rachel had left on her desk. The school was quiet; just the sounds of Mr Cook whistling as he walked around the school, securing all entrances and exits and muttering, 'You won't get past me a second time, you bastards', could be heard echoing along the corridors.

Suddenly, there was a knock at the office door. In strode Miss Thompson, chiffon scarves billowing around her neck as usual, and a series of box files in her arms.

'Sharon!' she proclaimed. 'How wonderful to find you still here. I thought this would be the perfect opportunity, now that the casting has been announced, to talk you through the plans for our great production. Do you have time?'

Without waiting for an answer, she sat herself down in the leather armchair opposite Mrs Goldman's and started rifling through her files. Mrs Goldman let out an internal groan. She had been hoping to get home in time for *Masterchef.*

'So, as you know, our story is based around a Real Life Disaster: that is, the attempted burning down of our much-loved school.' Miss Thompson let out a dramatic sigh and pulled out a crudely drawn picture of two characters. 'All told through the eyes of our two narrators: Mrs Goldman and Mr Cook.' She winked. 'I always told you I'd make you a star, Sharon.'

Mrs Goldman shook her head. 'I'm really not sure about this, Angela. I see no need for me to be immortalised on stage. And I thought the plan was for this to be an ensemble piece?'

Miss Thompson peered covertly around her, checking they were not being overhead. 'Of course, you're absolutely right: that was the plan,' she started. 'But that terrible woman Vivienne accosted me one afternoon as I was working through the choreography for the opening number – "Let's Burn That Bad Boy Down" – and told me in no uncertain terms that it was a mandatory condition of Fundraisers United supporting this production that her two children, Satin and Tartan, should take on lead roles. Apparently it had been formally signed off as part of the Fundraisers United's constitution.'

She tutted and pulled her chiffon scarves closer around her as Mrs Goldman pursed her lips in her attempts not to laugh out loud. She had to hand it to Vivienne: she had precisely zero shame when it came to getting what she wanted out of life.

'Oh well, that's that then,' Mrs Goldman agreed. 'And all of the children in the school are participating?'

Miss Thompson nodded. 'Apart from Ava and Simon in my class, that is. Simon' – she shuddered, memories of the Nativity still all too fresh in her mind – 'for obvious reasons. And Ava!' She threw her hands up in the air. 'It's completely impossible to get the child to do anything that she doesn't want to do. When I told her she would need to come along to the dance call I had scheduled for the ensemble auditions, she gave me the most scathing look you could imagine and told me she would not be coming to the auditions as she had been advised by her football coach that dancing could jeopardise her goal-scoring technique. I mean, really!' She looked outraged. 'Did you ever hear anything so ridiculous?'

Mrs Goldman hid a smile. 'I understand. But other than Ava and Simon … it's all cast? And you have everything you need from me and the rest of the staff?'

Miss Thompson looked coy. 'Well, I did wonder if we could perhaps talk about raising the budget the school makes available just a touch.' She pulled out another raft of papers. 'The trouble is, the few hundred pounds you've given me isn't going to get us very far. I mean, I've spoken to the London Palladium, and they are prepared to offer us a generous discount, but we're still talking tens of thousands of pounds. All of which should easily be offset by ticket sales, but there's the deposit to pay up front, of course. And then there's the professional cast members. I put in a call to Lin-Manuel' – Mrs Goldman looked blank, until Miss Thompson held up a programme from

Hamilton, the smash-hit musical, and she nodded vaguely in response – 'and he'd be happy for the current West End cast to come and lead the encores, but of course they'll need paying as well.' She tutted. 'Equity rates don't come cheap these days, you know.'

Mrs Goldman decided to stop Miss Thompson in her tracks before she went any further down this terrifying rabbit warren. 'Angela, let's just take a little step back for a moment and remind ourselves of the aims of this production.'

'To make my name as the up-and-coming theatre director, producer and writer of the moment, of course,' came back Miss Thompson, quick as a flash.

'And that might be a very lovely side effect,' Mrs Goldman said gently. 'But the real reason we've agreed to put on this production, Angela, is in order to raise the funds that the school so desperately needs, if we're not to close at the end of this academic year. The way you're talking, not only are we not going to end up making anywhere near the seventy thousand pounds we're aiming for, we're going to find ourselves running at an enormous loss! No, I'm sorry, Angela. This seems to have spiralled out of control. We need to rein things back in.'

Miss Thompson's shoulders slumped. She hadn't even mentioned the costumes she'd been planning to hire from the National Theatre's costume department, nor her ambitious plan to have the celebrity drag queen RuPaul come in and do hair and make-up.

Mrs Goldman was thinking. 'The school hall is perfectly well equipped for a theatrical performance – yes,

Angela, even one of this scale. And if you wanted to bolster cast numbers, why not have a chat to the local am-dram society and see if they'd be prepared to lend us a few bodies, in return for promoting their next show in the programmes.'

Miss Thompson shook her head. 'You are the boss, Sharon, but I don't think you know the first thing about theatre. Am-dram!' She clutched in horror at the large string of faux pearls she had looped around her neck. 'I really don't think that we need to sink to quite those depths. And there's not a hope in hell a little school production like you're suggesting is going to raise seventy thousand pounds.' She gathered up her box files and got to her feet. 'I think I'd best be off. I'm going to have to rewrite the entire second act this weekend now that you've told me we're not going to be able to have a stage revolve. Goodnight, Sharon.' She swept out, and Mrs Goldman could hear her muttering to herself, a phrase that sounded very like, 'So *selfish.*'

Relieved that at least she wouldn't be spending her Friday night stuck in the office being submitted to a blow-by-blow walk-through of the entire script, Mrs Goldman was thoughtful as she put on her coat and locked her office door, saying goodnight to Mr Cook as she left the building. Miss Thompson might be mad as a box of frogs at times, but there was one thing she'd said that was only too true. There really wasn't a hope in hell that a little school production like this would raise seventy thousand pounds. Sighing, she made a mental note to put in a call to the grey-suited men at the LEA first thing on Monday morning. It looked as though she had better get ready to meet the Head of St Catherine's . . . and start to make the plans for merging the two schools together a reality.

Becky was making the speech of her life. She'd finally, after several months of phone calls and emails, managed to get an audience with the Board of a FTSE 100 company in the heart of London, to talk to them about the business benefits of ensuring flexible working was the standard within their organisation, not the exception. She'd woken up that morning with her brain buzzing, full of every statistic possible about the proven impact on productivity, recruitment costs and attrition rates, what it meant for the gender pay gap and the benefits of being an employer of choice as a result of their clearly communicated strategic focus on diversity.

Despite her outward confidence, she had been secretly terrified as she'd signed in at reception, then taken the lift twenty storeys up, to walk into a boardroom that could not have been less diverse if it had tried. Ten sets of eyes stared back at her; they belonged to an almost identikit set of white, fifty-something men, whose expressions varied from the mildly welcoming (Darren, the HR Director, who'd been her point of contact and the reason she'd managed to wangle her way in there in the first place) to the downright hostile.

This was Becky's first client visit where she was flying solo. Previously she'd always had the lovely Alison – the lady who had set up the charity, and Becky's boss – by her side, but Alison had another client meeting that morning and had told Becky that, based on what she'd seen when they'd been out together previously, she had total confidence in Becky's ability to do just as great a job as she would, if not even better.

Which was both great and absolutely terrifying.

Having declined the proffered refreshments, on the grounds that, at nearly seven months' pregnant, drinking any amount of fluid would result in her having to run out of the room halfway through her presentation before she ended up pissing herself, which was so not the vibe she was going for . . . Becky thanked the Board for inviting her in, then launched into her presentation, which she knew backwards, and could have recited in her sleep. To her surprise, the initial nerves quickly wore off and she found herself having the time of her life. Changing the world of work was something that she wasn't just passionate about, it was a goal she was absolutely determined to achieve. With two daughters already – and who knew, maybe a third on the way, Becky and Jon having chosen not to find out the gender of their third child – this was a whole world of inequality that her kids were going to find themselves dumped right in the middle of, unless Becky could do something to make that change.

Research paid off, too. Becky was able to talk eloquently about the company's current – embarrassingly large – gender pay gap, which in line with current legislation was published on their website, and how introducing flexible working for all would be a real and very effective way of starting to close it.

'It's not about paying both genders the same for doing the same role.' She cut off the inevitable comments. 'That's called equal pay, and of course you do that already, because it's been the law for a number of years.' A couple of them smiled, somewhat sheepishly. 'But it's about making sure that, across your organisation as a whole you've got diversity at all levels which reflects the diversity of the general population.' She deliberately looked around the room. 'Which, I'm sure you don't need me to tell you, based on this meeting room alone, very clearly isn't the case.'

They had the good grace to laugh, even the po-faced CEO, who Becky was actually starting to warm to. She finished her presentation and then opened a round-table discussion about some of the practical things they could be doing. 'And you need to lead by example,' she told them all sternly. 'There's no use telling your staff that they can leave early to do the school run if they need to, and then staying in the office until ten o'clock at night. Employees will model their behaviours on their leaders, and so it's up to you to do the right thing.'

She looked around. 'I'm guessing some of you have families, yes?' They all nodded. 'Wouldn't it be nice to get home some nights in time to give your wife a night off from making the dinner, or be the person who comes into work late because it's you who's taken your son or daughter to their dentist appointment, not automatically defaulted to the woman in your relationship to do it.' A few nods of recognition. She was getting through; she was being heard. Change didn't happen overnight, but Becky closed the meeting with a plan to work with the company going forwards, and with a genuine belief that there would start to be a different approach to how people worked. Baby steps, but they would all add up to change the world.

Thanking the Board members profusely for their time, Becky turned to walk out of the room.

And that was when it happened.

One moment she was striding triumphantly towards the exit in her four-inch heels (Becky held no truck with sensible shoes, just because she happened to be pregnant) ... and the next, she wasn't.

Instead, her foot caught on the strap of her handbag, which she'd forgotten to pick up from where she'd placed it underneath the table, and she went flying across the wooden floor.

A thud, and a sharp pain.

And then a merciful blank.

Gemma had been at work, arguing with Siobhan over the necessity to still include a strapless bra in their range –'But they're fucking instruments of torture, there's no way even we can produce one that's vaguely comfortable and actually stays up.' 'We have to, Siobhan. Women wear them all the time.' 'Then they're sadomasochistic dicks.' 'That's as may be, but they still need strapless bras.' 'They should just go braless.' 'If I went braless, I'd be dragging my nipples around in my slippers.' – when her mobile had rung. It had been Jon, hoarse with panic. Becky had had a fall, he had told her, while out seeing a client. She'd been rushed into hospital and they had no idea if the baby was okay. Could she possibly go and collect Ella from the nursery, and then take Rosie back with her after school? He didn't know what time he'd be able to get back to them, but he'd keep her posted.

Of course she could. Quickly, Gemma cancelled her appointments for the rest of the afternoon, telling Siobhan she would need to hold the fort.

Pale-faced, she drove to collect Ella, who was delighted to see her, solemnly holding out her hand to walk alongside Gemma as she informed the toddler that she'd come to collect her 'while Mummy and Daddy are busy at work'. The nursery lent her a car seat and they drove to collect Sam, Rosie and an extremely suspicious Ava from school, arriving just as the school bell rang for the end of the day.

'Has somebody died?' Ava had clocked her mum out in the playground and come out with the rest of her class instead of going to after-school club.

Gemma winced at her choice of words. 'No, sweetheart. Nobody has died. Becky and Jon are a bit ... busy. They asked me to come and pick you all up this afternoon, so I've finished work early and we're going to go back to ours for a bit.'

'Okay, great!' Ava turned to Rosie, who was just behind her. 'We're going back to my house. Maybe we can talk some more about what we were chatting about earlier.' Had Gemma been somewhat less distracted, she might have thought more about the surreptitious whispers the two girls were exchanging; as it was, she had far too much on her mind to think about anything other than getting everyone into the car, and wonder what in the world was happening with Becky.

CHAPTER FOURTEEN

The children finished their pizza and Rosie and Ava headed out into the back garden to play yet more football. Ella was still chewing on some pizza crusts and Sam sat next to her, patiently picking them up and passing them back to her. Not for the first time, it struck Gemma what a lovely manner her son had with small children; his patience and compassion were miles ahead of hers. Which is what made his outburst the other night so horribly out of character.

She'd sat down with him the very next day, her primary focus on ensuring he was okay. Mortified by his outburst – not that he would ever have let on – Sam sat and took her gentle admonishment at the way he'd behaved towards Tom, and agreed that he would go and apologise to him. On the topic of his allocated secondary school, Sam had told her that it was 'Fine'. It clearly wasn't, but Gemma still believed that Catswells would be the right school for him and did everything she could to reassure him of that.

Sam had begged her not to contact the school about what the other kids in his class had said to him – 'Because if you do, Mum, I might as well just leave and go and live by myself in a cave now, because basically no one will speak to me ever again.' Reluctantly, she had acquiesced, on the proviso that he could reassure her they hadn't behaved like that again. Mercifully, the topic of conversation in Year 6 had rapidly returned to the usual focus areas of YouTubers and who in the class had a mobile phone, and the moment had been forgotten. Mostly. Something still didn't seem quite right with Sam, but Gemma couldn't put her finger on it, and in the absence of him offering up any further information she had had to put it down to the mysteries of pre-pubescent boys.

Ella finished and Gemma asked Sam to take her into the front room and put on some CBeebies for her. The little girl's face lit up at the mention of her beloved 'Beebies', and she willingly took Sam's hand as he led her through. Gemma heard the sounds of *In the Night Garden* start up.

Gemma looked at her phone for approximately the fifty-eighth time in the last ten minutes. It remained ominously silent.

She looked out of the window at the girls playing, shrieking with laughter as Ava did a particularly aggressive tackle, which had poor Rosie on the floor in the mud. Laughing, Rosie pulled herself back up, neatly tackling Ava back and regaining possession of the ball in order to fire it into the goal. The little girl had no idea what her parents were going through right at that moment; Gemma felt a surge of love and protection towards her.

Outside, oblivious to what was happening with her mum, Rosie was plotting with Ava. There had been another play rehearsal that day, and although Ava wasn't involved, Rosie was.

'So, what do you think?' Ava relied on Rosie as her play insider. 'Is it going to raise the money we need to be able to keep Redcoats open?'

Rosie, a loyal child, who, despite her chronic shyness, thoroughly enjoyed performing, and always wanted to think the best of her teachers, reluctantly shook her head. 'I don't think so. It is good fun, and Miss Thompson is actually a really good director ... but the Year Rs kept falling over in their dance together, and Satin sounds like a dying duck with an American accent when she sings.' Her face lit up with optimism. 'It might, maybe, raise ... two thousand pounds?'

Ava shook her head. 'It's not enough, not nearly enough. Which means ... it's going to be time for us to put Operation Hazard into action. Rosie, are you in?'

Rosie nodded her head.

'Then Operation Hazard is GO GO GO!' Ava was triumphant. 'We don't need any stupid play to save our school. Come on, let's go up to my room and get started. We haven't got much time left.'

Groggily, Becky sat back against the pillows one of the nurses had propped up behind her. Jon sat next to her, waiting to hear what the senior obstetrician who had come over to speak to them had to say.

'It's good news.' She nodded her head and looked at

them kindly over the top of her metal-rimmed glasses. 'Baby looks to be absolutely fine. We're going to keep that monitor on you, just to make certain, and keep you in overnight – that's standard protocol in the case of head injuries – but there's nothing I've seen on the ultrasound or observed when I've examined you that is any cause for concern.'

'But the bleeding? The sharp pain?' Jon gently squeezed Becky's hand. 'And the reduced movements? Do we know what caused any of those?'

She showed them a small patch on the ultrasound, which she told them was an area of bleeding. 'Probably just some of the blood vessels getting a bit of a knock, from where you hit the deck. They should heal up nicely. In terms of the reduced movements, we will, as I say, keep an eye on those through monitoring overnight, but you've felt a good few strong kicks since you've been lying here, haven't you?' Becky nodded. 'Then I'm not worried; the heartbeat is nice and strong and there's nothing at all suggesting any major damage to either you or your baby. The pain that you felt was likely just a mild tear to one of your muscles as you fell.'

Becky put one hand to her forehead, eyes still bright with tears. 'I'm such a klutz.'

The doctor smiled. 'You're not the first, and you certainly won't be the last.' Her eyes widened slightly. 'I do have to ask, though. Were you really wearing four-inch heels in the seventh month of pregnancy?'

Becky had the good grace to blush. 'When you struggle to clear five foot, those extra four inches are really important.' Jon sniggered. 'Don't tell me: you think I've brought it on myself.'

'Not at all,' laughed the obstetrician. 'I simply wanted to salute you: I'd struggle to walk in those now, let alone in the third trimester of pregnancy.'

'I do have my standards,' Becky quipped. Jon, looking at her closely, saw the first sparks of light in her eyes, which suggested the feisty, invincible Becky that he so loved was still in there. Not for the first time, he wished he could just wrap her and the baby up in cotton wool and protect them so that he knew they'd be safe.

They thanked the doctor as she headed off on her rounds. Exhausted, Becky turned her head to look at her husband, who gently kissed her hand.

'It's been one hell of a day,' she exhaled. 'One hell of a day.'

It was almost nine in the evening by the time Jon finally felt comfortable to leave Becky and head back to Gemma's. Gemma had laid Ella down to sleep on Ava's bed, where the little girl had fallen asleep almost immediately. Sam had volunteered to sit upstairs next to her and read his book while she slept. 'Because we haven't got any stair gates, Mum, and we don't want her to wake up and fall down the stairs.'

Her heart bursting with love for her son, Gemma made her way downstairs and into the lounge, where the two girls were curled up next to each other like kittens, watching the highlights of the Chelsea friendly that Ava had recorded earlier in the week. 'I wonder when my mum and dad will be back,' Rosie yawned sleepily.

Before Gemma could reply, Ava was straight in there. 'Don't worry. If they are dead then you and Ella can come and live with us. I would love to have a sister, not just a stinky brother, and Sam can look after Ella, because Mum doesn't like children, apart from me and Sam, and probably you a little bit, Rosie, although obviously not as much as us, because our heads came out of her actual front bottom, which is one of the most disgusting things I have ever heard ever, can you imagine, Rosie, your head coming out of a VULVA?'

Rosie's mouth fell open. On the plus side, Gemma supposed, at least Ava's talk of vulvas had distracted Rosie from her friend's extremely unhelpful suggestion that her parents might be dead.

Ava was still thinking. Her face furrowed. 'Mum, are you and Mr Jones going to have a baby? You might be, you know, because your stomach is getting extremely big.'

Jon's knock at the door could not have come at a more welcome moment.

Later that night, having been able to speak to Becky on the hospital phone and reassure herself she was okay, Gemma lay in bed, adrenalin still coursing around her body. What a day. Belatedly, she realised she hadn't spoken to Tom. It was too late to call him now; instead, she sent him a short text, telling him that she'd had some stuff going on, and that she'd explain in person if he wanted to let her know when he was free to meet.

Usually her boyfriend replied within seconds; today, much like earlier, her phone stayed ominously silent. Gemma felt a knot in her stomach, which had nothing to do with the cold pizza she'd eaten before she'd come upstairs to bed, and everything to do with her concerns over quite where she and Tom were in their relationship right now. So much for Ava's suggestion that they might be having a baby together.

She stared out the window at the stars, her mind racing.

Tom was at home; his phone, Gemma's text open on the screen, lay on the coffee table in front of him. Sighing, he attempted to turn his focus back to the pile of unmarked Year 2 homework sitting in front of him. It was no good: even the distraction of the poem written by a little girl called Sara – the children had been asked to write a poem about something they loved; Sara's was entitled 'My Poo' – was insufficient to prevent the doubts and insecurities he had been attempting to hold back flooding through his mind.

He loved Gemma. Loved her so much, loved her more than he'd ever loved another human being, ever. But Georgina's words at Christmas kept coming back to him. About not wanting him to be hurt. And right now, if he was honest, with Gemma having asked him to leave her house the other night, and not having talked to him properly since about what was going on in her head ... hurt was exactly how Tom felt.

'God, why does life have to be so bloody difficult?' he groaned, slamming his head on to the pile of exercise books he still had to work his way through. And, a split second too late, sincerely hoping that the material Sara had used to colour in her illustration for 'My Poo' was indeed the brown wax crayon he'd made the assumption that it was; or he was going to have brought a whole new level of meaning to the phrase 'being in the shit'.

Forty-eight hours later, Becky had been discharged from hospital, and was back at home, with strict instructions to rest for at least two weeks. She had phoned Alison, apologising profusely for her unscheduled time out of the office; her boss couldn't have been more understanding.

'Of course you must rest, and you've had great feedback from the company you presented to. They'd like you to go back in and present to their wider management team – when you're better, of course. They've passed on all their best and have had some flowers sent to the office for you; I'll drop them off at yours.' Even down the phone, Becky could hear her boss smiling. 'It's working, Becky. We're really getting through to people. I honestly believe it.'

Becky hung up after thanking Alison, her mind racing. Back in the early years of her career, she'd had no idea that a job could be anything more than a means to making money and supporting your life outside of work. Now, for the first time, she understood Gemma's passion for her work and that genuine sense of making a difference.

Which made it all the worse that her *stupid* body had let her down like this. Alison had taken such a chance on her, and this was how she'd repaid her. By getting put on compulsory bed rest. For fuck's sake. It was okay for men, having children barely impacted on them – they weren't the ones having to act like a walking incubator for nine months and then getting saddled with the lion's share of the childcare. Okay, so that was unfair: Jon was more than happy to take shared parental leave and look after their baby so that she could get back to the office. She still didn't really think he understood what it felt like to feel you were constantly letting people down, though. Motherhood was like one long juggling act. One where there were so many balls, you didn't have a hope in hell of not dropping some of them. Where you were destined to never really succeed.

She heard Jon's key in the lock and Boris bounced over to greet him, barking furiously and shedding enormous chunks of yellow fur absolutely everywhere.

'All right, mate, calm it down,' soothed Jon ineffectually as Boris put his paws up on his chest and stood on his hind legs to better lick his face. For an animal who could be so stupid – he had once got his head trapped in a saucepan in his attempts to lick out the remains of a spaghetti bolognese Jon had made, and had run howling around the house for a good twenty minutes looking like some kind of strange dog/saucepan hybrid, before Becky and Jon had managed to get their laughter under control sufficiently to grab him and release him from his metal prison – he demonstrated a surprising sensitivity to understanding when and to whom he needed to curb his inherently boisterous tendencies. Around Ella and Rosie he was never anything other than gentle – if not exactly calm – and since Becky had been pregnant – in fact, now she thought about it, before she herself had even known that she was pregnant – he had never once jumped up at her.

'Hello, love, how are you doing? Girls are all dropped off safely.' Jon pushed Boris gently off him and came over to Becky, who was lying on the sofa, her laptop on the table next to her. 'What can I get you? Something to eat? A cup of tea? Do you fancy a nap? I could read to you?'

'You could *read* to me? Jon: I had a fall, I didn't lose the part of my brain that has rendered me capable of reading for the last thirty-seven years.' He looked contrite, and she felt immediately guilty; this had been just as tough for him as it had for her. 'I'm sorry. No, I'm fine. I don't need anything, thank you.' She gestured at her laptop. 'I've got plenty here to keep me entertained.'

Jon looked stern. 'Absolutely not. You know what the doctor said. Total rest for the next two weeks. Which means no working, of any kind, at all.' As though reading her mind, he continued. 'And yes, that does include emailing, calling clients or reading endless articles on the internet about how companies have made flexible working work for them, on the grounds that it's "research".' His eyes twinkled. 'I could always ask Andrea to come round and chat to you, to "relax" you.'

'Please, God, no.' Becky sat up, cradling her bump protectively. 'If you so much as allow Andrea to cross the threshold, we'd be verging dangerously on divorce territory.' She shuddered at the very thought. 'That aside, I can't literally lie here and do nothing for two weeks. I'll go stir crazy.'

'But you have to.' Jon was unmoving. 'The doctor said. I love you, Becky, and I love our baby, and I'm not prepared to do anything that might jeopardise the health and well-being of either of you.'

'Yes, well, you're not going to,' Becky retorted in exasperation. 'You're going to go off to work as normal, getting to do exactly what you want to do, your entire life not inconvenienced in any way, while I have to just lie here, craving all the things I can't eat and drink and do because my sole purpose in life appears to now be boiled down to being a uterus on legs.' Angrily, she wiped the tears from her eyes. 'I'm sorry: I'm not having a go at you, I'm having a go at the situation. It's just so frustrating, you know?'

Jon held her hand. 'It is frustrating, I know. But the main thing is that you and the baby – and the girls – are all okay. In the grand scheme of things, nothing else really matters.' He passed her the remote control. 'Here you go. Knock yourself out on daytime TV. I'm going to go and clear up the kitchen from breakfast, and then I've got a tender for work to get started on.'

Becky groaned as she pressed the power button, and *Homes Under The Hammer* burst on to her screen. 'Enough already. I'm going to make myself a countdown chart. Roll on getting back into the office.'

Jon had been on his way into the kitchen, but he paused as she said that and turned back, a slightly unfathomable expression on his face.

'Everything okay?'

He stood there, looking over at her. 'The thing is, Becks . . . I'm worried about you. I worry about you all the time, but I'm particularly worried about you at the moment. I've said to you before, you've been taking on so much stuff. Work . . . the kids . . . the fundraising that you've been involved in. It's less than two months now until the baby's due, and so what I thought was . . . why don't you just take some extra time out? Don't go back to work; take it as holiday, or unpaid leave, or whatever. Then you can properly rest, have time to relax and enjoy yourself, and keep yourself in the best possible health for the baby arriving. What do you reckon?'

Becky crossed her arms and looked at him sternly. 'Jon, what have I told you? I absolutely love my job – in fact, I love it more now than I've ever done. I was just feeling like I was starting to make a real difference, before – well ...' She gestured to her current position, laid on the sofa. 'And I cannot wait to get back to doing what I now know I can do so well.' Her face softened. 'I know you're worrying about me. And it's lovely, it really is. But my health is about more than just my physical health, you know. Mental health is just as important, and for the first time in I don't know how long, this job's helped me to recover my sense of self, to remember who I really am. To not just be someone's mum, someone's wife, you know? Not that those things aren't important, or that I don't love doing them. But there's more to me than that, Jon. There really is, so much more. And for the first time, I'm starting to remember that.'

Her husband still looked unconvinced, but he wasn't going to argue with her.

Which was just one of the many reasons why Becky loved him.

CHAPTER FIFTEEN

'And a FIVE SIX SEVEN EIGHT!' Seated behind the school piano, Miss Thompson counted in both cast and orchestra members for the opening number of *Phoenix!* ('Because,' as she'd explained to a shell-shocked staffroom, 'we are emerging from the ashes; our school is being reborn.') 'Firelighters ... GO ... boxes of matches ... GO ... arsonists ... GO! Lovely, and then we bring in the smoke machine ... that's right, Mr Cook, crank it up to max ... maybe not quite that much max ... all right, Daisy, no, you're not going to die, I know you can't see anything, could everyone just calm down please, I said CALM DOWN, don't worry, Laeticia, we'll find your inhaler, I appreciate it's an emergency, could I have a first-aider please, FIRST-AIDER TO THE STAGE, PLEASE; I REPEAT, FIRST-AIDER TO THE STAGE!'

Seated at the back of the hall, away from the performers, allegedly completing maths worksheets but in reality deep in thought about Operation Hazard, her Top Secret Plan to save Redcoats, Ava was watching the activities unfolding on stage in horrified fascination.

She'd updated Rosie at break time on how their plans were going. 'So, Wave One is go, and we need to complete Wave Two this week. Then ...'

'Then ...?' Rosie prompted her.

Ava folded her arms decisively. 'Then we wait.'

'And will it all be okay?' Rosie asked.

'It will all be okay,' Ava had confirmed, with absolute confidence.

The smoke had been dispersed on the stage and children were emerging from the gloom as Mr Cook ran around, opening windows. 'Right then, we'll take that one again,' Miss Thompson instructed. 'Starting positions, everyone, please.' She played a chord on the piano. 'And a FIVE SIX SEVEN EIGHT.'

Ava groaned and slammed her head down on the table in despair.

Becky, who had been going stir crazy on her compulsory bed rest, had been delighted to come up with something that would break the monotony of these seemingly endless days. She'd been in regular contact with Geni, Violet, Sophia and Jason, from the antenatal classes, and had decided that now was the perfect opportunity to give in to their requests for her to tell them 'honestly, what parenting is *actually* like'.

Having brought Jon around to the idea – 'Truly, nothing is more relaxing for me than sitting and telling people the truth about what you go through when you have a baby – you need to think of this as a kind of therapy for me. If anything, it will be positively good for my blood pressure' – they'd agreed to invite the four expectant parents around to theirs that evening.

Arriving on cue, the two couples gushed over Becky and Jon's home – 'How can you possibly keep it this tidy with two children?' 'We gaffer tape the children to their beds,' quipped Becky, following up rapidly with, 'I'm joking, I'm joking!' to reassure her horrified-looking audience – and expressed to Becky how sorry they were to hear about her fall. Jon provided drinks for everyone, and before long they were all sat around in the living room, looking at Becky expectantly.

'Right then.' Becky bounced on a birthing ball; she loathed being such a cliché, but it was the only way she could get comfortable these days. Even if Boris did have to be physically restrained from diving over and sinking his teeth into it, thinking it was some strange, grey, alien intruder. 'Ask me anything. And I do mean anything. Obviously every baby is different, every parent is different, yadda yadda yadda. But I'll tell you how it was for me, warts and all.'

'I'll start,' said Sophia, raising her hand eagerly. 'When the baby comes out, does it stop hurting straight away?'

Becky stared her straight in the face. 'One word: placenta. It's the bit the baby books all seem to kind of gloss over. "Oh yes, and then several pounds of raw flesh fall out of your front bottom, but don't worry, you'll be so wrapped up in your new baby you won't even notice." I'm telling you now: if there's ever a time in my life when I don't notice several pounds of raw flesh falling out of my front bottom, then all I can say is that something has gone very seriously wrong.'

'What about afterpains?' Geni spoke up. 'I've heard that you can get them after you have the baby?'

'I never had them with Rosie,' Becky recalled. 'Then Ella turned up, and BAM. I thought I was in labour all over again. Don't be a hero: take the painkillers. They're there for a reason. And speaking of being in labour all over again ... has anyone mentioned the first post-birth poo to you?'

They all shook their heads. 'Well, let me just tell you that that bad boy ... by the time I finally birthed that thing, having had to bite down on my toothbrush to stop myself from screaming, I was so impressed that I called Jon in to have a look at it. We even momentarily thought about taking a photo of it and having it framed next to our newborn photos of the girls. It felt like just as much of an achievement, if not more so.'

Everyone howled with laughter. 'Can I ask about breast-feeding?' It was Sophia again. 'I'd really like to breastfeed, but most of the information out there seems a bit vague. What's it like, and is it easy?'

Becky thought back to the breastfeeding journey she'd been on with Rosie. The undiagnosed tongue tie, the hours and hours of frustrated suckling, the piece of Actual Nipple that had fallen off in Rosie's mouth, the sheer blind pain that was a baby desperately sucking on a nipple that was red raw, and the unimaginable hell that was mastitis.

But then the brilliant support she'd had from the breast-feeding helpline and the counsellor they sent round to help her, the amazing feeling when it had finally clicked for Rosie and her, and how easy it had been with Ella by comparison.

She talked them through every part of the process, sparing no details. 'One of the hardest things I've ever done: and yes, that does include childbirth. But oh, so worth it, and there is so much support out there, so if you want to breastfeed, then don't feel like you need to get it right all by yourself and without help. And if you can't breastfeed, or even if you don't want to: don't let anyone out there try to foist their unwanted opinion on you and treat you like a second-class citizen. You do what's right for you and right for your baby. And everyone else, frankly, can fuck the fuck off.'

Over the course of the next couple of hours, Becky answered questions on everything from nappy changing ('fucking grim, I don't care how much you love your baby, you're still regularly having to get your hands covered in someone else's shit'), sleeping ('maybe you'll be lucky enough to give birth to the Incredible Sleeping Baby, in which case, you'll be laughing. Let's just say, I did not; and there's a reason they use sleep deprivation as a form of torture'), and sex after having a baby ('my best advice: shit loads of lube, and try to avoid asking, "Is it in yet?"'). Finally, Violet, who had stayed quiet for most of the evening, spoke up.

'I don't mean to sound rude, Becky – you've been so amazing answering all of our questions. There's no way

Daphne would have been so honest with us.' Smiling, the others nodded in agreement. 'But having a baby sounds unimaginably tough. Is it really worth it?'

Becky thought for a moment. Back through the years of sleep deprivation so acute she felt ill with tiredness, back through the screaming toddler tantrums and the terrible twos. Back to her ravaged vagina, her sagging tits and her once washboard stomach, which these days looked like it could double as a waterbed.

'I can honestly say,' she announced decisively, 'that having children is one of the single greatest things I've ever done. And I'm telling you now: you'll never know a love like it. It's absolutely unreal, right, Jon?'

He nodded his head. 'Like nothing I've ever experienced in my life. I don't have words for how much I love my kids.' He paused. 'Mind you, I could also say the same about what they've done to my home and my bank account.'

Laughing, the little group broke off, the couples thanking Jon and Becky again and again for their hospitality as they headed out into the night.

Jon looked pleased and proud. 'That went well, didn't it?'

'Fuck,' Becky responded. 'It's just hit me: we're about to put ourselves through that all over again. What the hell were we thinking?'

'It'll be worth it, though,' Jon reminded her, folding her into his arms, the baby gently kicking between them. 'Oh my goodness, it'll be worth it.'

Just as Becky and Jon had been welcoming the two couples into their home, Gemma's mum and dad had arrived at

Gemma's to look after Ava and Sam while Gemma went to meet Tom for dinner at a local restaurant. This was getting ridiculous, she had decided. She was an adult, and she just needed to face things head-on and tell Tom exactly why she had thus far completely avoided his entirely reasonable question of: *Do you reckon that living with me . . . might be something that you fancy giving a go?*

She thanked them profusely as she put on her coat and found her car keys. 'Thanks so much for babysitting, I really do appreciate it.'

They shook their heads to tell her that really, it was no problem at all, as Ava loudly declared, 'I am NOT a baby, they are NOT babysitting. I am a footballer, so if they are doing anything, they are footballer-sitting.' She paused to consider what she'd just said. 'Which wouldn't make any sense, because you don't sit when you're a footballer, you run around, because it's very important to keep fit. Come on, Granddad, let's go and play some football before it gets dark and Granny makes us come inside.' She looked pained, and Gemma's mum asked her if she was okay. 'I'm fine, Granny. I'm just a bit full after tea, so I'm trying to make myself need a poo, so I can fit some more cake in. Bye, Mum. Enjoy having DIRTY SEX in the restaurant with Mr Jones.'

She ran out the back door before anyone could respond to this startling train of thought and Gemma turned to her mum, her cheeks flaming red. 'Just to be really clear, I am not going to be having dirty sex – or sex of any kind, this evening. We're just going for a meal.'

'You don't have to explain yourself to me, dear,' reassured

her mum, kissing Gemma on the cheek. 'Goodness, the things you young people get up to today . . . it's like another world to me.' She looked at her husband. 'Sex in restaurants, eh? Whatever next?'

Gemma left before she could dig herself any further into the hole Ava had so neatly set her up to fall into.

The restaurant was packed by the time she arrived, but she spotted Tom immediately, sitting right at the back with a glass of wine. He waved to her and she made her way towards him. Not for the first time, she was struck by just how utterly gorgeous he really was. 'He could have any woman in this restaurant,' she wanted to cry out, 'and yet the one he wants is me.' A thought occurred to her, and she corrected herself. 'At least, I hope it still is.'

Over a dinner of fresh pasta, seafood and a sensationally good panna cotta for dessert, which they shared, Gemma and Tom caught each other up on the last few weeks.

'And so Sam's doing okay?' Tom asked as he forked up pasta.

She nodded. 'I think so. I finally got him to talk and we had a long, long chat the other day. He's apologised, of course – and he said that he'd come and said sorry to you too.'

'He has.' Sam had approached Tom awkwardly one break time, the week after his outburst. Staring at his shoes, he'd muttered something that at first Tom hadn't even heard.

'Did you say something, Sam?'

'Mmmmppffffhhgmm,' said Sam.

'Look, I'll be honest, mate,' said Tom. 'You could be

telling me Mrs Goldman's walking around the playground in a bikini, for all I can hear.'

The thought of the Head in a bikini did the trick; for the first time, Sam sniggered, before looking up and meeting the teacher's eyes.

'Mrs Goldman is definitely not wearing a bikini. But I wanted to say sorry. I was a dick, and I shouldn't have been mean to you and said what I did.' He crossed his arms and scuffed his foot on the ground, clearly uncomfortable.

'Sam, thank you for saying that. It means an awful lot. But it's okay, you know. We all have moments when everything gets a bit much. Even me. Next time, though, do me a favour? Just come and have a chat with me, or your mum, or your dad, rather than going all Incredible Hulk on us and crashing round your room swearing.'

Sam had the good grace to look abashed. 'Yeah, sorry about that.'

'We're all good. Go on, off you go. I'll catch you later.'

And Sam, his expression unreadable, had sloped off, to go and walk round and round in continuous circles in the playground with his mates, which was apparently how eleven-year-old boys kept themselves entertained these days.

Gemma was beyond relieved to hear that Sam had indeed followed through with his promise. She told Tom how, while she'd kept her vow to her son not to go to the school about what had been said to him, she hadn't been able to resist having something of a no-holds-barred conversation with Vivienne, who had stood there, arms folded defiantly. 'I'm really not sure what your problem is, Gemma. Tartan is simply stating the facts. Sam *will* be going to an inferior school, and Tartan *will* have a better start to his life outside of education.' She held up her hands in mock confusion. 'I don't know what you expect me to do about that.'

Almost choking herself from the efforts of writing 'FUCKING WANKPOODLING COCKWOMBLE TWAT' on the roof of her mouth with her tongue, Gemma walked away, though not before promising Vivienne that if Tartan came anywhere near Sam for the remainder of the term, there would be hell to pay.

'Is he feeling any better about going to Catswells?'

'I think so.' She bit down on another prawn, chewing and swallowing before continuing. 'Mmm, these are delicious. It turns out, when he said there was "absolutely NO ONE" in the class who was going there, that wasn't entirely true. There're actually four or five of them who have got in – just none of Sam's close friends. I've tried to reassure him that he'll make new friends once he's there, and that he can still see his current gang as often as he likes on the weekends and in the holidays, but of course you know what this age group are like.' She rolled her eyes. 'Everything's the End of the World!'

Tom smiled in recognition. 'Just imagine what it's going to be like when Ava gets to that age.' He winked, and Gemma recoiled in horror.

'Please, no. I'd really rather not.'

'So.' His face became serious, and she could feel the butterflies starting up in her stomach once again at the thought of what he might be about to say. 'We need to talk.'

She nodded, her face belying the nerves that she felt. 'We do.'

He reached across the table and took her hand. 'I love you, Gemma. I really love you. I love you so much that sometimes it scares me. And I would love, love to be spending more time with you. I felt like moving in together was the natural next step, but it seems like, from the way you've totally been avoiding the question so far, that that's something you're not quite ready for. And that's fine: I would never want to push you into anything.

'But, Gem ... I'm going to be honest with you. This isn't working for me, not like this. You keep doing your disappearing act on me, which means I'm spending half my life panicking that you don't love me, wondering why you can't tell me what's going on, wondering why we don't just talk things through.

'So I need you to be honest with me. Do you love me?'

She didn't take her eyes off his. 'I love you so much. Oh my goodness, I promise you, you never, ever need to panic that I don't love you. I adore you.'

He wasn't going to let her off that easily. 'Then the disappearing acts? The total avoidance of the question I asked you about moving in together? What's that all about?'

She took a deep breath. 'It's the kids, really. The thing is, Tom, if it was just you and me – I'd have said yes to moving in together before you'd even finished asking me. But it isn't just about me. Ava and Sam have got to come first and, well, with recent events ...' She trailed off, reliving the night Sam had gone postal in his room, and the time Ava had screamed at Tom. 'I'm just not sure if us being together ...' She gulped, refusing to give in to the tears that were threatening to overwhelm her. 'If it's the right thing for them.'

'And have you asked them?' Tom's voice was gentle as he held her hand, rhythmically stroking her thumb.

She shook her head. 'I don't think I can. I don't think it's fair. I'm sure they'd say yes – because they like you, and they want me to be happy ... most of the time, that is, so long as Ava's not busy planning my funeral. But that doesn't mean it's the right thing for them. It would be asking them to make an adult decision, when they're not even out of primary school. And I just don't think that's right.'

Tom was torn between not wanting to push her, and feeling desperate to prove her wrong. 'I think you under-estimate them, Gemma. They're bright, switched-on kids who know what they want. Is it not even worth the conversation?'

For a moment, she wavered. Was she protecting them too much?

Before she could reach a decision, her phone rang. It was her mum. Her heart thumping with adrenalin, as it always did when she feared anything could have happened to the children, she answered it. Tom, his brow furrowed with concern, watched as she took the call.

'Shit.' Her face was filled with concern as she hung up.

'The kids? Are they okay?' He was half on his feet, ready to rush back to hers with her.

'Sorry. Don't panic: the kids are fine. Mum was ringing

to tell me that she's just had the date through for the funeral of a friend of hers. She felt awful interrupting us but she wanted to let me know as soon as possible as she knew I'd need to make new plans. It's the Thursday after next and, sod's law, it clashes completely with that trade show Leroy has asked me to go to with him – the one in Manchester, so I'm going to need to stay overnight. My parents were going to have Ava and Sam for me, but there's no way they can not go to the funeral, and I can't really ask Becky and Jon given Becky's supposed to be avoiding exerting herself – five minutes in Ava's company and I feel like I've exerted myself, so goodness knows what twenty-four hours with her would do to a pregnant woman. Fuck, why is it that every time I think I've got a plan coming together it collapses around my ears?' She slumped on her elbows, looking genuinely like she might burst into tears.

Tom made a split-second decision. 'I'll have the kids.'

Gemma looked up at him. 'What do you mean?'

'I mean, I'll look after them. I can come to yours, so they'll be in their own space – and it's only for one night. Means you can get to the trade show, and who knows, it might give us a bit of an indication of how they'd feel if I was around on a permanent basis.'

Gemma wavered. On the one hand, it was the perfect solution.

On the other hand . . .

Tom squeezed her hand reassuringly. 'I promise you, sweetheart. It'll be fine.'

She nodded, tentatively at first, then more confidently.

'It will, won't it? It will be fine, and that's incredibly kind of you, thank you so, so much. Phew, what a relief. Another crisis averted, thanks to my knight in shining armour.'

They paid the bill and walked home, kissing all the way, and for the first time, Gemma thought to herself that maybe she had got this all wrong. Maybe she had been overreacting, and everything was going to work out to be absolutely fine.

CHAPTER SIXTEEN

It was the night before the trade show, and Gemma had just finished packing; she would be leaving at the god-awful time of 4 a.m. the next morning. Her mum and dad, who didn't have to leave for the funeral until after the school run, had offered to stay over that night, meaning they could take the children to school and Tom would only need to do one night. This had given Ava, who had never been to a funeral, ample time to grill her grandparents over quite what it entailed as they'd eaten dinner that evening.

'So, will you get to see the body?' she asked in ghoulish fascination, ignoring completely the chicken casserole on the plate in front of her.

'No, Ava, you don't get to see the body at funerals. Shush, and eat your dinner,' Gemma told her.

'That's not true,' Sam chipped in. 'What about that awful film you made us watch, Mum, the one with that boy with glasses in, where he gets stung by bees and dies a horrible death and then he's lying there dead in his coffin at the funeral and everyone can see him and that girl comes running in and starts yelling and screaming because he's not wearing his glasses.'

'Yes!' Ava was triumphant. 'Then you could see the body.'

'Oh. Well, that's America. They do things differently in America,' Gemma confirmed.

'Okay.' Ava thought about this, as she swirled her chicken casserole around the plate. 'If it was me, I would really want to see the body. Does it get dragged in in one of those big black bags that they put bodies in, so that all the guts and blood don't come pouring out, and then does everyone start screaming because they are scared of dead bodies?' She paused, reflectively. 'I would *love* to see a dead body.'

Gemma's mum had turned a whiter shade of pale. 'Ava,' Gemma told her daughter, 'if you don't shut up and eat your casserole, you'll be in danger of turning into a dead body yourself.'

'No,' Ava informed her, her mouth now full of food. 'I will only be in danger of turning into a dead body if I eat this, because your cooking is so very very bad. What?' She looked at the faces of the rest of the table, apart from Sam, who for once was united with his sister. 'Mum's cooking is the worst cooking I have ever eaten. Even worse than Becky's. And her cooking makes the food go *black*.'

There were times, Gemma mused to herself, when a night away from your children came at just the right time.

*

Kissing her sleeping babies goodbye, she crept out the house in time for the taxi that would take her to the airport the next morning. The sky was already starting to turn from black to navy, golden streaks of light doing their best to burst through. She'd explained to the children how they would be coming home from school with Mr Jones, and that they would need to show him where everything was.

'And will he be sleeping in your bed?' asked Ava suspiciously.

'Yes, he'll be sleeping in there,' Gemma confirmed. 'The sheets are clean on; there's no need for him to go into the spare room.'

'That's not very fair,' Ava had muttered to her brother. 'I was planning to sleep in Mum's bed while she was away.'

The trade show was a great success. Leroy was effervescent, entertaining company as always, as was Natalie, their Sales and Marketing Director, who had been supporting Gemma with the early sales and marketing strategies for Pert. The three of them toasted their success with a glass of champagne in the hotel bar, and then, to Leroy and Natalie's surprise, Gemma announced she was heading off to bed.

'What?' Natalie raised one of her perfectly arched eyebrows. 'Surely a night away from the children's the perfect excuse to go nuts and dance until dawn?'

Gemma shook her head. 'You've got to be kidding me. I get woken up pretty much every night by Ava arriving in my bedroom in the early hours of the morning, sprawling out across the entirety of my king-sized bed, and then kicking me in my episiotomy scar until I give up on sleep entirely and lie there waiting for the sun to get up. A whole, uninterrupted night to myself, without anyone else having designs on my bed? You're absolutely mad if you think I'm going to waste a single second of it.'

Natalie shook her head, as Gemma said her goodnights and made her way upstairs. 'Parenthood,' Natalie sighed, 'Seems to make you completely lose the plot.'

Had she still been within earshot, Gemma would have been in total agreement.

The plane descended steeply into Gatwick, and Gemma – never the greatest flier – held her breath. As was usual, she'd left home thrilled to get a break from her children . . . and was returning absolutely desperate to see them again.

They hadn't spoken the previous evening; she'd been tied up in seminars and meetings until gone seven in the evening, and when she'd texted Tom to ask him if everything was okay he'd simply replied with an, *All good. Don't worry. Love you xxx.* She'd smiled, imagining Ava putting Tom through his paces without Gemma to keep her in check. He'd probably spent the entire time out on Ava's makeshift football pitch in the back garden.

The street was quiet when the taxi pulled up, shortly after 5 p.m. that evening. Paying the driver, she put her key into the lock, expecting the children to come running.

To her surprise, the house was silent. Had they gone out? She'd texted Tom when she'd landed to let him know she'd be back within the next hour or so, he'd replied with a heart emoji but nothing else.

Before she had any more time to wonder, Tom emerged from the kitchen, arms outstretched towards her. 'Hello, beautiful.' He kissed her lightly on the lips. 'How was your trip?'

She exhaled, relishing being back his arms. 'Good. Really good. Thank you so, so much for holding the fort. How have the kids been?'

Was it her imagination, or did his arms stiffen slightly as he responded? 'Um ... fine. Yep, fine. Sam's in his room. Ava's gone next door for tea, Becky came over and asked if it would be okay and I didn't think you'd mind. You don't, do you?'

She shook her head. 'Of course not. She and Rosie are inseparable these days.'

'Yes. Yes they are.' His voice was inscrutable.

She stepped away and looked more closely at him. Something was definitely up. 'Tom, what's going on?'

'Okay.' He paused. 'Listen, why don't you pop upstairs and say hi to Sam, and I'll pour you a glass of wine, and then we can sit down and have a chat. There are ... a couple of things that I need to update you on.'

She looked at him. 'Um ... Okay.'

As she walked towards the stairs, he halted her. 'Oh, and tell Sam that I'm going to speak to you, okay, before he says anything.'

What the hell was going on?

When she went upstairs and knocked on Sam's bedroom door, she found him not, as she'd expected, plugged into his computer, but lying on his back on his bed reading his Minecraft annual. He sat up when she came in.

'Oh. Hello, Mum. Did you have a nice time?'

'It was fine, thank you. Hello, love.' She sat down next

to him and kissed him, relishing having at least one of her babies back in her arms again. 'No computer?' She raised her eyebrows.

Sam's face darkened. 'No. Has Mr Jones spoken to you yet?'

'Not yet, no. Why? What's happened, Sam?'

He rolled over: the conversation so far as he was concerned was over. 'You'd better speak to Mr Jones. I don't want to talk about it.'

She was about to leave the room when he called after her. 'Oh, and Mum? You'd better ask him about Ava, too.'

'She's okay?'

He nodded. 'She's fine. Mad, but fine.'

It said volumes about Gemma's preconceptions of her daughter that she took Sam's description of her as 'mad' to be simply that she'd been demonstrating yet another example of slightly unhinged, off-the-wall behaviour.

She didn't even consider that, this time, it might just have had another meaning.

Tom was sitting at the kitchen table when she came back downstairs, two glasses of chilled white wine poured and awaiting them. She sat down next to him and looked him in the eyes. 'So? What's been going on?'

It transpired, despite Tom's reassuring texts, that things had very much not gone as either he or Gemma had hoped in her absence. Not that he and the children had got off to a bad start. On the contrary. Ava had told everyone who would listen that Mr Jones would be taking her home from school that day, 'because he likes to sleep in my mummy's bed', and Tom had had to explain to more than one

224

concerned-looking parent that it was because he and Ava's mum were actually in a committed, long-term relationship, and not that he had some strange fetish about sleeping in the beds of the parents of kids at the school.

They'd arrived home and Ava had, as predicted, dragged Tom immediately outside to play football. Tom had encouraged Sam to join them, but he'd told them he was okay, that he had some homework that he was going to do up in his room.

If Gemma had been there, this would have immediately aroused suspicion; she could count on less than one finger the number of times Sam had gone to do his homework without being repeatedly begged, pleaded, threatened and cajoled to do so. Tom, however, saw no reason to disbelieve the boy, and so, after checking he had everything he needed, he had followed Ava out into the garden and prepared to get his arse kicked.

After half an hour or so he had told Ava it was time to start getting tea ready, and the two of them had gone into the house. Ava had happily slumped in front of the TV, and Tom had popped upstairs to check on Sam.

Gemma always, always knocked on both of her children's bedroom doors before she entered them, wanting to ensure they had the privacy she had craved as a child, in their tiny, bursting-at-the-seams council house, and had never quite managed to get. Thanks to Sam's headphones, she quite often had to knock two or three times, increasingly firmly, before she got a response. But she always waited for him to acknowledge her and to tell her it was okay for her to come in.

Tom, on the other hand, came from a family where bedroom doors were always kept open, and where it was the exception, not the rule, for him or his sister to spend time alone in their rooms. Consequently, while he did knock, he did so lightly, and when he didn't hear anything from Sam, he gently opened the door and peered in.

Sam was totally absorbed in what he was doing, sitting in front of his computer, staring at the screen and then typing furiously. Out of habit from work, Tom glanced at the screen to ensure that the website he was on was suitable.

And then he had to stifle a gasp of horror, because open on the browser tab in front of Sam was a website that he recognised by sight, just from its branding and the bold, primary-coloured logo. To the untrained eye, it might look exactly like a homework support site, designed to assist Year 6 and above pupils with their homework.

But to Tom, who had recently sat through a full day's workshop run by the local constabulary on internet safeguarding for children, it was all too recognisable as one of the better known chat websites, used almost exclusively by groups of children in order to single each other out, point out perceived failings and – well, bully. That's what the site was used for. Bullying.

Sam still hadn't clocked Tom was standing behind him, and Tom wasn't going to stay there spying on what the boy was up to. Gently, he tapped him on the arm and Sam shot into the air with fright. The moment he clocked it was Tom, not Ava, he immediately started trying to close down his browser windows, but not before Tom stopped him.

'Sam.' Tom's voice had been gentle; he didn't want to scare him into not talking. 'What are you doing?'

'Homework!' Sam immediately replied. 'I told you. Homework. That's what I was doing.' He cast a sideways look at the screen. 'And you shouldn't be in here, anyway. This is my bedroom. Did you not see the sign on the door? It says KEEP OUT.' He folded his arms defiantly.

Tom sighed. 'Sam, I think both you and I know that you weren't doing your homework just then. The thing is, unfortunately for you, I've just finished a training course that was run by the police, which told me all about some of the websites that were causing problems for kids like you at the moment. And that site you were just on, just then' – he gestured to the computer screen, with the logo of the website still clearly visible – 'that was pretty much top of their list. They've dealt with some horrendous cases of bullying via that site. One lad, only a couple of years older than you, tried to kill himself as a result of what some of his so-called friends had been saying to him on there. Can you imagine that? Feeling so desperate that the only way out was to think about taking your own life?' He shook his head. 'So we can do this the easy way, Sam, or we can do it the hard way. Either you can tell me what's going on ... or I can sit down and take a proper look at your internet browser history. What's it to be?'

Sam was pale faced. 'Fine. I'll tell you. But you're not to tell Mum.'

Tom shook his head. 'Nope. Sorry. It doesn't work like that. Your mum and I don't have secrets from each other, the same as you and she shouldn't have secrets from each other. So, what's been going on?'

It transpired that, at the start of that term, Tartan had come into Year 6 full of excitement over a website that his older cousins – who were in secondary school – had been showing him in the holidays. Tartan, self-proclaimed leader of Year 6, immediately announced that everyone in the class had to join and prove it by showing him their user name.

Sam, who thought Tartan was a total dickhead and usually ignored him completely, had told Tartan to 'piss off, you hairy penis', but had found it harder and harder to ignore the increasing pressure from not only Tartan but also the rest of the class, as they joined and gradually found themselves caught up in the tsunami of peer pressure to call out each other's failings. Bully, or be bullied, it seemed. And Sam, who had tried for so long to be strong, had eventually capitulated – around the time that the secondary school places had been announced. Tartan's face-to-face attacks on Sam over the fact he was going to Catswells had seamlessly transferred across to the internet, where there was no danger of a teacher overhearing, and where others in the class were willing to back him up behind the cloaked security of their anonymous keyboards. And Sam, not knowing quite what to do, being told every day by Tartan that he was going to 'be sorry' if he didn't see him online that evening, had spent more and more time on the site, desperately trying to defend himself and retain the small group of friends he had left.

It had been a horrible, terrible time, and despite the trouble Sam knew that he would inevitably be in for having gone on the website in the first place, he couldn't help feeling a very small, minuscule, tiny amount of relief that now, at last, somehow, this nightmare might get sorted out and he could stop spending every second of every day feeling like he wanted to burst into tears.

Not that he was going to let Tom know that, of course. 'I hate you, Mr Jones,' Sam told him, his face twisted into a mixture of fury and abject mortification. 'I hate you, and I hope that my mum comes back soon and that I never have to see you again.'

'Oh my God.' Gemma had her head in her hands. 'Oh my God. My poor boy. My poor boy. I thought I was doing everything right. I knew Sam was on his computer all the time, but I had no idea that anything sinister was going on. Every time I checked in on him he was playing Minecraft or staring at that maniac DanTDM. I can't believe I could have been so naïve.' Tears pricked her eyes. 'Thank goodness you found him. Thank goodness.'

'I wouldn't thank me too much.' Tom took a sip from his glass of wine. 'Sam's basically refused to speak to me, or even acknowledge my existence since that all kicked off last night. I told him that I wasn't going to do anything else about it other than to ban him from using his computer until you came back, and that you'd sit down and have a chat with him once I let you know what had happened.' He looked at her. 'But I had to let the school know, today. You understand? This is clearly a much wider issue, affecting far more than just Sam. Mrs Goldman's handling it personally; she's already spoken with most of the class and I believe they will be taking formal action with Tartan. Vivienne's on the warpath, as you can probably imagine.'

Gemma could. Her poor boy. 'And Ava?' Sam's earlier words flooded back to her. 'He said I needed to talk to you about Ava, too?' God, please tell her that her daughter hadn't also been dragged into this underworld of bullying.

Tom looked serious. 'Ah, yes. I'm afraid Ava and I also had something of a run-in. She's absolutely furious with me, which is partly why she's gone round to Becky's for tea. You see' – he took a deep breath – 'I finished off the last of the Coco Pops.'

'Oh, Tom.' Gemma knew only too well how that would have gone down; Ava's possessive approach to the household Coco Pops supplies was legendary. She'd once nearly taken off Sam's little finger when she'd threaten to bite him after he'd finished the only box in the house off.

He smiled wryly. 'Tell me about it. Really, I should have known better. I've worked with kids for years; it still never occurred to me that eating the last of the breakfast cereal would result in such a meltdown.' He decided not to mention to Gemma what Ava had called him when she'd discovered the empty box; her new vocabulary that she'd picked up when visiting St Luke's was clearly being put to good use.

Gemma shook her head, half laughing, half close to tears. 'I'm so sorry. You've had so much to deal with.' A thought occurred to her. 'And I can't believe you didn't mention any of this to me, that you didn't let me know what was going on.'

'I'm sorry.' Tom looked genuinely contrite. 'I truly thought I was doing the right thing. There was nothing you could have done from up in Manchester, and I'd promised you that I would hold the fort. I guess it was a pretty stark insight into what being a step-parent would be really like.'

'Whoa whoa whoa. Have I missed something? You're talking about being the kids' step-parent?' Not knowing quite what to think, she got up from the table, a roller-coaster of emotions surging inside of her.

'No!' Tom could see the expression on her face and immediately backed off. 'I didn't mean it like that. I'm not trying to rush you into anything, Gemma, I promise. I just thought . . . I mean, this was the perfect opportunity to see how the kids got on with me looking after them, to see what it would be like if we were all living together.'

'Yep, well, I think we can safely say that plan fell at the first hurdle.' Distress at the thought of everything that had happened in her absence made Gemma's tone sharper than she'd intended. 'I think . . . you should probably go.'

'Gemma.' His face was grave. 'You're doing it again. You're running away. You can't keep doing that. We're in this together.'

'No.' She shook her head, not meeting his eyes. 'To be honest, Tom . . .' She sighed heavily. 'I don't know quite what to do right now.'

For a moment, there was silence. Tom opened his mouth to say something, thought better of it, and closed it again. Gemma, staring at the floor, didn't move.

'Okay.' Tom gathered his belongings, opened the door and walked down the path, turning at the end to look at her, sadness in his eyes. 'I love you, Gemma.'

He did. She knew that he loved her; just as much as she loved him.

The trouble was, neither of them knew any more if that was actually enough.

CHAPTER SEVENTEEN

Honestly, thought Mrs Goldman to herself, if it wasn't one thing this term, it was another. She wondered if it was a sign that she should retire from teaching and go and do something more relaxing, like bomb disposal.

Having listened carefully to Tom's account of what he believed had been happening within Year 6, and then having spoken to Mr Andrews, the Year 6 teacher, along with several of the students, she had called both Vivienne and Tartan in to meet with her that morning. Vivienne listened stiffly as Mrs Goldman showed her what she believed Tartan to have instrumented, and provided screenshots of some of the conversations started under Tartan's alias, BigDickVI.

'This is absolute nonsense,' Vivienne retorted, tossing the printed screenshots back on to the Head's desk. 'Of course my precious angel hasn't been writing these.' She kissed him indulgently on the top of his head, and Tartan squirmed away in embarrassment. 'BigDickVI. Really?' She leaned conspiratorially over to Mrs Goldman, whispering under her breath. 'It'd be wishful thinking on his part: I'm afraid he's likely to take after his father when it comes to endowment, and there were certainly no Big Dicks there.' Tartan hid his face in his hands.

Mrs Goldman was losing patience, not least because she had the grey-suited men from the LEA arriving to meet her shortly. 'The evidence would suggest otherwise, I'm afraid.' She handed over another screenshot, one in which AngelFaceXXX had asked SparklyGlitterz who BigDickVI was in real life, at which BigDickVI had responded, 'r u stupid? It's me, Tartan, the one and only.'

Vivienne was dismissive. 'That could be anyone. There's bound to be loads of Tartans out there.'

'I can confidently say, in my forty-odd years in education, that I have never encountered another Tartan. Let alone' – Mrs Goldman passed across another screenshot – 'one who also confirms his surname, and the fact that his little sister Satin will be starting this up in Year 3 as well. It would be something of a startling coincidence, don't you think?'

Vivienne was silent for a moment. 'Fine,' she countered at last. 'Okay, so what if it is Tartan? He's been messing around on the internet, he's been a very naughty boy, I'll have a word and we'll take away his internet access, okay?' She sighed. 'I really do feel this is yet another storm in a teacup from Redcoats.'

'On the contrary.' Mrs Goldman stood up, towering over the woman and her son. 'I can tell you now that, as per our internet and social media code of conduct, use of that site by any staff or student is prohibited. And to have not only used it, but to have encouraged it, indeed, enforced it, for a much wider student population ... well, that, I'm afraid, necessitates formal action being taken against Tartan. Action which, without wishing to prejudge the outcome, has a strong possibility of resulting in expulsion.' She crossed her arms and looked sternly at them both.

Vivienne was appalled. 'Expulsion? My Tartan? Surely ... surely not.' She turned on Mrs Goldman. 'After all of the work I've put into this school over the years, all of the fundraising efforts I've made. You can forget about any more of that if you're going to walk Tartan out of the door. I shall well and truly wash my hands of this school.'

'Actually,' Mrs Goldman's voice was mild, 'I was going to talk to you about allowing Tartan to remain at school, given how close we are to the end of term, in order to take his SATs. He would of course need to remain in isolation from the rest of the class, and I would have been looking to discuss with you about how we provide the appropriate supervision for him, for example, looking at you financially contributing to perhaps providing a private tutor. But, if you're determined to wash your hands of Redcoats, then I suggest that we don't delay. I will ask Rachel to write to you to confirm the formal details for the meeting which will be held to agree what sanction will be taken.'

'No.' Vivienne's voice, for the first time since Mrs Goldman had known her, sounded almost ... pleading? 'No. I think ... if that's something the school would be prepared to do, that would be ... excellent. And I could certainly look at funding a private tutor.' She picked up her iPhone. 'I'll get on to it straight away. Come on, Tartan.'

He stood up, and looked directly at the headmistress. Behind his perfectly styled hair and supercilious smile she thought she saw, perhaps for the first time, a genuine look of contrition. He cleared his throat, before speaking in what was little more than a whisper. 'I'm sorry, Mrs Goldman.'

She nodded her head. 'I understand, Tartan. And I'm sorry too, that your time at Redcoats has to end tarnished like this. Not to mention the fact that you'll no longer be able to participate in the gala performance.'

He nodded, as though expecting it, but Vivienne's composure vanished in an instant, replaced with abject horror. 'What do you mean, Tartan won't be participating in the gala performance? But he is the star! How can the show possibly go on?'

'The show will go on,' Mrs Goldman continued patiently, 'but it would be entirely inappropriate for me to allow a child, who by now the whole school will know was behind such widespread use of this website, to walk on stage in one of the lead roles.' She sighed. 'I don't know how we shall get around it, but we shall.' Her heart sank at the thought of having to break the news to an already histrionic Miss Thompson. 'And I'm sure Satin will be more than up to the challenge.'

'Oh, of course she will,' Vivienne beamed, her concern that Tartan wouldn't be taking his rightful place in the spotlight immediately replaced by her delight that she still had one child up there to lord it over the rest of the school.

'Which reminds me, I need to go and arrange for her profes-sional make-up artist to perform a trial on her this evening. Come on, Tartan. You won't object, Mrs Goldman, if I take Tartan home with me today? After all, the whole thing has been a terrible trauma for him.'

Very early in her teacher training, Mrs Goldman had learnt the art of smiling politely in front of parents, students and officials, never revealing the true thoughts going on inside. As she showed Vivienne out, and invited the two grey-suited men from the LEA in, she thought she had probably never been more grateful for such a skill than she had been so far this academic year.

Gemma had spent hours sitting with the children the pre-vious evening, trying to understand just what had gone so horribly wrong in her absence. She had tackled Ava first. The little girl, knowing what was coming, had stood defi-antly in the middle of the living room when Gemma had collected her from Becky's, her hands on both hips.

'I know what you are going to say to me, and I would like to tell you that it is definitely, *definitely* not my fault,' said Ava, getting the first word in as usual.

Gemma sighed. 'But do you think you might possibly have ever so slightly overreacted? It was only some Coco Pops. Mr Jones didn't mean to finish them off.'

'Yes he did!' Ava was outraged. 'If he hadn't meant to finish them off then he wouldn't have eaten them all.'

Gemma tried again. 'I just think, Ava, that your behav-iour was extremely unreasonable.'

'And I think,' retorted Ava, 'that Mr Jones's behaviour

was extremely unreasonable. They are MY Coco Pops, and he was NOT to eat them.'

Gemma persevered in her attempts to get her daughter to understand why behaving like that was simply not acceptable, and eventually got her to agree that she would write a letter of apology. It was perhaps fortunate that she didn't overhear Ava, running up the stairs to her room to write her apology letter, announcing that she was 'going to make absolutely sure that Mr Jones is very sorry *indeed*'.

One down, one to go. Bracing herself for what was to come, Gemma ascended the stairs Ava had just run up, knocking on Sam's door and waiting for his confirmation that she could come in.

To her surprise, her son seemed remarkably upbeat, the strain of the last few months having lifted with the knowledge that, at last, the grown-ups had found out what was going on and everything would get better again. He moved along his bed so Gemma could fit on, and she sat down side by side with him.

'What I'm most disappointed in, Sam . . . is actually me.' The heavy weight that had landed on her chest when Tom had broken the news of what Sam had been going through still sat there, uncomfortably. 'I thought I'd brought you up to know that we don't have secrets like that from each other. That we tell the truth. And that you know you can tell me anything.' To her horror, she felt tears starting to form; her voice wobbled as she continued. 'It's the thing I've most prided myself on as a parent, feeling that you and Ava can always come to me. Except this time, you couldn't. And I can't help thinking I've failed.'

Sam recoiled slightly at her visible emotions, in the way that pre-teen boys generally did. Awkwardly, he patted her on her shoulder. 'You haven't failed, Mum. You're a really good mum.' He looked embarrassed. 'I just did it because everyone else was doing it. It seemed like a good idea at the time.'

She sniffed loudly. 'And if everyone else walked off the edge of a cliff, would you think that was a good idea too?' They both smiled at her use of the classic Parenting Bingo line.

'I really am sorry, Mum.' It was clear that he meant it. She looked at him, sat there, his hair tousled, his voice just beginning to break, in that strange halfway house between childhood and becoming an adult. Sometimes, she couldn't believe how grown up he seemed; at times like this she realised that he was still her baby, who needed her now more than ever.

'Next time, just come and chat to me, okay? I've told you before and I'll tell you again: if there's a problem, no matter how bad it seems, we'll work it out together.'

He looked abashed. 'I do know that, and I will. I promise. And I'll say sorry to Mr Jones, too. I was pretty horrible to him. Although' – he looked proud – 'at least this time I didn't tell him to fuck off.'

Baby steps, eh? Pulling her boy close – he tolerated a brief hug – Gemma wondered what all of this meant for her and Tom's future. Then, before she had a chance to think too much more about it, the door burst open and Ava marched in, wanting to know 'how much does a box of Coco Pops cost, because I am trying to do the maths so

I know the percentage Mr Jones took and then I can work out how much money he needs to give us back so that I can buy some new Coco Pops', and it felt like some kind of normality had been restored. Whatever normality meant in Gemma's household these days.

In class at Redcoats, Ava looked up sharply when the headmistress entered their classroom. Something was clearly going on. Since their first day of Year 3, back in September, when she had seen Mrs Goldman cross herself and announce that on pain of death, she would not be going back in there with Year 3 again, the Head had stuck to her promise. And yet now, here she was, making a beeline for the beleaguered Miss Thompson, who was currently draped in fluorescent vests, which she was working with the class to turn into costumes for the various 'flames' in the production.

'Good afternoon, Year 3,' Mrs Goldman announced.

'Good afternoon, Mrs Goldman,' the class chorused back dutifully, all except Ava, who was eyeing the Head with suspicion. Something was going on, and she was determined to be the first to find out.

'Miss Thompson, I wonder ... could I have a very quick word?'

'Of course.' Miss Thompson looked around the room for a suitable candidate to take over from her holding of the fluorescent vests; Ava quickly stuck her head under the desk so that she wouldn't get picked. 'Simon! Come on, up you come. I appreciate how disappointed you are not to be allowed to be in the play with everyone else' – from the look on Simon's face, she'd somewhat misjudged how he was feeling – 'but you can hold these while the others stick the flames on to them.'

Ava shook her head. Simon Barnes? In charge of wardrobe? Really? She'd thought for some time that Miss Thompson must have had a breakdown, and it seemed that here was the proof she'd been looking for.

The Head and Miss Thompson walked towards the back of the room, standing in the little ante-room that held the children's coats and PE bags. Craning her neck, Ava attempted to hear what they were talking about.

'Oh NO!' she suddenly heard Miss Thompson wail. 'No, no, no, not at this late stage. It's impossible, it really is, Sharon' – Ava sniggered, it was always funny to hear the teachers pretending they had real names and weren't actually referred to as Mrs Such-and-Such outside of work – 'I beg you, you have to reconsider. Where am I going to get an understudy from at this late stage?'

Ava felt a sudden sinking feeling in the pit of her tummy. It was the same feeling she'd had when she'd missed that penalty in training the other day and she'd just known that she wouldn't be picked for the game on Sunday. And, sure enough, she wasn't. Ava's sinking feelings were usually spot on.

Nothing else happened that afternoon, apart from Simon Barnes managing to superglue himself to Miss Thompson's desk, necessitating a first-aider being called and Mr Cook having to sand down the part of the desk that was now attached to Simon. But that didn't fool Ava one little bit.

It was the calm before the storm.

She was right, as always. The next morning, when Gemma dropped the children off at school, Miss Thompson was waiting at the KS2 door for them. 'Ah, there you are, Ava. I was wondering . . . could I possibly have a word with you and your mum?'

It was worse than Ava could even have imagined. The only good part was that that fool Tartan had been found out for what he really was, and was no longer going to be allowed to take part in the show.

But on the other hand . . . it was her, Ava, who was being asked to step in. 'You're the only child in the school – other than Simon, and our insurance won't cover him performing any more, not after the Nativity – not in the production,' Miss Thompson implored her. 'There simply isn't anyone else we could ask to step in without completely throwing out all of the dance numbers. And you've sat through all of the rehearsals; you must know most of the choreography off by heart.'

It was true. Ava had sat through a *lot* of rehearsals, watching Tartan and Satin prance around the stage pretending to be Mrs Goldman and Mr Cook. Which, she would like to add, they were *terrible* at. Tartan had been playing Mr Cook as though he was Zac Efron, which, if you asked someone who knew Mr Cook well to think of what he was like, and then think of the opposite, might have been what they would have come up with. And Satin's Mrs Goldman was clearly on drugs. The illegal kind.

Secretly – something she wouldn't have confessed to anyone in the world, at least not without the promise of a million pounds and a full-time playing contract with

Chelsea at the end of it – Ava quite liked acting. Her dad had been in a few plays, and sometimes when he looked after them, before he went to Berlin, which was NOT in America, both Ava and her dad knew that now, he and Ava and Sam would put on funny voices and pretend to be people that they knew. Ava would never have told Gemma, but her dad did an absolutely brilliant impression of her mum, pretending he was running late in the morning and telling Ava and Sam to do their 'TEETH! HAIR! SHOES!'

But that was beside the point. This play was stupid and Ava didn't want to be in it, particularly not if she had to be in it with Satin.

'No.' Ava shook her head stubbornly. 'I don't want to do it. I told you that I don't want to do it, and I'm not going to do it, and you can't make me. So there.'

Despairing, Miss Thompson came into school the next morning determined not to give up. They had a full run-through that afternoon, with the cast in costume and make-up for the first time. Which, looking at Satin, she'd decided to go ahead and put on before she even came into school. Sitting unusually quietly at her desk, it was obvious even from the other side of the classroom that the girl's face was completely caked in make-up. Miss Thompson was a great subscriber to the school of thought of More is More, but the child was eight, for goodness' sake! It was a bit much.

She went over to Satin, not wanting to upset her only remaining star. 'Satin, darling … Oh!' Close up, Satin looked really quite peculiar. And also extremely miserable.

She looked at the teacher through big, sad eyes. 'Satin, what's wrong?'

'I've got chicken pox,' Satin muttered. 'Mum put this make-up on me so that I could come in anyway and do the play. She thought no one would notice. But I look stupid. And I feel really poorly.' A solitary tear rolled down her cheek. 'Miss Thompson, can I go home please and go to bed?'

Vivienne said very little when she was called to collect Satin, just arrived at the school office, wearing a similar layer of make-up across her own face.

'Ooh, have you got chicken pox as well?' asked Rachel as she saw her. 'Did you not have it as a child? It's supposed to be really nasty. A friend of mine had it, she was in bed for *two whole months*.'

'I'm perfectly fine,' snapped Vivienne, who was clearly anything but. 'Now, where's Satin? She's just got a nasty rash, I'll get her home and into bed and she'll be back in time for the rehearsal tomorrow.'

It was at this point Mrs Goldman materialised from her office, which was next door to reception. 'I'm afraid not, Vivienne. I have seen Satin, and she's clearly unwell and needs to be in bed. Chicken pox, as you know, is highly contagious, and I cannot possibly allow either Satin or yourself back into school until all of the spots have fully scabbed over. So we will see you both back in two weeks' time.'

'*Two weeks*?' Vivienne was so horrified she was almost lost for words. 'But ... the play's next week! Satin will miss it! One child out of the limelight, I could have lived with ... but both! Satin's going to be an Oscar-winning actress, you know. This is a pivotal opportunity in her dramatic development. I can't possibly allow her to miss it.'

Mrs Goldman, who had witnessed Satin's 'dramatic development' at many points over her school career to date, and felt primarily sorry for any future film director who would have to attempt to bring her under control, was having none of it. 'Vivienne, you are being ridiculous. Now, take your extremely unwell daughter home, put her to bed and, for once in your life, try to think of somebody other than yourself.'

There was a stunned silence.

'Fine,' retorted Vivienne, collecting a subdued Satin from the medical room and preparing to depart. 'Satin and I will indeed stay away from the school for the next two weeks. And I wish you the best of luck finding not only two brand-new leads' – she turned to leave, and spat her final remark over her shoulder – 'but a brand-new stage manager.' The door slammed behind her.

Mrs Goldman rarely swore, but had she had less control over her composure, right then would have been when she'd have let out an unapologetic 'FUCK'. She had completely forgotten that Vivienne was also the stage manager and, along with Miss Thompson, was basically running the production.

From behind her, she heard a round of applause. It was Rachel, sitting behind the reception desk. 'I have to say, Sharon, I've spent my last few years working here wondering when you were finally going to tell that woman to get knotted.' She bowed her head in approval. 'I've never been prouder to work for you in my life.'

That was something, Mrs Goldman supposed, as she went off to break the news to Miss Thompson that not only was she minus both leads ... she now needed to find a replacement stage manager. For a production that opened in less than a week.

When they spoke about the joy of teaching, this was surely exactly what they meant.

CHAPTER EIGHTEEN

Becky and Gemma were holding a crisis Fundraisers United meeting at Gemma's. They'd invited Kristin to join them, but she'd declined, saying that she must be there for Vivienne 'in her hour of need'.

'Which basically means that she's washed her hands of the whole bloody thing and has left us two mugs to pick up the pieces.' Gemma took a swig of the glass of wine in front of her, leaving Becky practically salivating. 'Sorry, lovely. You're welcome to smell it, if you like.'

'No, you're all right. Should be less than a month to go now before I can enjoy me a giant glass of the most expensive fucking champagne money can buy. In the meantime, I'll crack on with this lovely glass of' – she examined the label on the bottle she'd poured it out of – 'orange and mango squash. Mmmmm! De-LISH-ious!'

Gemma shook her head. 'I don't know how you're doing it, having a third. I really don't.'

'La la la la la.' Becky put her hands in her ears and sang loudly. 'Don't remind me. I keep telling myself that this time I surely must be due the two-hour start-to-finish labour and a baby who sleeps through the night from Day one. Don't even think about telling me that I'm kidding myself.'

Her friend laughed. 'In the meantime ... we have the tiny matter of a huge, enormous, absolutely fucking critical-to-saving-the-future-of-our-school production to put on. The production is now minus its two leads. And its stage manager. Which, much as I loathe her, Vivienne was bloody good at.'

'Okay. Let's work through this logically.' Becky pulled out a sheet of paper and started writing on it. 'First up, we need to replace our leads. Surely it's as simple as just pulling out two kids from the rest of the cast and telling them they've been promoted?'

Gemma shook her head. She had been in to ask exactly that question of Miss Thompson when she'd picked the children up from after-school club that afternoon, keeping a careful eye out for Tom, who she'd been completely avoiding since the day of their argument. Miss Thompson, still hysterical, had told Gemma in floods of tears how it simply wasn't possible.

'They've all been concentrating so hard on learning their own parts, they simply haven't had the opportunity to watch what Satin and Tartan have been doing. The principals and ensemble are very rarely on at the same time, other than the big chorus numbers. And, even if they had been, taking two of them out would *totally* ruin all of my choreography. We might as well not bother going on at all.'

'Okay, so that option's out.' Becky chewed the tip of her pencil. 'What about cancelling the show altogether? Could we do that? Or postpone it until Satin and Vivienne are better? Then we'd just have the one lead to find.'

Gemma shook her head. Back before everything had gone tits up with her and Tom, he'd told her that the absolute deadline for them to have confirmed they had the seventy thousand pounds needed for the rebuild project to the LEA was the end of April. This would allow time both for the plans to merge the school with St Catherine's to be shelved and for the rebuild to be fully completed ahead of the new academic year starting in September. 'Postponing isn't an option, and Vivienne knows that, otherwise she'd have been the first to not just suggest it, but to positively demand it. And surprisingly ticket sales have been really strong. Kristin gave me the figures earlier. Your idea to encourage people to pay what they could afford to fund the school was a great one. We've raised almost fifteen thousand pounds already. It's obviously still nowhere near what we actually need ... but it's a really good start.'

They sat there, drinking their wine and squash, neither saying what both were thinking, which was that it was a bit bloody late for a good start at this point in the year. It was a strong finish they needed, not a good start. Admitting that, though, would be admitting failure, which they simply weren't going to do. And who knew? Maybe there was still time for a miracle to happen.

'Okay, so the show must go on,' quipped Becky. 'The problem of the stage manager ... well, I think we can solve that. I'd be happy to step in, if it means we might be able to save Redcoats. I've got quite a bit of annual leave to take which I was going to tag on to the start of my maternity leave, but it's no big deal to move some of it around so that I can be there for the rest of the rehearsals. So that solves that problem.'

'Are you sure?' Gemma looked uncertainly at her friend's enormous bump. She looked like a caricature of a pregnant woman: still model-slim from behind; a danger to shipping and looking like she'd eaten an oversized beachball whole from the side and front-on. 'It seems a bit much to be taking on when you're eight and a half months' pregnant. The last thing we want is a live birth halfway through the show!'

'Would probably ensure none of the kids ever want to have sex, if they had to witness a live birth,' shrugged Becky. 'The best sex education we could provide.'

'I'd love to tell you that we've got a viable alternative, but I just can't get the time off at the moment, plus ...' Gemma trailed off. She hadn't quite found the opportunity to tell Becky about what had happened between her and Tom. They hadn't spoken since he'd walked out of her door a few days earlier; he'd tried to phone her but she'd rejected his calls, not knowing what to say. There was certainly no way she could spend a whole week in his company; it would be farcical the two of them not speaking, and, if she was honest, it was just going to hurt too much.

'Plus ...' Becky prompted her.

'Plus ... you'll be a brilliant stage manager!' Gemma tried to sound enthusiastic, even though her heart was breaking at the thought of Tom.

'I will, you know.' Becky nodded confidently. 'I stage

managed a production of *Cat on a Hot Tin Roof* at uni. Did the final performance on the Saturday night after we'd spent all afternoon drinking. I was supposed to be the fire officer and do all the checks before the show: I went into the auditorium and shouted, 'Are there any fires in here?' and ticked the box in the book to say that I'd completed them. I then spent the whole play trying not to puke in the wings. If I can get through that, I can get through anything.'

'So, that's our stage manager crisis resolved. Tick. Now . . . I don't suppose you'd also like to double up as both lead roles, would you?'

Becky laughed. 'Sadly I think my singing and dancing days are well behind me, particularly now that I'm roughly the size of a monster truck, and about as easy to manoeuvre. Okay, so all of the kids in the school are in this already? There's no one else we can get to step in?'

Gemma shook her head. 'Apparently the risk of Simon Barnes on stage is greater than the show going ahead minus a lead. And the only other person is Ava, and she's point-blank refusing to do it.'

'Why?'

'Because she's Ava.'

'And because I am DIFFICULT.' Ava, who had clearly been shamelessly listening at the door again, burst into the room, accompanied by both Rosie and her big brother, who was looking much more like his old self. After the conversation they'd had that night, and with Tartan removed from Year 6, plus Sam's access to the website cut, not to mention Gemma keeping a close eye on his browsing history, both she and Sam felt better about things than they had done in ages. Sam had even been spending time outside of his bed-room, occasionally stepping in as goalie for Ava to practise penalty kicks against or, more commonly, just annoying the hell out of his little sister.

'Ava, have you been listening outside doors again?' Gemma's face was stern.

'Yes!' said Ava delightedly.

Gemma shook her head. 'You've been told before not to do that. Eavesdropping is not something you want to grow up getting into the habit of doing.'

Ava looked perplexed. 'But then how will I find out the things people are talking about that they don't want me to know?'

Gemma buried her face in her hands and laughed out loud. 'Come on, then. As the three of you have been listening in, that means you're now official committee members' – 'Members of FUC,' Sam sniggered under his breath – 'and so you can help us sort this show out. We're trying to work out who can take on the roles that Satin and Tartan were playing, but apparently everyone else is in the show apart from you, Ava.'

Ava shook her head. 'Not just me. Simon is not in it either.'

'I know,' replied Gemma. 'Miss Thompson won't let him be in the play.'

'That's right,' agreed Sam, 'because of what happened in the Nativity, and also because he keeps on eating the props.'

Ava nodded. 'It's true. So far Miss Thompson has had to buy twenty-seven new sliced loaves to replace the ones Simon has kept eating in the "We're Going To Be Toast" song.'

Gemma dismissed that as a minor detail. Surely Ava and Simon could step into the two main roles, and then that would be the problem solved!

Ava shook her head. 'I know what you're thinking, but it's not going to work. Miss Thompson won't let Simon be in the play, and anyway, I won't be in the play if Simon has to be in it with me. Simon,' she announced decisively to her mum and Becky, 'is an absolute fucking liability.'

'AVA!' Gemma reprimanded her daughter, as Sam killed himself laughing. 'We do *not* say the F word, do we?'

'Yes, *we* do,' retorted Ava. 'I hear you saying it all the time.'

'Anyway.' Becky attempted to move the situation on, before Ava could announce that she'd picked up the phrase 'absolute fucking liability' from Becky, who could frequently be heard yelling it at Boris after he went on one of his rampages. 'It doesn't sound like Simon is an option. Which leaves us . . .' She put her hands in the air and then let them slump, down by her sides, looking totally defeated. 'I don't know where it leaves us.'

'I could do it,' a little voice piped up. It was Rosie.

'You could do it?' Becky stared at her daughter. 'But you're in the play already, aren't you? And there's so much to learn, all the choreography, all the songs.' Inwardly, she was shell-shocked. Rosie, in stark contrast to her mum's gregarious nature, had always seemed far happier taking a back seat and blending into the background. Becky would never have dreamt of voicing what she really thought, which is that she imagined her introverted daughter would keel over in fright if she had to take the lead role on stage in front of several hundred people; nevertheless, she couldn't imagine how she could possibly do it.

'I know them.' Red-faced yet determined, Rosie stood her ground. 'I really like acting, Mum. I was so jealous of Satin and Tartan, getting to play the leads. And neither of them are very good, either. Some of Miss Thompson's script is really funny, if you do it right. And I could do it right. I've watched every single scene; I know exactly how I would do it. I'd be a brilliant Mr Cook.'

'She would.' Ava nodded in clear approval. 'Rosie would be brilliant. You should definitely pick her.'

'But . . . Mr Cook's a boy. And Rosie's a girl. So how will that work?' Sam looked utterly perplexed.

'Oh, Sam, it's called *acting*,' Ava told her brother in her most scathing tones. 'Something you clearly don't know anything about, based on the bit you're in,' she muttered under her breath. 'Besides, Rosie might want to *be* a boy. How do you know she's not transgender? You are very . . . DISINTIGRATORY,' she told him, while Gemma and Becky nearly cried laughing and explained to the little girl that the word she was looking for was actually 'discriminatory'. Which no, Sam most definitely wasn't.

The room had a palpable sense of excitement, as Becky looked Rosie straight in the eyes. 'You really want to do this?'

Rosie nodded. 'I really want to do this. I think I could be really good.'

'She definitely could,' Ava confirmed loyally.

'Okay. So it sounds like we have a replacement for Tartan. Which just means ...' Gemma looked at her daughter. 'If Rosie is going to play one of the leads ... then will you play the other one? And replace Satin? So the two of you can play the main parts together?' She held her breath.

Ava thought for a moment. 'Oh, o*kay*. I will do it, even though I don't want to do it, because I would like them not to close Redcoats down, and also because I do like Rosie a lot and so it will be okay if we are doing it together. But my conditions are that, if there is any money left over after they have sorted out the burnt-out bit, that you get Mrs Goldman to agree to make a proper football pitch on the back field for us to play on.'

'I think if you manage to save Redcoats, you'll find that even Mrs Goldman is agreeable to a football pitch on the back field,' Becky said mildly.

Gemma was looking at her daughter. 'I'm really proud of you, Ava. I know how much you didn't want to do this play. Stepping in at the last moment like this is an amazing thing to do.'

Ava shook her head in despair. 'No it isn't, Mum. Scoring two hat-tricks in the final of the Champions League against Real Madrid would be an amazing thing to do. This is just a play. Besides,' her eyes sparkled as she looked at her brother, 'Sam has to wear a rainbow costume and pretend to be a rainbow and shout out, "I'm a little rainbow, I'm a little rainbow!" with the rest of his class, and I *definitely* wouldn't want to miss out on him having to do that.'

Sam's face blazed scarlet. Gemma turned to him, her

own face a picture. 'You have to be a rainbow? You kept that one quiet.'

Sam shook his head in despair. 'This term's been really shit, Mum. I can't wait to get to secondary school.'

It had been harder than Becky had thought it would be to get Miss Thompson to agree to having Rosie and Ava step into the lead roles in the production. 'I'm sure you can see how this will look,' Miss Thompson warned her new stage manager. 'Putting the children of two of the members of Fundraisers United straight into the lead roles, without even giving anyone else a chance to audition.' She shook her head and tutted. 'Really, we should be looking to run the whole audition process all over again.'

Mrs Goldman was more pragmatic, pointing out that they had already established there was no one else who would be able to step in. It was only Rosie's love of acting that had meant she'd studied the script sufficiently to be able to pick up the many complex song and dance numbers at such short notice; Ava, of course, had been made to watch every single rehearsal and could consequently recite most of it backwards in her sleep.

'We can't, it goes without saying,' she warned Becky, 'risk a repeat of the Nativity.' Becky shuddered at the very thought. 'I'm relying on you to ensure everything runs smoothly backstage.'

'It will be absolutely fine,' Becky reassured the Head, with a confidence that she really didn't feel.

'Then it's done,' Mrs Goldman confirmed. 'Ava and Rosie will step into the leads; Angela, I suggest you set up an intensive rehearsal schedule to give them the best possible chance of succeeding.'

'Honestly,' Becky heard the Year 3 teacher muttering as she swept dramatically off, chiffon scarves flying, 'I'm sure they never had these problems on the set of *Harry Potter*.'

In what seemed like no time at all, it was opening night. Becky had been at the school since early that morning, having arranged for one of the nursery staff to babysit for Ella after nursery closed that evening. Jon had apologised profusely that he wasn't going to be there; they'd had a sudden request from one of their major prospects to go and pitch to them in Milan, and he'd had to take a forty-eight-hour trip over there.

'Now, no having that baby before I get back,' he told her sternly as he'd left, before the sun was even up.

Becky shook her head. 'Not a hope in hell. Still two weeks to go, and if you remember, both Rosie and Ella went two weeks overdue and ended up being induced.' She kissed him softly. 'Safe flight, and I'll see you tomorrow night.'

'I love you, you know.'

'I love you too. Now go, or you'll miss your flight.'

He left, and Becky sprang into action, ensuring the kitchen was clean and tidy and the house was in perfect order before the girls woke up. She'd even found time to unpack the couple of bits they'd bought for the new baby that weren't going to be hand-me-downs from Ella and Rosie (if he was a boy, he would be wearing a lot of pink, that was for sure), and make a start on her hospital bag. Not that you really needed much to have a baby apart from a metric fuck-ton of drugs.

Final rehearsals that day had been predictably chaotic, but Miss Thompson had remained calm amidst the chaos. 'It's a bad rehearsal, which means a great first night,' she had cooed to the panic-stricken cast members. 'You're all going to be just marvellous.'

'Miss Thompson has been on the gin,' Ava told Rosie knowingly.

The curtain was due to go up at 7.30 p.m. sharp, which meant letting audience members in shortly before seven, encouraging them to purchase items from the merchandise stall, which Gemma would be manning. Leroy and Zero had generously sponsored a range of *Phoenix!* merchandise, and Gemma had somehow managed to persuade both Leroy and Siobhan to accompany her, promising Leroy that he could combine selling the items with pitching Zero's consumer product. His boyfriend, Jeremy, was backstage, having stepped in at the eleventh hour to do hair and make-up for the children after Vivienne had called up the school to delightedly announce that the professional hair and make-up artist she had booked was now mysteriously 'indisposed'.

'Fucking hell, this is bonkers, this is.' Siobhan looked around the hall with wild eyes, at the orchestra tuning up, at the (toned-down) smoke machine, and at Mr Cook conducting an under-the-chair security check on every seat in the auditorium. 'Are all school productions like this?'

Gemma hid a smile. 'Maybe not quite like this. Here, why don't you pop over to the refreshments stall and grab yourself a wine? Possibly two. I feel like you might need it.'

Backstage, Becky was expertly marshalling her cast members into ordered lines, ready for their opening number. Ava and Rosie had been in costume for a good hour now and were quietly playing football Premiership Top Trumps in a corner.

'Should you two not be running through your lines?' Becky asked them.

Ava shook her head. 'Rosie gets worried if she thinks too much about her lines, so we're not thinking about them. We're thinking about how much I'm going to beat her by in Top Trumps instead.' She grinned slyly and Rosie thumped her gently on the leg. 'What? I'm helping you!'

Smiling, Becky left them to it, bumping into Tom as she walked away. 'Oh! Hello!' She hadn't spoken to him properly for ages, she realised; she'd not seen him at Gemma's, and although he'd been at rehearsals, they'd both had their hands far too full to exchange anything other than a quick hello or goodbye.

Tom smiled, a tired smile. 'All set, Mrs Stage Manager?'

'About as set as I'm going to get, I imagine.' She looked around nervously. 'Just as long as you don't let Andrea backstage. She sent me a text today telling me that she was really sorry that we hadn't been able to enjoy each other's company more as "pregnancy BFFs", and that she would make sure she found me this evening to see if we could arrange a joint bump casting session.' Tom looked perplexed. 'Apparently it's where we take off all of our clothes and rub clay over our naked bodies. Like if Demi Moore had decided to combine her *Vanity Fair* cover when she was pregnant with that scene from *Ghost*. Basically, the stuff of nightmares.'

She laughed at the look of horror on Tom's face. 'No, so long as you keep Andrea far away from me then we're good to go. Another hour and a half and it'll all be over, and we'll be able to relax with a nice big glass of wine.' She screwed up her face. 'Or, if you're me, a nice big glass of orange and mango squash, which just doesn't hit the spot in quite the same way. Have you and Gemma got plans for after the show? You could all come back to mine for a drink? I'm on my own tonight; Jon's away in Milan, so you'd be keeping me company.'

His face fell. 'I'm not sure what Gemma's plans are tonight, I'm afraid.' When Becky raised an eyebrow he went on, 'Has she not told you? It's just . . . we haven't seen much of each other recently.' In response to Becky's blank look he told her briefly about what had kicked off between him and the children, and the fact that he and Gemma hadn't really spoken since.

'But that's ridiculous. You two are perfect together, and Ava and Sam are absolutely fine. I'd be stunned if they had an issue with you being around. Go make things up! Seize the day!' she encouraged him.

He shook his head. 'No. The kids have got to come first. Believe me, I'd love it not to be this way. But it turns out, not all fairy tales come true.'

He was gone, back to his charges, before Becky could tell him what absolute bullshit that was, that of course he and Gemma were meant to be together, it was just simple common sense. Sighing, she found her headset and clipboard, then made her way towards the sound and lighting desk that had been set up backstage. Her lower back twinged as she walked: she'd spent yesterday evening bouncing a fractious Ella around on her hip and was clearly paying the price for it now. She couldn't *wait* to collapse into a hot bath and get to bed.

It was time. The audience were in place, the performers were waiting in the wings. Ava and Rosie stood in the middle of the stage, looking at each other. From her vantage point, Becky could just see Ava lean across to a terrified-looking Rosie and tell her, 'Don't worry. You're going to be brilliant.'

Tentatively at first, then more confidently, Rosie nodded her head. 'We are. We really are going to be brilliant, Ava, aren't we?'

Ava grinned. 'Of course we are. We're *superstars*.'

And they were. They really were, from the moment the opening chords crashed out and Ava, bringing the house down with her caricature of Mrs Goldman, told the assembled parents, friends and relatives what they were about to witness. 'A tragedy ... an utter tragedy' – 'It's like *Romeo and Juliet*,' Leroy had sobbed to a baffled-looking Siobhan – 'followed by triumph, as we rose from the flames ... like a PHOENIX!' At which point the reflective-jacket-clad students step-ball-changed on to the stage, and Ava and Rosie headed backstage as the ensemble launched into 'Let's Burn This Bad Boy Down'.

Really, thought Becky, they couldn't have got off to a better start.

And then her waters broke.

CHAPTER NINETEEN

For a moment, Becky wasn't sure what had just happened. With both Rosie and Ella, her waters hadn't broken naturally at all, and a delightful midwife had had to shove some horrendous instrument of torture in the style of a crochet hook up her front bottom in order to tear the sac of waters and get things moving.

Consequently, for thirty hideous seconds she stared in horror at the water pooling underneath her, steadily trickling out the bottom of her black maternity jeans, and wondered how in the world she'd managed to wet herself without even feeling like she needed the toilet.

And then she realised.

Okay, so it was going to be fine, Becky persuaded herself. Sure, her waters might have broken. But didn't all the books tell you that could quite easily happen hours, if not *days*, before labour started. The production was only an hour and a half long, and they were ten minutes in already.

She'd finish up here, help clear up, then pop into the maternity ward on her way home, just to make sure everything was okAAAAAARRRRGGGGHHHHHHHH.

With impressive self-control, Becky managed not to scream out loud as a vice-like grip tightened itself around her middle. An unstoppable pain that felt horribly like . . .

No. Surely not.

She couldn't be having contractions?

Could she?

The audience applauded wildly as the curtain came down for the interval, a twenty-minute opportunity to raise more money for the fundraising efforts as hordes of thirsty parents flocked to the refreshments stand and to buy some of the merchandise that Leroy was parading up and down with, rather as though he were a candidate on *The Apprentice*. 'Just look at the colours on this one,' he exclaimed, sporting a hot-pink and lime-green *PHOENIX* sweatshirt. 'Simply *fabulous*.'

Gemma's phone buzzed in her pocket; she'd clearly forgotten to switch it to silent during the performance. Quickly taking it out to turn it off, she saw to her surprise that she had a WhatsApp from Becky. Shouldn't she have her hands full, stage managing?

It was a short message, and said simply: 'Can you come here a sec?'

Gemma sighed. The hall was thronged with audience members; it was going to be a nightmare to push through from the back where she was and get to the stage. Plus, she really, really didn't want to risk running into Tom.

She replied quickly: 'Absolutely rammed here. Is it urgent?'

The two blue ticks showed her that Becky had read it immediately, and was already replying.

'Yes.'

Asking Leroy and Siobhan to hold the fort, and wondering what in the world was going on with her friend, Gemma sorry'ed and excuse-me'ed her way through the crowd, until she reached the steps up to the stage and was able to access backstage. Immediately, she spotted Becky in the gloom, sitting down next to the sound and lighting desk. There was a Wet Floor sign next to her, Gemma noticed. From behind the stage she could hear the cries of excited children, but to her relief there was no one else in sight. It looked like she was unlikely to run into Tom for the time being.

'Hey.' She raised one hand to Becky in greeting. 'What's up?'

In response, Becky showed her an application she had open on her phone.

It was called Contraction Master.

And, according to the timings Contraction Master had been recording, for the past twenty minutes Becky's contractions had been almost exactly three minutes apart.

'What the ... ?'

Becky nodded in response to Gemma's unfinished question. 'I know. I know. What are the chances, eh? Two weeks early, Jon in another country, halfway through the school production ... and that's the time my waters decide to break.' She gestured to the large puddle on the floor, which Gemma realised with a start wasn't the result of one of the Year Rs failing to go to the toilet before the show, but was clearly Becky's waters.

'Oh my God.' Gemma put her hand to her mouth. 'You've got to be—'

She was cut short from asking Becky if she was joking, as another contraction gripped her friend, who stood up, holding on to the desk in front of her for dear life and making noises that sounded as though they belonged more in a farmyard than on a stage.

'We need to get you to a hospital,' Gemma announced. 'Come on. Put down that script and follow me. I'll drive you straight there.'

'Nu-uh.' Becky shook her head, the worst of the pain having passed. 'No way. I promised I was going to be the stage manager, and it's a promise that I'm going to keep. I'm not going to be like Vivienne, flaking out and leaving everyone in the lurch.'

'But, Becky, this is ridiculous. You're in full-blown labour,' Gemma protested. 'Someone else can step in and do this. You need to get to hospital.'

'They can't.' Becky was unmoving. 'You know how bloody complicated this production is; you know the amount of dance numbers and quick changes and special effects Miss Thompson, in her wisdom, decided to put in. It took me studying it all for the best part of a week to be able to pick it up. So don't try to tell me there's someone else who can do this. Because there isn't.'

It was clear she wasn't going to budge; and Gemma had a fairly strong feeling that it wouldn't be a good idea to start arguing with a woman in full-on labour. Capitulating, she held up her hands. 'Okay. So what do you want me to do?'

'Stay here,' Becky breathed, as another contraction began to hit her in earnest. 'If it does all go horribly wrong and I start pushing back here, I'd like someone I know and love on hand. I don't want to risk ending up with Mr Cook as my birthing partner.'

It was a fair point. Sighing, Gemma pulled up a chair next to her friend and texted Siobhan to tell her she'd see her at the end of the show.

Are you bailing on us? Siobhan texted back immediately. *You can't miss any of this. It's the most fucking batshit brilliant thing I've seen in ages ... and I go clubbing in Brixton!*

The next forty minutes were some of the longest of Gemma's life. And not, incredibly, because of the action on stage. Had she had time to do anything other than keep her eyes firmly fixed on Becky, and her hands poised at any moment to catch a baby, Gemma would have been able to marvel at her daughter and Rosie's natural rapport, the way their confidence grew and they held the audience in their hands with their performances as the Head and Mr Cook (whose reaction to Rosie's performance Gemma was yet to observe; possibly just as well). She would have realised that, despite her foibles, Miss Thompson really had written, directed and put on a quite remarkable production, particularly given the ages of the children involved. And she would have felt some optimism that maybe, just maybe, the miracle they had all been hoping for would have occurred, and they might somehow have managed to raise the funds needed.

As it was, all she felt was cold blind panic.

Becky's contractions continued at a steady three minutes apart, right the way through the second half of the performance. By the time they reached the closing number, 'Rising From the Flames', most of the audience were in tears . . . and Becky, to Gemma's horror, suddenly dropped to her knees and started mooing like a cow, eyes squeezed tight in pain.

'Oh my God, is it coming? Becky, we have to get your trousers off.'

Her friend managed to shake her head. 'No . . . we . . . fucking . . . don't.' The contraction subsided and she glared at Gemma. 'You thought that time you threw up on your date was bad. That'd be nothing compared to the tale I'd have to tell if I actually did end up giving birth on stage, in front of a two-hundred-strong audience and the entire student population and teaching staff of this school.' Staggering a little, she made it to her feet, as the final chords rang out and the audience rose to their feet as one, cheering and applauding. Gemma just had time to see her daughter and Rosie at the front of the cast, beaming from ear to ear.

'Gem? I hate to drag you away from our daughters' triumph, but . . .' She was beginning to groan again. 'If I don't want to give birth on the stage, we really do need to move. And fast.'

Gemma had always prided herself on being a law-abiding citizen. She never dropped litter, always wore her seatbelt and immediately corrected anyone serving her in a shop if they happened to give her too much change. That was all about to change, though, as she ran to retrieve her car from the school playground and sped round to the school entrance, where Becky was hanging on to the railings, looking increasingly desperate and wild-eyed.

'Here, in you get.' She tried to gently steer Becky into the front seat, but Becky shook her head violently. 'Back . . . seat . . . more . . . room,' she managed to gasp. Gently, Gemma fastened the seatbelt around her friend, who had her eyes closed and was starting to pant.

'Just keep your legs closed back there,' Gemma muttered as she jumped into the driver's seat and sped off, trying her best to keep to the speed limit whilst also being hideously conscious of the noises Becky was making behind her.

'Oh . . . oh . . . oh,' Becky whimpered as Gemma took the speed bumps out of the road the school was situated on at pace. 'What're you trying to do to me?'

'I'm doing my best,' said Gemma through gritted teeth as she indicated left and turned on to the main road. 'Just as well the hospital's only a five-minute drive away, eh?'

'Too bloody right,' groaned Becky. 'Oh shit, that's some more of my waters. Your car's going to be trashed, Gem. I'm so sorry.'

Despite her panic, Gemma found it in her to laugh. 'Trashed? You mean more than the damage my kids have already inflicted on it? I'm surprised you noticed your waters amongst the sea of water bottles and empty sweet wrappers.'

The welcoming bright lights of the hospital were just in front of them: Gemma thought she had never been so relieved to see anything in her life. 'Almost there, Becks.

Just hang on.' A thought occurred to her. 'Shit, do you want me to phone Jon? Tell him what's happening?'

Becky shook her head. 'He'll be wining and dining his clients, and I know how important this pitch is to him.' Her face softened. 'He's been nothing but supportive of me and my career; I want to do the same for him.'

'Yes, but I think this is a bit different,' Gemma protested. 'His baby's about to be born.'

'No it's not. I'm probably not even in labour proper yet. I remember with Rosie and Ella, we had about fifteen trips to the hospital each time when I was screaming in agony and each time they just gave me a quick look, shoved a cursory finger between my legs and told me I still wasn't dilated enough and to go home and rest. Rest! Like that's possible when you're in so much pain you're throwing up every few minutes.' Becky sighed. 'No. I just don't do quick labours. Jon will have had time to get to and from Milan ten times over by the time this one comes out.'

'If you're sure?' Gemma eyed her friend uneasily as she parked the car. 'In that case, do you think you can walk to the hospital from here, or should I go and get a wheelchair?'

Becky smiled confidently. 'I'll be fine.' Gemma opened her door and she swung her legs around, standing up on them somewhat shakily. 'Okay then, let's— OHHHHHHHHHHHHHHHHHHHHHHHHHHHHHHHH.' Gripped by the largest contraction yet, she was down on all fours in the middle of the car park, desperately grappling with her flies. 'Oh my God, Gem, it's coming, it's coming, IT'S COOOOOOMIIIIIIIIIIIIIIIIIIING.'

*

Gemma thought she'd never been so exhausted in her life. And it wasn't even her who'd just had a baby. Little Sofie Ivy lay contentedly in her mother's arms, already breast-feeding like a pro, completely oblivious to the drama she'd just caused. Becky's eyes were closed; Gemma couldn't tell if she was sleeping or not. Gently, she brushed her friend's still damp hair away from her face.

'Thanks, Gem.' Becky opened her eyes and smiled sleepily. 'Fucking hell. Did that really just happen?'

'Tell me about it!' Gemma thought back to just an hour and a half previously, when Becky had dropped to the ground in the car park, screaming that the head was coming out, and Gemma had genuinely never felt more terrified in her life. Telling Becky to just hang on, she had sprinted over to the hospital building with an athleticism she didn't realise she possessed, screaming to the first person she saw in reception that her friend was having a baby, and it was coming 'RIGHT NOW!' The amazing NHS staff had jumped into action, running out with a stretcher which they had gently lifted Becky – still on all fours – on to, and wheeling her at pace into the reception area and through to the maternity ward.

'And I didn't give birth on a stage! Or in a car park! Yay me!' Becky stroked her daughter's head and beamed with pride.

'Not for want of trying, mind.' Gemma had thought the baby was going to come out there and then, but the midwives had managed to pull Becky's trousers and pants down once they were in the birthing suite and even get her off the stretcher before, half standing, half crouching, she had given one great groan, yet more waters had poured out from between her legs, and little Sofie's head had emerged, to be very quickly followed by her body and legs, in what all seemed to be one giant involuntary push. Becky had collapsed into a sitting position on the floor, and her daughter – who one particularly on-the-ball midwife had somehow managed to catch – had been gently handed to her before being weighed and wrapped in blankets.

'Next time, when I tell you we need to go, that there isn't time for you to stage manage the second half of a sodding performance – you need to listen to me, okay?' Gemma shook her head in mock admonition as Becky laughed and told her friend that, if she thought there was going to be another one, she really did have another think coming.

The midwives had thoughtfully brought Becky over a phone, so she was able to call a shell-shocked Jon herself and give him the good news. Gemma smiled as she left the room while they spoke and gave Leroy a quick ring – he and Jeremy had offered to take Sam, Ava and Rosie back to Gemma's until she got back from hospital – and checked everything was okay. She imagined it was going to take Becky at least ten minutes – and probably a few photo messages – to convince Jon that she wasn't joking, that their third daughter really was there.

It was gone 10 p.m. by the time Becky assured Gemma she was going to be absolutely fine, that the wonderful girl from the nursery was going to keep Ella overnight, and so if she just wouldn't mind having Rosie for an impromptu sleepover then that would be amazing. 'I'll be home first thing tomorrow,' she promised, 'but with the birth having been so quick, and with Jon being away, they'd rather I stayed here tonight. You head on home, though. Get some rest. After the day we've had, I imagine you need it.'

Now there was the understatement of the year. 'And Gem?' As Gemma turned to go. 'Thank you so much. I know you never intended to be my birthing partner, but I couldn't have asked for anyone better. Last time around, Jon kept telling me he was bored and asking if I was going to get on with it in time for him to get home for the ten o'clock news.' She rolled her eyes. 'Quite how we're still married, I have no idea.'

'It's no problem at all.' Gemma smiled. 'It was an absolute honour to see this little beauty come into the world. Not to mention really really fucking amazing that it wasn't me doing the giving birth bit this time around.'

'Yes.' Becky winced. 'I'd kind of gathered that I ended up with such a birth because my vagina had assumed wizard's sleeve proportions. Ending up with stitches as well means I feel like I've got the short end of the wedge on every front.'

'Ah well.' Gemma shrugged sympathetically. 'You've still got the "blood clots the size of rodents dropping out of your front bottom" bit to come. Isn't childbirth a fucking miracle?'

'Yeah, you can fuck off as well,' Becky laughed as she blew her a kiss. 'Night, Gem. Thanks for being such an utterly amazing bestie. I have no idea what I'd do without you.'

Gemma smiled all the way home.

CHAPTER TWENTY

'Settle down, settle down.' Mrs Goldman clapped her hands together to quieten the – usually orderly – staffroom the following Monday. It was time for the weekly staff meeting, the first since the triumphant gala performance.

Gradually, the teaching staff each found themselves a chair to perch on or a wall to lean against and, clutching their mugs of coffee, listened to what the Head had to say.

She beamed round at them all. 'So, as you will know, most of you having been involved in one capacity or another, the gala performance took place last week and, I have to say, it exceeded my wildest expectations.' She looked around the room. 'You should all feel rightly proud of yourselves, but I do think that a particular round of applause needs to go to Angela Thompson, who has devoted her evenings and weekends – the little of her evenings and weekends that she has left, that is, when not marking, lesson planning or jumping through the latest

Government-sponsored hoops – to writing, organising and directing such a beautiful show.' There were wry smiles of recognition at her words as the staff applauded Miss Thompson, who appeared genuinely overwhelmed, curtseying and accepting with delight the large bouquet of flowers Mr Cook presented her with.

Mrs Goldman moved things along before Miss Thompson could go into full-on Oscar-acceptance mode, which would leave the rest of the staff with not a hope of making it to their classrooms any time before lunch. 'I really can't thank you all enough. I'm meeting with the parents' fundraising team later this morning, and hope to have an update for you all then as to the total amount of money we've raised.' She bowed her head. 'As you know, there are just days left until I need to confirm to the LEA whether we have been successful in raising the seventy thousand pounds we had been hoping for. I will keep you all informed.'

The children were eating tea at Becky's – Jon having cooked, which meant, for once, no smell of burning filled the kitchen – Becky's cooking prowess being legendary, in all the worst ways. Ava was staring, fascinated, at Becky, who was breastfeeding Sofie while the children ate.

'I'm glad I don't have to get my nipples out at teatime,' she announced brightly. Sam put his head in his hands.

'Me too,' agreed Rosie.

'Sofie would be pretty sad if I didn't,' Becky told them both.

Ava looked as though she disagreed. 'How do you know

that she likes that milk? She might just want some normal milk, out of the fridge, not Nipple Milk.'

'Nipple Milk.' Sam was in danger of spitting his fish-fingers and chips across the table. Gemma gave him a stern look.

Becky laughed. 'I think Sofie's okay with Nipple Milk.' She stroked her daughter's soft head.

'I wonder if one side is main course and one side pudding,' Ava mused. 'Or if you can tell the nipples what flavour you want to come out.' She thought about it for a moment. 'I would choose . . . Left Nipple: Pepperoni Pizza; Right Nipple: Strawberry Ice Cream.'

'Well, that's good news,' Jon announced, 'because strawberry ice cream is exactly what we've got for pudding.'

Ava looked briefly horrified. 'I don't want to be rude, Becky, but I don't want to have the strawberry ice cream if it's going to come out of your nipples.'

Leaving the adults still laughing, the three older children headed out into the garden to play football as Jon took Ella upstairs to change her nappy and Becky winded a milk-drunk Sofie. Gemma stacked the plates into the dishwasher, her mind in a million different places. Becky watched her closely. With the excitement of Sofie's birth, the conversation she'd had with Tom backstage at the gala performance had slipped her mind. Now it suddenly hit her that this was almost certainly the reason that her friend looked like she was perpetually on the verge of tears.

'Gem? What's going on with you and Tom? He mentioned something to me just before I went into labour with

Sofie. Don't tell me the Couple of the Year have hit another rocky patch?'

Her tone was light, but she was horrified to see Gemma turn round from the dishwasher with tears in her eyes.

'Gem, what's up? Come on, sit down. Here.' She proffered a chair to Gemma who collapsed into it gratefully, then thrust Sofie in her direction as she crossed to the fridge and pulled out wine and two glasses. 'Just watch out for projectile puking, okay. That's Sofie, not me, although based on my early pregnancy I can see why you might need me to clarify that.

She passed her friend a filled glass, and watched as she sipped it sadly. 'I knew something was going on. You can't have split up, though, surely? You guys are the ultimate romance! I mean, he's even saved in your phone as Love of My Life!'

Gemma managed a wry smile. 'He's saved in my phone as Love of My Life because you got pissed the night of my fortieth and changed his name on there to that, much to my utter mortification.' She sighed heavily, thinking how much had changed since then. And not all of it in a good way. 'No, we haven't split up. At least, I don't think we've split up. God, Becks, I love him so much I can't think straight. But . . . well. It's just not that simple, is it? When we were in our early twenties, before we had kids, dating was easy. We'd find someone we liked, kiss them, shag them, move them in and that was that. The most we had to worry about was if they'd leave their dirty pants on the floor and whether they'd leave the door open when they took a shit. In the case of my ex: a yes on both fronts.

276

'But the rules of dating change completely when you've got kids to consider. If it was just me to think about then Tom and I would be together twenty-four-seven, shagging round the clock without a care in the world. With everything that's happened this school year, though – with Sam, in particular – it just feels too much, too soon. And so I keep him at arm's length, to make sure I protect the kids, which means he worries that I'm not serious about him, which makes me feel terrible, which makes the time we do spend together all about trying to work out all over again how we feel about each other, and what kind of future this relationship really has ... and we just end up stuck in some miserable cycle in which I don't feel like anyone is really getting what they want.' A tear ran down her cheek and dropped on to a sleeping Sofie's head; the baby, dreaming, no doubt, of Nipple Milk, didn't even stir. 'Oh, Becks.' Her voice broke. 'Why does adulting have to be so damn hard?'

Out in the back garden, completely oblivious to the emotional turmoil their mum was going through, Ava and Sam – who Ava had reluctantly brought into the plan, having accepted that she was going to need his help, even if he was a smelly boy – updated Rosie on the progress of Operation Hazard.

'So you really think it's worked?' Rosie's eyes were wide.

Ava nodded. 'I really do.'

'When will we know for sure?'

'Friday. Our post usually comes before we leave for school, so I can check it then.'

'And then what?' asked Rosie.

Ava folded her arms triumphantly. 'Then we go and tell Mrs Goldman. And I bet we get at LEAST a hundred house points each.'

Mrs Goldman sighed as she opened her first email of the morning, sitting in her office after the end of assembly. It was the final totals from Fundraisers United. Vivienne's chicken pox had developed into shingles and it was thought unlikely she'd be back at the school until after the May half-term; Gemma had therefore temporarily stepped into the role of Chair, and had dropped by the previous evening to give Mrs Goldman the heads-up on what she thought they'd managed to raise.

It was an amazing, really quite staggering total for a school of their size, coming in at almost twenty thousand pounds. But it was still absolutely nowhere near enough. Even Mrs Goldman, for all her bravado, couldn't pretend to the LEA that the other fifty thousand pounds was in the bag. Particularly given she had not a clue where it would come from. She had actually thought they might, somehow, have managed to achieve a miracle. But it seemed like the dream was over.

Steeling herself, Mrs Goldman picked up the receiver to put in the call she had never wanted to make to the LEA. David Haines, the Head of St Catherine's, had been hounding her with almost daily phone calls, telling her that they really must meet up to agree on a shared approach to discipline and staff management for the new merged school. Thus far, she had managed to prevent herself from screaming down the phone to tell him to go stuff himself, but it had been a close-run thing.

A knock on her door interrupted her as she was dialling the digits. Tutting, she put down the phone and called for whoever it was to come in.

To her surprise, it was Ava who stood there, a sheaf of papers in her hands.

'Hello, Mrs Goldman,' said Ava happily. 'Can I come and sit down please. You're going to want to hear what I've got to say.'

Mrs Goldman ran one hand across her forehead. 'So, let me get this straight. You're telling me . . . that you've raised the money we need to save the school.'

'Yes,' said Ava, swinging her legs on the chair where she sat. 'All of it.'

'And you've done this . . . by yourself?'

'No.' Ava shook her head. 'Rosie helped loads. It was our plan that we made up together. We called it Operation Hazard, because Eden Hazard is my favourite footballer, even though he decided to leave Chelsea, which was very irritating of him. And I suppose Sam helped a bit. He told me how to buy stamps, and lent me some of his pocket money to buy them, and looked up the addresses on the internet, and told me that if I stuck the Queen's head on upside down when I did the stamps that she would make sure my head got cut off, so I was very careful indeed when I did that bit.'

'Right.' Mrs Goldman felt like she must have been dreaming. 'So you wrote all these letters.'

'Loads of them,' Ava confirmed. 'Loads and loads. To

everyone we could think of. Even' – she looked disgusted – 'West Ham, because they are Sam's favourite team, and so it wouldn't have been fair otherwise.'

'And you wrote to all of these football clubs and told them that we were trying to raise money to save the school?'

'Not just clubs!' Ava bounced in her seat. 'Clubs, but also players, and managers, and even the girls' teams, even though they don't get paid as much and so probably don't have as much spare money because for some stupid reason they pay the boys more just because they have penises.' She caught the look on her headmistress's face. 'Sorry, Mrs Goldman, for saying the P word in your office, but it's true. It's the gender pay gap, you know.' She nodded knowledge-ably. 'But it's okay, because Rosie's mum Becky is going to get rid of it, when she finishes getting her nipples out and goes back to work, and then they'll make sure all of the footballers get paid the same, whether they've got a penis or a vagina. Apart from me: I'll always get paid the most, because I'm the best.'

Temporarily, Mrs Goldman glossed over a Year 3 student reeling off the names of the private parts of bodies in her office, and got back to the point in hand. 'And they replied?'

'No.' Ava shook her head crossly. 'Hardly any of them, which is *very* rude, and I expect they will get into lots of trouble with their mums and dads, because I know how cross Mum gets if I get a present and don't remember to write a thank-you letter.'

'But some did?'

'Some did!' Ava crowed. 'All of these ones here.' She scanned through the letters in her hand. 'This one is going to pay us ... two thousand pounds ... this one is going to pay us ... seven thousand pounds.' There were five more, all in a similar vein. 'And this one' – she waved it triumphantly – 'look at this one here.' She gave the Head a stern look. 'Do you not keep an eye on what happens to people who used to go to school here, Mrs Goldman?' She held out a signed photograph of a player, a footballer even Mrs Goldman immediately recognised. 'They came to this school as well, and look in this letter, they say it was the best school that they ever went to. They definitely do not want Redcoats to get closed down, and they have loads and loads of money because of all the goals they score, and so ...' She paused for dramatic effect. 'They are going to pay us THIRTY THOUSAND POUNDS!'

Mrs Goldman nearly fell off her chair.

'You just have to keep persevering,' said Ava, nodding her head. 'It is no good giving up, Mrs Goldman, if you don't succeed straight away.' The Head looked at Ava in disbelief, and she pointed at the school values, displayed prominently on the office wall. 'Perseverance is one of our values, you know, Mrs Goldman.'

Wondering quite who was running this school, Mrs Goldman quickly did the maths in her head. 'So that makes ...'

'Fifty-five thousand pounds,' Ava said witheringly. 'Did you not do maths when you were at school? *Plus* this morning I had a letter from the Chelsea Women's team ... and they have offered to come and play an exhibition match for us, on the field, and if we're really good then we get to have a kick-around with them, and I, I get to be mascot!' Her composure deserted her completely and she stood up and actually punched one fist into the air. 'ISN'T THIS THE BEST DAY EVER, MRS GOLDMAN?'

Sitting, genuinely flabbergasted, at her desk, Mrs Goldman thought that the little girl might just be right.

The news of the success of Operation Hazard and the saving of Redcoats spread fast. By the next morning the local paper had dispatched a reporter to the school, and Ava was appalled when she was told by Miss Thompson that she wasn't going to be allowed to speak with them.

'But it's me and Rosie – and Sam, only a little bit – who did the saving of the school! Why am I not allowed to speak to them?'

Miss Thompson didn't pass on what the Head had said when she'd told her that the press were intent on interviewing Ava: 'For goodness' sake, don't let her out of your sight today. It's not her I'm worried about; it's the chap who's come from the paper. He looks about twelve years old; I dread to think what it would do to him if Ava starts haranguing him over the disparity of the gender pay gap and the inequalities between men and women's football.'

Gemma, for her part, had been absolutely stunned when Mrs Goldman had called her at work to tell her what her children had done. Lost for words, she'd put the phone down to see Siobhan staring at her expectantly, and had recounted the whole affair to her.

'I've said it before, and I'll say it again,' Siobhan declared. 'Your kids are fucking BATSHIT.'

She certainly wasn't going to argue with that.

CHAPTER TWENTY-ONE

It was the last day before the May half-term, and a triumphant celebration had been arranged by a somewhat reformed Fundraisers United. With Vivienne still absent, recovering from shingles, and Kristin at her beck and call, Sarah Hardcastle, Noah's mum, had stepped into the breach and had proved impressively effective when it came to organising large-scale catering and entertainment at relatively short notice.

Now, having cheered on an absolutely stunning Chelsea Women in their exhibition match – Ava, to her delight, having been given the opportunity to take some penalties against them and even getting one past their frankly superb goalkeeper – parents, children, teachers and families were congregating to celebrate having successfully raised the money they needed to keep Redcoats open.

It was a beautiful early summer's evening and the catering team manned the barbeque and provided a seemingly endless supply of canapés and both alcoholic and non-alcoholic drinks. Gemma, surrounded by her friends, her children and their children, couldn't help reflecting on how much had happened in just nine short months. Not least the somewhat dramatic arrival of Sofie, who was sleeping peacefully in Becky's arms, Jon with a protective arm around them both.

The only blot on her horizon was, of course, Tom. She knew they were rapidly hurtling towards the point of no return: the two of them needed to sit down and have a serious conversation. Adopting the 'head in sand' approach, she had briefly considered not coming along at all that evening, but Ava had flat out refused to accept the idea of her mum not being there. 'You will miss me playing in the most important football game of my life, and next term Sam has his SATs, which he is probably going to fail, and then you will be too embarrassed to ever go into school again, so you might as well make the most of it for now.' She looked coy. 'Besides, Rosie has a letter for you.'

'She has a letter for me?' Gemma was confused. 'Why has Rosie got a letter for me?'

'It's a thank-you letter,' Ava nodded.

'To say thank you for what?'

'For letting her come to our house tonight for a sleepover.'

Gemma ran her hands across her face. 'But Rosie isn't coming to our house tonight for a sleepover.'

Ava sighed. 'Well, I told her she was allowed to.'

'Why didn't you ask me first?'

The little girl sighed even more heavily, as though the

answer was obvious. 'Because I really want her to come. And if I'd asked, you might have said no.'

I mean ... why bother with the tedious process of seeking consent, when you could simply present a fait accompli?

When it came to her concerns that Tom might insist they stopped avoiding one another and talked all this through, though, the school grounds turned out to be so rammed that she had barely seen her boyfriend all evening, other than from a distance. Just now he was over on the other side of the field with Ava, Rosie and a number of the other kids, organising an impromptu football match.

Maybe she should give up on dating. Tom was her perfect man; Becky was right, he really was the love of her life. But she just didn't see how she had the capacity in her life to be the perfect girlfriend, on top of being the perfect mum, the perfect employee and the perfect friend. One way or another, she was going to end up letting someone down.

She sighed heavily as Jon gently removed Sofie from Becky's arms to take her and change her, and Becky moved her chair over to Gemma's and elbowed her.

'What's up, birthing partner? Missing having me leak waters all over your car?' Becky smirked. 'Valet guys did a good job, didn't they?'

They really had, even if they'd come straight back to the front door after Gemma had given them her car keys, to ask, 'Um, all those water bottles in there ... can we just check: do you want us to take them out, or is it some kind of ... installation, thing?'

'No.' Gemma shook her head. 'Really not missing that seminal bonding moment between us even slightly.'

'And everything's okay at work?'

Even despite her concerns about Tom, Gemma felt her spirits lift. 'Everything is very okay at work.' Pert was looking in line to be one of the fastest growing start-ups of the year, and Leroy had even talked about entering them for a couple of awards. More than that, when he and Gemma had gone out for lunch recently, he'd told her that he was giving her an increased stake in the shared businesses, that he couldn't imagine working with anyone he trusted as much as her, and that he was insanely excited about what the two of them were going to achieve together over the next few years. For context, Leroy had also been 'insanely excited' over the new pale blue belt that he'd found in Joseph the other day, and 'insanely excited' over the fact he'd found a milk supplier who would deliver milk 'in real glass bottles, Gem: it's the future!'. But it was still a compliment that Gemma treasured, and proved to her beyond all doubt that she really was making something of herself with her new venture.

'And the kids are good?'

Gemma smiled. 'The kids are great.' Ava had clearly had one of the best days of her entire life, and Sam was back to his usual, carefree self. Gemma could see him over by the fence with his best mate Jacob, laughing their heads off about something, which, knowing what eleven-year-old boys were like, she was much better off not knowing about.

'Excellent.' Becky clapped her hands together. 'So it's not the kids, it's not your job, your disaster of an ex and his too-small pants seem to be well off the scene these days, which means . . .' She followed Gemma's gaze over to where

Tom was explaining to a protesting Ava the reasons why no, she wasn't getting a free kick, and no, he wasn't going to send all of the opposing team off, even if one of them had 'looked at her in a mean way'.

'Ah. The delectable Tom.' Gemma shot round in an instant and her face flamed red, telling Becky everything she needed to know. 'Have you two not sorted it out yet? Right.' She made as though to walk over to him and Gemma physically grabbed her to pull her back.

'No, Becky. It's not that simple.' She sighed. 'I told you. The kids have got to come first. And so the best I can offer Tom is the opportunity to occasionally see me on the side, in between me being a mum and an employee and a friend. Do you think an amazing guy like that is going to settle for that as a relationship? Because I sure as hell don't.'

'You baffle me, Gemma. You really do.' Becky was looking at her, bemusement etched all over her face. 'In every other area of your life you throw yourself into it and refuse to even consider the possibility of defeat. Whether it's your job or the kids or even sodding Fundraisers United. You never give up. And yet, when it comes to Tom, it's like you're scared. It's like you're frightened to get too close to him, for fear of what will happen.' She shook her head. 'I don't get it.'

'Me neither.' Gemma linked her arm through her friend's, never betraying the fact that Becky had inadvertently hit the nail right on the head. 'Come on. You've gone nine months without anything with a percentage proof to its name. Let's go and find ourselves a G&T.'

*

It was much later that evening and the crowds had started to disperse. Becky was slightly shell-shocked, having been accosted by Andrea Barnes, who had marched over to her, a sheepish-looking Nigel in tow. She had been relieved to see that at least he'd exchanged his cycling leggings for a pair of cords.

'Becky! There you are!' Andrea thrust her face in Becky's direction, air kissing her flamboyantly. 'I've been looking for you all evening! Anyone would think you'd been avoiding me!'

Becky had. Andrea had ended up going overdue with baby Clifford, who was asleep in a sling that Nigel was wearing. Having announced Clifford's safe arrival on the class Facebook group – 'Little Simikins is besotted with his baby brother!', alongside a photo that appeared to show Simon attempting to roll his baby brother off the sofa – she'd sent Becky a series of messages suggesting that they should meet up 'for Baby Ring Sing Ding time, it's at the local community hall, all of the mummies and daddies sit in a circle and sing Baby Ring Sing Ding to their babas while the lady who runs it plays the recorder. Becky, you would love it!' Becky was pretty fucking certain that she wouldn't.

'No, no, not avoiding you . . . just a bit busy.' She gestured at Sofie. 'How are you, Andrea? How did the birth go? Did you get the natural birth that you wanted?'

Andrea's face fell. 'Not exactly.' She lowered her voice. 'I actually ended up having to have an induction, I went so overdue.'

'That's a shame.' Becky was sympathetic; she knew how much Andrea had wanted to give birth out in the open, despite that being the action of a genuinely crazy person. 'Did you at least get to have your whale music and your water birth?'

Andrea's eyes narrowed, as though weighing up whether to tell Becky something. Glancing quickly around them to ensure they weren't being overheard, she leant forwards. 'Actually, I had every drug going. I'm beginning to think you were right all along, Becky. Childbirth hurts like a bitch.'

Much later, Gemma and Becky were sitting around one of the tables in the hall, sharing a bottle of surprisingly okay red wine. Becky had recounted the usually prim and proper Andrea proclaiming that 'childbirth hurts like a bitch', tears of laughter in her eyes. Jon, meanwhile, had said his good-nights and disappeared home, taking Sofie, Ella and Rosie with him – thwarting Ava's sleepover plans – and telling Becky to stay and enjoy herself.

'He's quite a guy, your husband.' Gemma looked after him. 'You did all right there, didn't you?'

'I really did.' Becky beamed. 'Although, if he could work on being able to lactate, then we'd seriously be talking.'

Gemma looked around for her kids, who were nowhere to be seen. Sarah Hardcastle, who had a new partner and was looking radiant in a hot-pink summer dress, saw her looking and sought to reassure her. 'Looking for Ava and Sam? Don't worry. They're outside with my lot helping Mr Jones put away the football stuff. He said he'd bring them in once they were done.'

As if on cue, an excitable Ava ran into the hall, followed by a more sedate Sam. Tom was nowhere to be seen.

They ran over to the table. 'Oh, *there* you are,' said Ava. She looked disapprovingly at the wine on the table. 'I hope you're not going to get drunk and be sick on someone like you did on that man that you once went to the pub with, before you were in love with Mr Jones.' How Gemma was delighted that her daughter had somehow picked up on the details of her dating disaster, back when Becky had talked her into joining Tinder.

Having secured a promise that that would categorically not be happening, Ava grabbed her mum's hand. 'Anyway, you need to come with me and Sam. It's urgent and it cannot wait.'

'Ava, how urgent? I'm just sitting here and having a chat with my friend.' Having once been called by Ava because it was 'urgent', only to discover the urgent problem in question was that she thought someone had moved one of her shoes very slightly to the left on the shoe rack, Gemma felt that her daughter's definition of urgency and hers differed somewhat.

'VERY urgent.' Ava nodded her head. 'Isn't it, Sam?'

'Um ... yes. Yeah, it's very urgent, Mum.'

Oh, good grief. Reluctantly, Gemma allowed her children to drag her towards the exit to the hall, telling Becky she'd be back shortly, and not to leave without her.

'Is it a *bad* urgent thing?' she asked them as they led her outside. Ava had also once told her that she needed to come urgently, which had turned out to be because the bath had overflowed and water was pouring through the kitchen ceiling. It was sometimes good to set your expectations for these things.

'No, definitely not,' Ava confirmed, and Sam agreed. 'I mean, it is a bit of a gross urgent thing . . .'

The children giggled, and Gemma groaned. 'Oh no . . . please don't tell me one of you has been sick somewhere.'

The hall door slammed behind them and they were out in the playground, walking towards the school field. The sun had fully set, and there was nothing but pitch darkness in front of Gemma.

She turned, puzzled, to Ava and Sam. 'Kids . . . what's going on?'

They giggled again. 'Mum, you have to trust us,' said Ava.

'Oh, and by the way,' said Sam, 'we want you to know that we think this is a really, really good thing.'

And before she had a chance to wonder any further . . . the two of them had sprinted back off towards the hall, laughing hysterically . . . and a strong pair of arms that she knew only too well had very gently wrapped around her from behind.

She gasped, and the arms held her more tightly, before very gently letting her go, holding one of her hands, and pulling her further into the darkness of the field. Briefly, she really really hoped that she hadn't totally misjudged this and wasn't in fact being dragged by a murderer to her death.

'I hope you don't hate me for doing this.' Tom's voice allayed her concerns in an instant. 'I'd wanted to come and talk to you like a normal person . . . but, well, any time I got within about a half-mile radius of you, you seemed to instinctively notice me coming and make a run for it.'

She was grateful for the darkness and its ability to hide

her blushes. Tom had spotted exactly what she'd been doing. Gemma had always seen people in colours. Dull, uninteresting people were shades of grey. Not the erotic kind. People she knew well were greens and blues. Her close friends and family were warm reds and pinks. And her children and Tom were iridescent, gleaming bright gold. She didn't even need to keep a lookout for Tom to know when he was approaching . . . and to be able to immediately get out of the way.

'Any other guy would probably have given up by now, just assumed you're not interested,' Tom continued, 'but I'm not any other guy. I'm me, and I also happen to be madly in love with you, Gemma. And I thought you felt the same way. Which is why I had to do this. I can't go about the rest of my life pretending that we never happened, pretending that what we had didn't exist. If you tell me, here and now, that I was wrong, that you never felt anything for me, that you don't want anything to do with me, then I will go. I promise you. I will go, and I will never bother you again. But I love you, Gemma. And what I want to know is . . . do you love me?'

For a moment, she couldn't speak. 'Of *course* I love you. But it's not fair on you. I can't give you a proper relationship. I've got about twenty minutes to call my own each week which I can commit to coming and spending with you, but if the kids aren't okay with you being in the house then we're going to spend most of that trying to have standing-up sex in an alleyway somewhere like teenagers without any-where to go.' Her voice cracked. 'And I'm really really bad at standing-up sex; I just don't think my body bends that way.'

'Gemma. Gemma, Gemma, Gemma.' He reached out in the darkness and she felt him take her other hand, gently holding them in the warmth of his, pulling her closer towards him. 'I love you, yes? No ifs, no buts. I understand that you have a ton of other stuff going on in your life. And I love that about you, I love your energy, and your passion. I love the fact you're a kick-ass businesswoman. I love your kids. I love everything about you, Gemma. I came into this relationship with my eyes wide open. So please, stop trying to convince yourself that you're not good enough for me. Because, in my wildest dreams' – now it was his voice cracking – 'I never, ever thought I'd be lucky enough to meet someone as amazing as you.'

There was silence; the darkness lay all around them, heavy as velvet.

Gemma exhaled. 'But the kids. I've been so worried, Tom, so fucking worried about them. With everything that's happened with Sam this year, and then Ava going on about us having dirty sex, even though chance would have been a fine thing, and then I thought, is me moving a live-in boyfriend in going to fuck them up even more than they're probably already likely to be because they've got two divorced parents, one of whom doesn't know that Berlin is in Germany, even though he's now living there?' She let out a sob. 'I am so scared, Tom, so fucking scared. I don't know how to be a great parent. There is no instruction manual, no cast-iron guaranteed way to get it right. I cannot tell you how much it scares me, every single day, that I might be failing them. That I might be letting them down. I love them so much. And I love you so much. And I just don't know what to do.'

She sobbed now, and he held her, rhythmically stroking her back, not telling her to stop, just being there. When her sobs had slowed to gentle gasps, he spoke again.

'Gem, the kids have been to see me tonight. They asked to chat to me, because they wanted to know why I hadn't been round recently, and they said you'd been making up excuses.' There was the hint of a smile in his voice. 'Apparently you told Ava I might be directing the next school play?'

Gemma shrugged nonchalantly, her total fib having been uncovered. 'It could happen.'

'Yeah, and pigs might fly. But I was honest with them. I said to them that you'd been worried about them, about how they'd feel if I moved in properly. And – and I promise I'm not exaggerating for dramatic effect here – Ava said it would be almost as good as the time Chelsea won the Premiership.'

'What about Sam?' Sam was her main concern, after everything he'd been through that year.

'Sam apologised again for how he behaved. I told him for the tenth time not to worry about it; he's clearly had a tough year. But then he said – oh God, he'll kill me for telling you this, and you're not to tell him that I've told you, or tell him off for his language – he said, "To tell you the truth, Mr Jones, Mum's been a really miserable dick since you've stopped coming round, so it would be all right with me if you started coming back again."' Tom's voice broke slightly, when he told her that he'd followed that up by saying: 'Actually, Mr Jones, please could you come back. Me and Ava really miss you.'

294

Gemma exhaled; the sound slid away from her into the night. She hadn't realised until that moment just how heavily the thought of her children not wanting Tom around had been playing on her mind.

'So, Gemma, the children are okay with us being together. More than that, they're happy for us. And so what I want to know' – she felt him take a step backwards, still clasping both of her hands – 'is how you feel about that? Are you willing to give us a go again? Are you willing to stop running away; to trust me that we'll work it out together?' He paused. 'And are you willing . . . to stop beating yourself up about not being perfect? No one is perfect. No one. No one gets it right all of the time. But you, Gemma, are an amazing person. You are an amazing mum. An amazing friend. Amazing at your job. To me, in fact, you are just about as perfect as they come.'

She responded by filling the six inches between them, reaching upwards until her mouth found his, and they kissed until their lips were raw, and her legs shook, and if you had ever tried to tell Gemma that it would be possible to be this happy, she could tell you right now, she'd have never believed you.

And then an enormous beam of light swung towards them, halting as it picked out the pair of embracing bodies, and stopping dead.

'I'VE FOUND THEM!' The disembodied voice of Mr Cook came towards them through a loudhailer; so dazzled were they by the brightness that they were unable to identify where he was. 'HERE THEY ARE, MRS GOLDMAN. BRING IN THE POLICE! CALL

999! SUMMON COBRA, MI5, MI6, THE SECRET SERVICE! I'VE DONE IT!' His voice was histrionic with nervous excitement. 'I ALWAYS KNEW MY COMMITMENT TO WATCHING BACK-TO-BACK EPISODES OF *SHERLOCK* WOULD PAY OFF, MRS GOLDMAN.'

His footsteps came closer, and the blinding beam from the torch wobbled as he stepped towards them. 'I'M APPROACHING THE SUSPECTS, MRS GOLDMAN,' he declared. 'THOSE LITTLE BASTARDS THAT TRIED TO BURN DOWN OUR SCHOOL. I'VE GOT YOU NOW! DON'T YOU DARE MOVE A MUSCLE, OR I'LL UNLEASH THE DOGS ON YOU!'

Patiently, Gemma and Tom waited, safe in the knowledge that Mr Cook's dogs were two laid-back Basset hounds who were about as aggressive as a bowl of custard.

The caretaker moved closer, the searchlight trained on his target. 'Right then,' he muttered. 'Let's be having— Oh. Oh no.' His distress and disappointment were palpable as he identified them.

'Good evening, Mr Cook.' Tom was charmingly polite; Gemma hid her face in his shoulder to smother her giggles. 'Can Gemma and I be of help, at all?'

'I don't suppose it was the two of you burnt down the school, was it?' he tried optimistically.

'I'm afraid not.' Tom shook his head. 'Sorry to disappoint you.'

The caretaker put his head in his hands. Gemma thought she heard him groaning something about a thwarted knighthood.

'MR COOK?' came back the voice of Mrs Goldman, having clearly located her own loudhailer. 'ARE YOU OUT THERE? ARE YOU HURT? SHALL I CALL THE POLICE?'

'No, no.' Mr Cook fumbled for his own loudhailer, raising it to his mouth once more. 'NO, MRS GOLDMAN. I'M AFRAID IT'S A FALSE ALARM.' He looked in utter disdain at Gemma and Tom, still entwined in each other's arms. 'IT'S JUST THOSE TWO BLOODY IDIOTS WE CAUGHT LAST YEAR. OUT HERE, HAVING INTERCOURSE. AGAIN.' He shook his head in despair. 'I DO THINK, MRS GOLDMAN, WE NEED TO RECONSIDER OUR SCHOOL POLICIES. WHAT'S THE POINT IN HAVING STRINGENT SECURITY CHECKS IF ANYONE CAN WALTZ IN AND START MAKING THE BEAST WITH TWO BACKS ON THE SCHOOL FIELD?'

And, faces flaming, Gemma and Tom walked arm in arm towards the school, back to Becky, who was absolutely killing herself laughing, and would no doubt take great pleasure in reminding them both of this moment for pretty much the rest of their lives.

CHAPTER TWENTY-TWO

After that, the summer term had flown past, and Gemma could rarely remember having felt happier. The children had been in their element: Ava had been telling anyone who would listen how she had played with the Chelsea Women's squad 'and I expect they probably will be phoning me up any day now to come and join the team properly', and, with Tartan virtually out of the picture, Sam had returned to the happy, relaxed, still rather more entertained by fart jokes than she would have liked, boy that she knew so well. Even his SATs had been less of a drama than Gemma might have imagined. 'It's okay, Mum,' Sam had told her, when she'd asked him if he was worried about them at all. 'Mr Jones told me that they're just a load of pointless tests invented by complete tossers to make them feel better about themselves.'

Gemma might have berated Tom for his choice of language, had she not been so utterly euphoric at him finally having moved in with them full time, not to mention how happy the children were to have him around again. Ava, no doubt remembering the brief period when Gemma had lost control of her senses and agreed to have Nick move back in with them, had solemnly asked Tom 'and when you go to the toilet, Mr Jones, you won't wee up the wall, will you, because my mummy doesn't like it', and Tom, straight-faced, had promised the little girl that he had never in his life weed up a wall, and wasn't about to start now.

'I wish I could wee up a wall,' said Ava wistfully. 'Front bottoms are stupid. You can't even wee in a straight line out of them, it goes all over the place and gets your socks wet.' She caught sight of her mum's face. '*Obviously* I have never tried to wee up the wall. But I am just saying. If I did.'

Both of the children still spoke regularly to their dad via FaceTime and on the phone, and frequently had Gemma in stitches regaling her with her ex's latest escapades. 'He told me that he met a pretty girl, and I think he probably wanted to have S-E-X with her,' Ava recounted, her eyes wide. 'But then he took her out for dinner and while they were eating some pasta with spicy sauce the girl told Daddy that she was actually a boy!' She nodded solemnly. 'I wonder what Daddy thought about that.'

Gemma had bitten down on her lip to stop herself from laughing, and had said to Ava that she really couldn't imagine what Nick had thought about that. She would have paid cold hard cash to have been able to have witnessed his face at that moment.

And Sam couldn't have made it clearer that he was

totally comfortable with his mum and Tom's relationship these days. He'd even, rather sheepishly, when they'd been sat out in the back garden one evening, confessed that he really quite liked their new family dynamic. 'It's just good, because he's always here when I need help with my homework,' he'd muttered. 'And you are much less grumpy Mum now Mr Jones is here. I'm just saying.'

'Yes, that is true,' Ava agreed, 'and I know why that is, it is because of SEXUAL INTERCOURSE.'

Jon, hanging out the washing in the garden next door, nearly choked.

Almost before she could believe it, the last day of the summer term had rolled around. Gemma had taken the day off work to attend the leavers' assembly. To her surprise, when she went downstairs to put the kettle on, Sam was already down there, dressed, hair brushed, and – my God – had he actually cleaned his teeth? Gemma clutched one hand to her chest as she walked into the kitchen.

'What? What's wrong with you, Mum?' Sam backed away, disconcerted, as his mum advanced on him in her dressing gown. 'Why are you being so weird?'

'I'm sorry, it's just ...' She put one hand to his head, as though to feel his temperature. 'Are you feeling okay? Are you actually dressed, washed and with your teeth brushed without me first having to scream "TEETH! HAIR! SHOES!" at you three hundred times?'

Sam looked sheepish. 'Yeah ... well. I thought maybe, just for once, I should try getting ready without you nagging me and see what it was like.'

'And?' She looked at him.

'And . . . I probably won't be doing it again, so you should make the most of this.'

'Git!' She flicked him with the tea towel and went to make a cup of tea. 'Want one?'

They sat at the table, drinking their tea in companionable silence. Gemma stole a glance over at her son. Seeing him sitting there, all grown up – it wouldn't be long before he overtook her in height – her heart felt like it might burst. How could it possibly be that this bright, switched-on, *fully dressed, halle-bloody-lujah* young man had once been her tiny baby? What was that saying again? The days might be long . . . but, oh my goodness, the years really did turn out to be short.

Sam saw her looking and screwed up his face. 'Uggh. Are you thinking all horrible soppy things, just because it's my last day at Redcoats?'

'Nope. Nope, absolutely not . . . Okay, maybe just a little bit.' She blew on the surface of her tea to cool it down. 'I just can't believe how quickly it's gone.' Surprisingly, her thoughts turned to Nick. He had been there on Sam's first day; it had been a rare moment of harmony between them. 'It's weird, not having your dad here.'

'Yeah.' Sam's face was unreadable. 'It is weird. I'm glad that you and Dad aren't together any more, Mum, because I don't think you were very good for each other' – understatement of the year – 'but I do wish a little bit that he was here for my last day.'

Much to her surprise, so did Gemma.

As she dismissed the thought and was about to challenge Sam to a game of Rock, Paper, Scissors to see which one of them got the unpleasant task of waking up Ava … there was a knock on the door.

'I'll get it.' Gemma smiled. 'Tom's in the shower. So you can get your sister up.'

She could hear Sam groaning at the thought of Ava's early-morning wrath as she walked down the hallway; a tall figure, silhouetted through the glass panes of the door, was haloed by the early-morning sun already shining through. Was it the postman? Jon?

It was Nick.

He held his arms wide as she opened the door. 'Babes! Look who it is!'

Gemma clapped one hand to her head as she took in the sight of her ex, clad in jeans so skinny that she thought even Leroy would have dismissed them as being a bit much. And that from the man who had once memorably gone clubbing wearing a pair of jeans that had one buttock fully cut out, for goodness' sake.

'Nick! This is a surprise. Um … what are you doing here?'

The last time her ex-husband had turned up on her doorstep, he had asked her how she felt about them getting back together. She crossed every single part of her anatomy that he wasn't going to ask her to give it another go.

Nick looked sheepish. 'I was just wondering. How would you feel …?' He looked at her expectantly and her heart sank like a stone. No, no, no. Not again. Not when everything else in her life was finally working so well.

'How would you feel,' he continued, and then surprised her with a sudden wink, 'if I came along to Sam's leavers' assembly today?'

If he'd told her he was thinking of entering the priest-hood, Gemma wouldn't have been more surprised. 'You remembered it's Sam's leavers' assembly?'

'Ava might have reminded me it was Sam's leavers' assembly.'

'She did?'

'She did.'

'Even so.' Gemma had been trying to get her ex to arrange a visit to the kids all year and had never managed to pin him down. 'What made you actually get on a plane and come over here?'

He looked abashed. 'Ava did. She can be quite scary when she wants to be, you know.'

'DAD!' Sam suddenly came flying into the hallway at the sound of voices, nearly knocking Nick off the front step with the force of his embrace.

'Steady on, son!' Nick held the boy tightly; Gemma could see from the look on his face and the sudden tears in his eyes how moved he was.

'You really came!'

'I really did.'

'Marvellous.' Gemma clapped her hands together sharply; this was all very well, but frankly her morning routine didn't leave time for emotional reunions on her front step. 'Perfect timing, Nick. Congratulations. You get the task of waking Ava up for the day. Good luck!'

Her ex groaned in horror and covered his face with his hands as, laughing, Gemma went upstairs to update Tom on their early-morning visitor.

The leavers' assembly was another Miss Thompson special; she'd even roped in Becky again as stage manager, and Rachel, the school secretary, on sound and lighting. Mr Cook, ominously, was on pyrotechnics. The hall was already packed by the time Gemma and Nick arrived, but her mum and dad, who had also come along for the occasion – and had been barely able to control their delight that Gemma 'had finally settled down with that lovely young man' – had saved them two seats at the front. The other classes filed in and Tom gave her a wink as he led Year 2 to their spaces on the floor in front of the stage.

She'd explained to Tom that morning, as she'd got ready – to the background sounds of Ava telling her dad about the gardening she'd been doing at school – 'We got all of these seeds, and then we suffocated them in the ground.' 'I think you mean you planted them, sweetie.' 'It's the same thing.' – about Nick's arrival. To her surprise, he couldn't have been more relaxed about it.

'Nick's the kids' dad, Gemma. I think it's great that he wants to come and spend time with them. And I think it's even more great that you tell me all the time what an utter dick you think he is, because it means I don't have even the slightest concern about him being around.' His voice softened. 'Have I mentioned any time recently how much I utterly adore you?' For several glorious minutes, Nick's arrival had been entirely forgotten, and suffice to say they'd nearly been very late indeed.

And now, as she sat there in the hall, listening to the noises of the audience, and the children shuffling in their seats, and Year 6 getting ready backstage, it struck her just how much her life had changed over the seven years Sam had been at the school. Seven years ago, her confidence had been at absolute rock bottom. She'd been in a terrible relationship – and knew it – had two children under the age of five and was really struggling to keep her house, job and family plates all simultaneously spinning without dropping any of them and seeing it smash into tiny pieces. The plates marked 'friends' and 'Gemma' didn't even get a look in, and Gemma couldn't imagine how they ever would. There simply weren't enough hours in the day.

As the curtains were pulled back, and Year 6 started singing, a song Miss Thompson had composed for them called 'We Are The Future, We Are The World', which immediately had ninety per cent of the audience pulling out their hankies (and Ava very deliberately turning around to her mum, dad and grandparents and pulling a face like she was going to be sick), Gemma wondered, just for a moment, what she would say to the her of seven years ago, if she had that chance to go back, to tell her what was in store for her.

Would she even have believed it if she'd said that it was all going to be okay? That, despite everything she feared, she was actually going to turn out to be all right at parenting. More than all right. That she was going to end up having brought up two children who she was so proud of she sometimes felt like she might burst.

That, despite the guilt, and the all too frequent feelings that you were failing on all fronts, making the compromises that she had to be a single working parent would be more than worth it. That the day would come when not only was she going to manage to find a way of effectively integrating work and home and life, but that she was going to turn out to be more successful in her career than she could have ever imagined, that she was going to be running her own business at the age of forty.

And that she wasn't doomed to struggle along in that failing relationship for ever, that there was actually, if she could just keep on going, the most incredible man on the horizon for her, who loved her for everything that she was, and never wanted her to be anything that she wasn't.

No, she thought, watching Sam stand up and furiously – he hated public speaking with a fiery passion – orate the things he would miss about Redcoats. 'My little sister beating me at football and telling everyone else in the playground that I am a loser is a thing that I will definitely not miss,' he announced, in an almost certainly unscripted moment. She was fairly certain that she wouldn't have believed any of that even slightly.

But it turned out ... it was true.

The biggest thing, Gemma realised, that had changed over the past seven years – since she'd first become a parent, in fact – was her. For so long, she'd convinced herself that everyone out there was winning at life, while she was falling short on every front.

When actually, it turned out, everyone out there – well, maybe apart from Vivienne – felt the same way. Everyone panicked about whether they were doing a good enough job, whether they were being a good enough parent, friend, partner, colleague, person.

For the first time, she realised: she believed in herself.

The assembly reached its climax, the Year 6 students

singing a reprise of 'We Are The Future, We Are The World', and the audience rose to its feet. Nick put his arm through Gemma's and gave her a squeeze. 'That's our boy, that is.'

And as Sam stood on the stage, mortification written all over his face at having to be the centre of attention; as her mum and dad beamed up at him; as Becky poked her head around the side of the curtains and gave Gemma a wink; as Tom mouthed 'I love you', from the other side of the hall; as Mr Cook set off a series of pyrotechnics which sounded like they were going to take the roof off and risk the other half of the school being burnt down; and as Ava loudly whispered to Rosie that next year, with the Year 6s gone, they were going to 'rule the school' . . . Gemma smiled, and smiled, and smiled.

ACKNOWLEDGEMENTS

Having the opportunity to have a book published is still a total 'pinch me' moment, and *Winning At Life* would never have come to fruition had it not been for the hard work and input of an incredible team of people. Thanks have to start with the team at Sphere/Little Brown: Gemma Shelley, who has once again delivered an amazing marketing strategy for me. Kirsteen Astor, who has done such a fantastic job on the publicity for *Winning At Life*. Hannah Wood, who blows my mind with her talent and with the beautiful front cover she has designed. Thalia Proctor, for overseeing the editing process (and for not being entirely thrown when a parcel wrapped in bright green tape landed on her desk after I'd lost my sellotape!). Alison Tullett, for the incredible job she did on copy editing. Adele Brimacombe, for her eagle-eyed attention to detail on the proof reading front. And, not forgetting my spectacular editor, Maddie West, who transformed my somewhat epic ramblings into something far more coherent and a million times better than I would ever have managed without her. Maddie also needs to be applauded for giving me the best note on a paragraph in *Winning At Life* that I have ever received on anything I've written: 'Too many cunty twats here'. Absolute gold.

Without my blog, there would never have been a book, and without all of my amazing blog readers, there would never have been a blog at all. Thank you so, so much to all of you: your love and support continues to completely overwhelm me and I am so ridiculously grateful for our mad little corner of the internet.

If the task of writing a book sounds terrifying, it's nothing compared to the moment you have to give it to an Actual Reader to Actually Read and hope that they don't entirely hate it. I couldn't be luckier to have my two brilliant beta readers in my life – both of whom pull no punches. Alice, thank you so much for your fantastic feedback, for your scarily expert knowledge on the life and times of RuPaul ... oh, and for the little tiny matter of gently pointing out that I might possibly have forgotten about one of my characters halfway through *facepalm*.

There's nothing like a sibling if you're looking for candid feedback, and Helen, as always you didn't disappoint on this front. Thank you so much for juggling work and life to fit in an early reading for me, for your fantastic – occasionally scathing ('You're still going on about the bloody school' being my personal favourite) – comments ... and for reminding me that *Trisha* was last on our screens almost ten years ago! Love you.

It would be impossible for any of us to parent without our villages, and I am as always so grateful to every single one of my friends and family who are ever willing to step in and help me juggle the various components of my batshit life. Particular thanks must go to the brilliant Vee, Vic and Clare – mainly because I'm looking forward to seeing the level of Vic's histrionic excitement when she sees her name in a book! – and to my work colleague Alex, who steps up almost every week to make a dash to the shops for a last minute purchase of whatever I've forgotten the kids need for school the next day. Legends, all of you.

Much of *Winning At Life* centres around a series of dramatic productions. While I don't think we ever put on anything quite as out there as *Straw! The Musical*, we probably weren't too far off, and therefore an enormous shout out to the Birmingham School of Speech and Drama Class of 2000 for the many, many moments of inspiration, randomness and spontaneous jazz hands. God, we had the best of times. (And, also, occasionally the worst of times . . . 8am Body Con after a night out, anyone?!) Love you all.

Speaking of drama . . . JAAAAAAAMS!!! My very best BFF, I am so utterly grateful to have you in my life, and equally grateful to have witnessed your stranger sartorial choices over the years: Leroy's pair of jeans with one buttock fully cut out being not even slightly inspired by one of your more outré clubbing outfits . . .! While *Man. Bat. Ball* is a fictional production, if it wasn't then I'm certain you would have starred in it. Here's to many more years of Cava drinking. Absolutely adore you.

Mummy, thank you so much for your love and support, and also for not grounding me for all the swears the last book had in it! Maybe the next thing I write will be slightly higher brow and contain fewer references to the F word . . . then again, maybe not! Oh, and particular appreciation for your dedication to the cause in going all the way to Hungary to photograph the Hungarian translation of *Absolutely Smashing It* in a bookshop for me! So grateful for everything you do for me, I love you very much.

Yo, Pop! Apologies for failing once again to get a reference to the Gear Box Story in ... but I kind of wanted my readers to stay awake! Thank you so much for always believing in me; for the Big Walks; and for ensuring that I was in my early twenties before I realised that it wasn't actually illegal to put the windows in a car down on a motorway! And don't even get me started on 'Insect Days'! You are the best and I love you very much.

Wrenfoe: I'm not quite sure what you were expecting when you entered into married life with me, but I'm guessing it involved slightly lower levels of total and abject chaos! Thank you so much for the way you consistently take it all in your stride, and for the endless love and support you've given me to follow my dreams. Thanks also for putting up with my 'corner', which I absolutely definitely will tidy soon. (Never going to happen!) I love you so much. I'm Spartacus!

And Jamie and Beth. Without the two of you, genuinely, none of this would ever have happened, and I am so so lucky that you're mine. Thank you for putting up with a mum who's a bit sweary, somewhat inept, frequently juggling seventeen things at once – and who still doesn't have a bloody clue what a fronted adverbial is – but who loves you more than she'll ever have words to properly tell you. Love you for ever, Mum xxxxxxxxxx

PS TEETH! HAIR! SHOES!

**Unmissable, hilarious and kind, this is the first
novel from Kathryn Wallace, who blogs as
*I Know, I Need to Stop Talking***

Gemma is only just holding it together – she's a single parent,
she's turning 40 and her seven-year-old daughter has drawn
a cruelly accurate picture which locates Gemma's boobs
somewhere around her knees. So when her new next-door
neighbour, Becky, suggests that Gemma should start dating
again, it takes a lot of self-control not to laugh in her face.

But Becky is very persuasive and before long Gemma finds
herself juggling a full-time job, the increasingly insane
demands of the school mums' Facebook group *and* the tricky
etiquette of a new dating world. Not only that, but Gemma
has to manage her attraction to her daughter's teacher, Tom,
who has swapped his life in the City for teaching thirty six
seven-year-olds spelling, grammar, basic fractions – and why
it's not ok to call your classmate a stinky poo-bum ...

It's going to be a long year – and one in which Gemma and
Becky will learn a really crucial lesson: that in the end,
being a good parent is just about being good enough.